ANAMNESIS

The Ability to Bring Back Memory

CASSIE GREUTMAN

ANAMNESIS

The Ability to Bring Back Memory

Cassie Greutman

Printed in the United States of America

First Printing, November 2020

Second Printing, March 2024

Published by Fully Invested Publishing

ISBN e-book: 978-1-964185-06-4

ISBN Print: 978-1-964185-07-1

CHAPTER ONE

Looking over my shoulder was a habit I just couldn't break. Probably good, considering how I'd spent the last year. My sister wasn't after me anymore, but now my dad was. Kind of funny when you thought about it. Not.

I hiked my bookbag over my shoulder and upped my pace down the alley, trying *not* to think about it. Those kind of thoughts led to thoughts of Faerie, which then went straight to Dan and Nina, my foster parents, and how my dad had forced them into a situation where their memories had been taken away.

Bye bye family.

Goodbye to everything I really cared about. Or mostly everything. I'd gained my sister in the mess. And I still had Jaden, whatever we were.

But no home. No parents. No stability. Poof. Because of the man I was supposed to call father.

Storm, my always disheveled street dog, showed up then, right as I was getting even more down. He bumped me in the leg. I smiled. It wasn't much, but more than anyone else had been getting from me lately.

If only we had a plan. At least a plan. Even if it was impossible, it would be better than this, wandering each day into the next without any hope. It had been more than a month. If I'd had any hope before, it was gone now.

Like he knew where my thoughts were going, Storm bumped me again.

"Sorry, buddy. I know, you're hungry."

Today he'd just have to put up with a to-go meal though. It was Jaimie's birthday, and I didn't want to be late.

Starren wouldn't let Storm in our apartment. She'd never even seen him. Whenever she was around he avoided me too. But she was at work a lot, and what she didn't know didn't hurt her. I always made sure to get all of the dog hair out of the shower. He'd filled out, and was clean, which helped his looks a lot. Cray still said he looked like a hellhound, but I thought he was handsome. Every day when I left for school, I locked him up so our landlord didn't find out about him, or the dog warden find him, but every day he somehow showed up in the alley, waiting for me. This dog had talent.

"Stay," I told him when I got to the Martan's apartment building.

He whined at me, giving me the puppy eyes. I didn't let him catch on to how much it affected me, and walked into the building. The elevator was broke again, so I shuffled toward the stairs, blowing on my hands. March was much warmer than when we'd gone adventuring in January, but I still wasn't a fan.

It was the scent I noticed first. Steps coming down the stairs, strong perfume ahead of them. My soul went happy for a second, right before Nina stepped around the corner.

"Hey!" She smiled, that big grin.

One word nearly sent me into a tailspin of happy.

"How's it going?"

And there was the devastating wreck at the bottom of the tailspin. Nina would never be so casual with me if she knew who I was. My foster mom still didn't remember me. She was just nice to everyone.

"Oh, good."

She started past me.

My mind frantically raced with things to ask. How was she? How was Dan? Did they feel like something wasn't right in their lives? Did they secretly miss me? "How's it going with you?" I asked. It came out rather lame, but I would have asked her anything to get her to stay here even a moment longer.

"Going good," she said over her shoulder, not really slowing down.

Why would she. This was just small talk. My heart shattered into a million tiny pieces, and I closed my eyes to hold back the tears. What was she doing here anyway? This was supposed to be my safe zone. Not that I wasn't glad to see her.

"You okay?" Her voice made my eyes pop back open. She'd paused a few steps down, and watched me intently.

"Oh, you know how it is as a teen," I answered, not being able to lie and say yes.

"Need to talk about it?" She was being her normal amazing self. She didn't even know me, but she was willing to listen to my problems. "Sometimes it's easier to tell a stranger how you're feeling."

A stranger. Talking with her would have been amazing, but the tears I'd been holding back were about to burst from their prison. "No, thank you," I got out, then tore off up the stairs. I hadn't seen her in over a month. Well, I'd seen her when I spied on her, but I hadn't interacted with her. Pushing down the need for my mom was so much harder when she was so close.

Thankfully she didn't follow me. The Martan's were just going to have to deal with me being late. I slid down the icky wall outside their apartment for a good cry. Jaden's sister Lucy was inside, and we didn't see eye to eye on anything. No way I would ever let her see me like this.

The birthday party went well. Jaden was the only one who seemed to notice my puffy eyes, but he didn't say anything. He was even kinder than normal, which I didn't think possible. I stuffed the questions down inside, wondering if Nina had been here. If I admitted I'd seen her in the hallway, Jaden would be all over me.

Thankfully Cray had to work. He might have noticed how I was feeling, and he didn't know about politely ignoring someone when they were hurting so you didn't embarrass them.

He was still pretty fae when it came to understanding emotion.

From all the happy and calm in here right now, she couldn't have been coming to see Rebecca, Jaden's mom. They were still friends, even with Nina not knowing me, but not in the way they used to be. Too many secrets between them now.

Nina did a lot of volunteering and charity work. There was probably someone in the building that had needed her today. Someone other than me.

"Time to open presents!" Rebecca announced, and Jaime squealed, just like any new eight-year-old would when presents were mentioned.

I slipped toward the door, grabbing my coat off the couch on the way. Not having parents made it really hard for a sixteen-year-old to get a job. And Starren wasn't much better off, being undocumented, so I hadn't had any extra cash to get Jaime anything.

"Leaving?" Jaden startled me. I'd been so intent on getting out of here without Jaime noticing that he'd apparently walked right up beside me without me having an inkling.

I slapped his arm lightly. "Don't do that. You of all people know how paranoid I can be. I might have hurt you."

He grinned. "Unlikely." His grin dropped. "What's going on? You've been upset all evening. Why are you leaving without telling anyone goodbye?"

"It's almost time for Starren's show to come on. We watch it together." Not a total lie. Every show was Starren's show. Surprisingly she loved TV, and learning about all the strange things humans did. She'd never admit it of course, but if she wasn't at work and we weren't training, that's where she was. I was worried about her being depressed, but I didn't know how to ask.

Jaden gave me a look that said he knew what I was doing, but he didn't push.

One of the reasons I liked him so much. But he didn't need to

know that. "I'll see you later." I threw my coat on and took off out
their door, making it down the stairs and outside with only a few tears
welling up.

Stormy was waiting for me just out of sight of the door. I crouched
down to give him a hug, and wipe the tears that had escaped off in his
coat.

My apartment was just two buildings over. Fort Wayne was a nice
city, so even though we were in the worst part, I still felt pretty safe,
and the buildings weren't too bad.

Plus, I had a little extra protection. I still didn't leave the apartment without my invisible sword.

Starren was watching some murder show when I came in. Her
favorite. Guessing who the killer was before anyone else made her
happy. One of the few things that did. That, and turning her nose up at
how inaccurate some of the deaths were.

I tried to bring Storm in with me, but he took off. "Storm," I called
after him half-heartedly, but he never listened. What was it about
Starren that he didn't like so much? He hadn't even been this weird
with Wade, and Wade was not a good dude.

My school stuff dropped to the floor by the island, followed by my
sword. I hated going to school like nothing was wrong, but I didn't
want Dan and Nina to get in trouble for losing a foster kid either. It
would happen eventually if they never remembered they even had a
kid, but if we could fix them first, we could nip it in the bud.

Starren looked at me, but then went right back to watching TV.

Long gone were the days where I came home to fresh baked
cookies and parents asking how my day had gone. "Foster parents," I
corrected under my breath, but I didn't know who I was kidding. Dan
was definitely a better dad than my actual dad, and Nina was an
amazing mom.

I dropped down beside Starren and covered my face with my
hands.

"What's wrong?" she asked.

I didn't have to look to know she was still watching TV. Emotions
were hard for her. Just the fact that she'd asked was a big deal.

"Missing Dan and Nina a little extra tonight." And the fact that I would admit that to her was an even bigger deal. We were changing, and it felt weird.

I could feel her gaze shift and bore into me. I dropped my hands and stared back.

She grabbed the remote and clicked the TV off. Right in the middle of some stupid guy going down a dark alley. This must be serious.

"I've been thinking about that. A lot."

I leaned closer. "Yeah?"

"And..." She paused.

I leaned in uncomfortably close. "Yes?"

"I think I know someone who could point us toward someone who could help."

I shrieked and grabbed her hand, which made her look extremely uncomfortable. But she didn't pull away. "Where is this person? What's their name? Can we leave now? How far away are they?" I bounced on the couch, that tiny ember of hope I was always trying to smack down completely bursting into flame.

"That's the problem. We'd have to leave Sanctuary."

I slumped against the couch, that raging inferno doused with two short sentences. How were we supposed to do that? We hadn't left Sanctuary since the whole Faerie fiasco where I'd met my evil father for the first time. "How many do you think are waiting out there for us? Did you just think of this guy?"

"I don't know. A lot. Father won't give up on you easily, and he's probably ready to kill me."

She was serious about that probably, unfortunately. Our father was not a good person. At all. But she hadn't answered my second question. "What made you think of him?"

She looked away, like she always did when she was guilty.

"Starren?" I asked. "Would you please answer me?" My voice started to rise, the temper that had been right under the surface since I'd lost my family bubbling out.

"I thought you'd stop caring. Stop needing them." She threw her hands up in the air. "I don't understand how all this 'family' stuff works!" Her air quotes would have made me laugh at any other time. But right now? I was spitting mad.

"You've known this entire time how to fix them?"

She leaned back. "No. I told you, I just know someone who might."

"How do we find them? Let's go!"

"It's not that easy, Trish. There's a chance he knows something, but if he doesn't, we'd have to go back. To Faerie."

I could feel the blood draining from my face, the anger swirling along with it. No wonder she hadn't brought it up before. Faerie meant Wade. And even worse for her, Father. Faerie held all things evil and scary. At least when it came to the two of us.

"We'd have to find a different way in than your tunnel, I'm sure that's heavily guarded by now. And as for portals..." she looked grim for a second. "Cumat owes me. A lot. If we go back to D.C., I might be able to get him to let us through."

"Yes! Let's leave now." Traveling to D.C., not great. Traveling to Faerie, terrible. Getting my parents back? Worth it.

A knock on the door stopped Starren from answering.

No way Jaden knew what we were planning already. I jumped up stalked over to the door. No way I was going to tell him either. He'd try to stop us. It was probably the landlord, after our rent. It was only a week late, not a big deal. Nah, the landlord didn't care enough to come in person. Had to be Jaden, here for something else. I'd open the door, tell him to get, and then we could go back to planning. Nothing mattered more at the moment.

I flung the door open, ready to tell him firmly but politely to go on his way so he didn't suspect anything was up, but instead of a tall, way too cute fae on the other side, there was a petite dark haired woman that looked enough like Nina to make my brain short circuit.

She smiled.

"Hello, Trisha. I'm your Aunt Wren. May I come in?"

CHAPTER TWO

Unintentionally, I blocked the door, dumbfounded.

She didn't care. She shoved right by me and moved inside, inspecting the entire crappy apartment. Once she noticed Starren, she zoned in on her, eyes narrowed.

I shut the door. "Uh... hi."

"Hi," Wren said, not taking her eyes off Starren. "Who's this?"

"That's... Starren." Something stopped me from adding my sister. This woman was a whirlwind, just like Nina. Only more forceful, if that was possible.

"Wren." She stuck out her hand toward Starren, watching her like she was trying to decide something.

"Nice to meet you," Starren said, moving from the couch to shake her hand. All of that TV was finally coming in handy. She actually knew how to act like a human. At least for the moment.

"It's really nice to meet you, finally, Trish." Wren's smile warmed my heart, something usually only Nina could do. But it dropped right away when I realized what was going on. Nina's little sister was here, in my apartment. Shoot.

"It's really nice to meet you too. Nina talks about you all the time." There was no use denying who I was. She totally knew.

"Speaking of my sister." Wren looked to me, to Starren, then zeroed back in on me. "How does she not know who you are?"

I let out a little, high-pitched giggle. "What do you mean?" Right to the point wasn't she? This was bad, so seriously bad. "Of course she knows who I am."

Wren stalked forward, and even though she was taller than Nina, she still had to look up at me. It certainly didn't feel like it. I could have been two feet tall, with how her look was taking me down at the moment.

"I don't like games, Trish. You're my niece, and because Nina loves you so much, I already love you like family even though we've never met. The problem I'm having at the moment is that every time Nina and I've talked in the last month and a half, you haven't come up. Before it was Trish this, Trish that, which I loved to hear about, but not anymore. So I asked her."

She started to pace a little, never turning her back fully on Starren. "I asked my sister how my niece was doing. And do you know what she said?"

I just stared at her, assuming it was a rhetorical question. She didn't move on with her questions. "No, ma'am," I squeaked out. Was this how Nina would be without her giant streak of kindness? All forceful? Or had whatever military job Wren had made her like this? I didn't know enough about her. Nina didn't even really know what she did, only that it was top secret, and that she was based just north of Chicago.

She stopped, right in front of me, dead still. "She said, 'who's Trish?' Who's Trish? Who is the person she has been gushing over for the last two years? Been planning her life around? You can see how I found this to be a problem."

Her combat boots thudded back and forth across the floor as I scrambled to find some type of explanation. There wasn't one.

"So I called Dan. My sister isn't one for pranks, so I was worried. But do you know what Dan said?" She paused in front of me, not even blinking as she stared. "He said, 'who's Trish?' And I suddenly got a bad, bad feeling. I don't like bad feelings." She stuck a thumb out toward Starren. "Now do you want to tell me who this really is? Because she is giving off some really strange vibes."

Ah, no, I did not want to tell her who that was. My panicked gaze went to Starren, waiting for her to interject and trying to tell her to stop the predator waiting to attack attitude.

"Can I just talk with her for a second?" I asked Wren. "You can have a seat on the couch." I didn't give her time to answer. I rushed forward and hauled Starren into the attached kitchen by force.

"What are we going to do?" I whispered. Somehow so far we'd been able to keep things under wraps while searching for an answer to the Dan and Nina problem. So much for that. "And you have to dial it down. She's already on high alert and you're just making it worse."

Starren was looking over my shoulder at Wren, who had not sat down, but was at least leaning against the couch.

"We're going to have to take care of her."

"Of course we are, she's Nina's sister. What do I say to get her to go away?"

Starren glanced at me and rolled her eyes before staring Wren down again. "That's not the kind of care I meant."

Not the kind of.. oh. Oh! "We can't kill Nina's sister!" I hissed.

She cocked her head. "I get the sense from her that it will be difficult. But with both of us, we'll be fine. Especially if we can lure her just out of the city limits. She wouldn't see it coming when the trees ripped her apart."

I grabbed Starren's shoulders and gave her a little shake. "We are not killing Nina's sister."

Finally she actually looked at me.

"Why not?"

"Because Nina loves her, for one, and for two it's horrible to just kill people! She might be a good person."

"No one is just good."

"Nina is."

She didn't argue with me on that one. Either because she knew it was true, or because she knew I'd throw a fit if she tried to tell me otherwise. Dan and Nina had only ever been patient and kind with me, even traveling to a foreign world full of monsters to help me save my sister. Another reason she couldn't really argue, since she was that sister.

"Fine, maybe a few people. But we don't know that this is one."

"We aren't killing her," I ground out. "Promise."

Starren stared down at me for a second. "I won't hurt her unless she tries to cause someone else harm."

It wasn't a full on promise, but it was as good as I was going to get at the moment, and eventually Wren was going to get tired of standing around in our musty apartment.

"What can we tell her?"

"Nothing but the truth. I'll be able to tell otherwise." I spun around to face Wren. She still leaned against the couch like she hadn't just admitted to eavesdropping. Had she heard the whole conversation? Surely not, I'd just been a bit loud on that last part.

I stuffed my hands into the pockets of my jeans, my shoulders hunching in. I couldn't tell her anything but the truth, or nothing at all. No fae could. But the truth was something I didn't tell anyone. Even Nina had found out the hard way. Talk about traumatic, seeing your sixteen-year-old daughter get shot in the gut with an arrow. And the nearly instant healing after may have been almost as bad.

"How about we order some pizza?" I asked. "We haven't had supper." I sent her a somewhat sickly smile.

"Or she could just leave," Starren said. "We aren't obligated to tell her anything."

I looked hopefully at Wren, who shoved off the couch with her hip.

"If I leave here, I'm going straight over to talk to Nina. I'm going through everything she has, and I'm figuring this out myself. I can't think of anything other than a head injury that could make a person forget something this important, and I find it really unlikely that both Dan and Nina had something like that happen, and they both just by chance forgot the same super important thing." Her eyebrows went up.

"Oh no, don't do that. Please don't do that." Her going over to Dan and Nina's and digging around could turn into a disaster. The food they'd eaten in Faerie had slowly started erasing any memories that pertained to the fae after the first bite, until there was nothing left. Not even me. It wasn't their fault they didn't remember. It was mine.

That hope wormed its way back in. The hope I kept trying to get rid of. Maybe if she went over and poked around, it would make them start thinking. Make them remember... something. Anything about me.

I crushed that worm under a ton of rocks. Rebecca had tried that. They hardly remembered her, with her connection to so many fae. She'd lost the only friend she had here, working her way back to where she was now with Nina. Friends, but only kind of.

My father had taken so much from me. From all of us. I tried to shove down the anger, but it bubbled its way to the surface so easily anymore. I wanted to hate him. But I wouldn't let myself.

"Oh, I've already been there. Three days, in fact. I've been very subtle so far, but that's about to end. I followed you home from school today. Sat out in the freezing cold while you were at that other apartment building. I was about to knock on their door and have this talk with you there, but then you came out and I followed you again, until we ended up here."

Ouch, that could have been bad, her confronting me in front of Jaden, Rebecca, Jaime, and yuck, Lucy.

Starren crossed her arms and scooted in front of me. "We don't have to tell you anything."

What was the worst that could happen? She could go and talk to Dan and Nina, and they would tell her they didn't know any Trisha's. I swallowed down the lump in my throat that thought brought up. They'd already been telling her that.

Wren shrugged. "True. I'll just be on my way then. Maybe Nina has regained some of that memory by now." She turned and headed for the door, opening it a crack. "And if not, I can always talk to Child Protective Services. Someone there will know something."

"No, wait!" I darted around Starren. "You can't do that to them! It isn't their fault!"

She turned back, honing in on my face. "Not their fault? Then whose fault is it?"

Crap. I internally scrambled for an answer, but didn't come up with anything convincing.

"Don't lie to me, Trish." She cocked her head. "If you even can."

I took a step back like I'd been physically hit by something. "What's that supposed to mean?" It came out weak. Stupid, stupid.

"Now will you let me take her out?" Starren asked.

Wren smiled, but it wasn't a joyful smile. More like a villain in a movie, getting what they wanted. "I'll leave if you answer one question for me."

That should be an easy request. Should. Then why did it freak me out so much?

She didn't wait for me to say yes or no.

"Are you fully human?"

Starren snarled and went for her sword. I grabbed her arm and pulled her back. Wren had better stop baiting her. Honestly it was kind of amazing she'd made it this long without murdering anyone, and I'd really like to keep the streak up.

"What are you talking about?" I asked. "What is there other than human?"

Wren shoved the door closed and leaned on it. "You tell me."

I shrugged my shoulders helplessly, like I had no idea what she was talking about. But she knew about the lying thing. Why was I keeping it from her? Maybe she could help. She was Nina's sister, Nina trusted her.

I'd never told anyone before. I didn't even know how to go about doing that. My mom had put a stop to me telling anyone for no reason. But if a person already knew... I tamped down the terror that jumped to the forefront whenever I thought of anyone finding out, of people knowing. Nina hadn't told her. Was that because she didn't trust her, or because she wanted to let me decide who to tell, and who to leave in the dark?

If I did tell her, I would be making the decision for an entire race, not just for myself. That didn't seem fair.

But Dan and Nina. I would do anything for Dan and Nina. I looked at Starren, and she glared back, tight lips, giving a sharp no with her head.

"Maybe she can help us. She's like a soldier or something. Nina wasn't ever very specific."

"That's even worse," Starren hissed, low under her breath.

"Nothing to see here."

"We're fae."

We both blurted completely different sentences out at the same time. Typical for us to be on total opposite sides of every single thing we came across.

"She's crazy," Starren said. "Doesn't know what she's talking about." She glared at me for a second, then went back to studying Wren.

"Fae?" Wren asked. Her posture had stiffened. She looked every inch a soldier at the moment. "What exactly does that mean?"

"Great job." Starren threw up her hands. "Now we really do have to kill her. This is your fault. I haven't had to kill anyone in awhile."

"Shut up, Star." I sent Wren a weak smile. "She doesn't really mean that." I went back to Starren. "You can't hurt her, even if you want to. I am not giving you permission. At all."

Starren smirked. "I don't need it. I'm saving your life."

"Wren, do you mean me or Starren physical harm?" I asked.

Wren looked at me like I was crazy. "No."

"Humans can lie," Starren said.

I hated it when Starren was right. She always sounded so smug. "Beside the point that she may not want to cause us harm, but if she goes around and blurts that out to anyone, we will come to harm anyway. I guarantee it."

"She doesn't have any proof."

"Can I stop you both there?" Wren asked. "Part of my job is dealing with weird. You got the right person here." Her hand had gone behind her back, and she was standing in an exaggeratedly easy stance.

"I don't care what your job is. I don't trust you." Without even looking, Starren leapt over to the couch and slid across the wood floor beside it, coming out on the other end with her sword. She lunged toward Wren.

But it was too late. Wren already had a gun in her hand. She raised it as Starren went into the air, sword up.

"No!" I screamed, jumping between them.

Much too late. The crack of a weapon firing sounded first. And yep, there it was. Pain ripped its way through my shoulder. I really needed to stop doing this.

CHAPTER THREE

Whyyyy. Why did this always happen?

"You've got to be kidding me," I ground out. First time for everything, this time I'd been shot in the shoulder.

I gritted my teeth and moaned.

"Oh crap, Nina's going to kill me." Wren dropped down beside me on the floor where I'd been knocked flat. She put pressure on my wound, making me hiss in pain.

"You shot my sister," Starren growled.

"It'll be fine, it'll heal," I said.

"Looks like it passed through your subclavian artery," Wren said as she examined the wound, blood flowing much faster than I'd have liked. "We need to get you in, you could bleed to death."

"You shot my sister!" Starren said, even louder.

"Not now, Star. Get me out." I didn't have to explain. She knew what I meant. I managed to sit up, woozy.

"You," Starren spit out in Wren's direction. "Do you have a car?"

"Yes, but an ambulance would be faster." Her phone didn't even make it to a 1 in 911 before Starren knocked it out of her hand with the tip of her sword.

"Car."

"Please, Aunt Wren," I said.

She looked between us, but grabbed her phone and slipped under my shoulder on my good side.

Starren ran to the kitchen and grabbed a couple towels, then moved up on the other side to keep me from keeling over.

Deep breaths. In through the nose, out through the mouth. You'd think I'd be used to this by now.

We got to the car with only a few waves of nausea blasting me. Apparently this non-mortal wound didn't bother my body nearly as much as it was bothering me.

They shoved me into a small dark vehicle and Starren jumped in the back with me. Aunt Wren got in the front and started the car.

"We need to get her outside of the city limits." Somehow Starren still had her sword. "Just start driving."

"Wouldn't a hospital be better?" Wren asked.

"Drive," Starren growled, sliding her sword up where Wren could see it.

"Great plan, Star. I'm sure she tossed her gun back at the apartment." I groaned as the car lurched forward, but didn't even feel like passing out. Yes, this was definitely much better than a gut shot.

"That was stupid," Starren said, whacking me lightly in the side of the head.

"Hey! Not like I'm not in enough pain already."

"You wouldn't be if you hadn't jumped in front of that shot."

"I wasn't even going to hit her," Wren said from up front. "That was just a warning shot."

"You wouldn't have hit me," Starren snarled. "And you wouldn't have had time for a second shot."

"Shut up, both of you. This is what got us in this situation in the first place." I adjusted my weight, trying to find a comfortable position. There wasn't one.

Both women went into guilty silence. "We're going to get this taken care of, and then I'll need something to eat, then we're going to talk. Like civilized people." The blood started to drip through the towel compress. "Sorry about your car, Aunt Wren."

"It's okay, sweetie, and you can just call me Wren."

"Okay." I closed my eyes for a second, the world spinning a bit. Not a problem. All this would be gone in a few minutes when we crossed the border. "You ready for this, Star?" I asked with my eyes still closed. "I really don't want to cross the line, but a hospital isn't an option."

Her hand gripped my good arm, for just a second. "You know I'm always ready for anything."

I didn't even know for sure what I was asking her if she was ready for. For Wren to see me heal? For us to cross the border? Were there fae out there, waiting for us? Father wanted me. Bad. With the way he'd tried to keep me in Faerie before and the few things Starren would say about him, I had no doubt he'd take me by force if he had the chance.

I felt it. The second we crossed the town line.

"That's good," I grunted out.

"Turn the car around and pull over," Starren told Wren. "We need to be as close to the city limits as possible."

Wren threw us an odd look, but obeyed.

I leaned against Starren while my skin knit back together, the stupid black floaters going across my vision. Apparently I'd lost more blood than I'd thought.

It took a moment, but the pain lessened until it was gone. I heaved a breath and poked at my arm. "All good." I looked up to see Wren staring at my arm, acting like she was about to climb into the back seat. "We better get out of here before someone notices we left-"

Bam. The car rocked.

"Great," Starren said.

The car rocked again, so hard the sides bounced off the ground.

"There's a human here, they aren't supposed to do this in front of humans!" I instinctively cradled my arm, but no pain.

"Get us back inside the city limits!" Starren shouted.

A light flashed outside, and there he was. Mister gorgeous. Bounty hunter Vilan. I hadn't seen him since he'd tried to stop us from leaving Jaden's place in California, months ago. Had he been after me this whole time?

"Move, Human," Starren said, poking at Wren with the dull side of her sword. "Get us out of here."

But Wren couldn't. She was mesmerized, the same way I'd been the first time I'd seen him. Part of his powers.

I reached forward and slapped her.

She jerked and grabbed her cheek. "What was that for?"

I didn't get a chance to answer. The car screeched and began to crumple. Starren instinctively shoved her door open just in time before the frame was too distorted for it to work properly.

I scooted over and she pulled me out.

Wren was not so lucky. Her door wouldn't budge, a piece of crushed bumper wrapped over it.

"Go through the back!" I pounded on her window. "Star, help her!"

Starren just watched.

I growled and shoved the back door open more, jumping in, fighting a bout of dizziness. Wren hadn't moved.

"My leg is pinned," she said, sounding totally calm. "Get out, it'll be fine. You help my sister with whatever's going on."

Uh, no. Nina would kill me if she knew I'd let her sister die. Okay, she'd probably never know, and okay, she wouldn't kill me, she'd just be glad I wasn't dead too, but still.

I stuck my head back out of the car. It had gone eerily quiet out here, and there wasn't any too bright men around. Worry about that when it became a problem. "Give me your sword," I told Starren.

Her eyes went into slits. "Are you finishing the human?"

I didn't answer, just held out my hand.

"I won't have anything to defend us with. We should go." She followed up saying that with a look around our perimeter.

"I'm not going anywhere until you give me that sword."

The car lurched a bit, and the grinding noise of it compressing wailed out into the night. He was pulling it toward where we'd seen him for a second.

"Shoot." I grabbed Starren's sword out of her hand and dove back into the car. "Here!" I shoved it at Wren.

Thankfully she seemed to know what I had in mind and didn't try to cut her leg off. She jammed the sword under the console, using it as leverage to move the plastic just enough, crying out as she pulled her leg free.

I grabbed her under her arms and yanked her into the back seat, right as the hood of the car mangled into a clump of twisted metal. Somehow she didn't lose her grip on the sword as we tumbled out of what was left of the vehicle.

Starren wrenched the sword from Wren's hand, and then pulled me to my feet.

The only sound in the night was the screeching of metal as the car turned into a ball of junk.

I reached for Wren and helped her to her feet. "We just need to get over the city limit."

It was farther than I'd expected. The car had moved quite a distance during its destruction. Wren struggled to walk beside me. I dragged her as quickly as possible.

A howl started up in the trees around us. Not a normal howl. I shivered. "What's that?" I asked Starren, working hard to keep the panic out of my voice.

"Get over the border, now."

We rushed forward even more quickly.

Two beasts burst out of the darkness, their eyes bright glowing white, bodies black and feathery. Dogish, but way too big.

Reflexively, I begged the trees for help. Branches lashed around the creatures to hold them in place, but withered and died the instant they touched the beasts.

"Death hounds," Starren panted out. "This was well planned."

I hardly blinked and they were between us and the border.

Wren's gulping breaths and Starren's little swishes with her sword were all I could hear over the hammering of my heart.

"Kill the other two. Leave the tree girl alive." The voice was breathy on the wind, sending an extra couple shivers down my spine. I shuffled Wren and Starren behind me, using myself as a shield. No one would die before I did, unless it was that stupid bounty hunter or his evil dogs.

"You two go. I'm immune to magic." Starren pushed around me. "I'll probably be fine."

"Probably?" my voice squeaked. "Even if those things didn't have magic, you 'probably' wouldn't be coming out on top."

A yip sounded from the right. I knew that yip. Storm came bounding toward us, rushing at the creatures who had started to advance. He didn't even weigh a tenth of what they did. Even though he was a big dog, he looked like the kind that people hauled around in their purse compared to the others.

"No, go back!" I yelled. There was nothing he could do, he'd just die for no reason.

But I was wrong. As soon as he leapt across the border, his body instantly changed. He morphed into a... dragon?

"What is that?" Wren asked, sounding very much like she wanted to vomit. I was with her on that.

"My dog?" I half asked.

"What?" Starren said. "That's not a dog. It's a dragon."

"Obviously, but he's a dog most of the time!" I'd been feeding a dragon this whole time? No wonder he was never full.

Starren just stood there, face blank. "Dragons haven't been seen in two hundred years."

Well yeah, the fae were awful, of course they didn't want to be seen.

Storm spewed out a stream of fire, and both dogs yelped. He'd grown when he'd changed, but he still was far out of his weight class. His deep gold scales winked in the light of the flames he spewed.

The heat warmed me down to my toes, and I stood spellbound as he swooped at the hounds.

"Don't touch them!" I screamed.

"He can fend for himself," Wren said, and jerked me forward with surprising force for a small, injured lady. "Let's get over that stupid border."

She was taking all this weird pretty well. If I'd had time, I'd have been impressed.

We scooted as a trio around the three beasts. One of the death hounds peeled its lips back and spit at Storm. The spit hit the ground and sizzled. Acid? We sprinted away, making a break for the city limits. The stench of burning earth was a great motivator to get out of the way, the clash of dragon and dog creating a din loud enough I couldn't hear myself pant.

I knew when we'd made it. Everything that made me special, made me fae, left my body. The extra spark of energy was gone. That part I missed. But I didn't care much for the fae, the reminder that I was one could stay gone as far as I was concerned.

Speaking of concern. As soon as we were safe I whirled around. Fire flashed, lighting up the sky for a second. That meant he was still alive, unless the hounds could do that too.

"Storm!" I screamed into the dark.

Starren gripped my shoulder, trying to drag me from the border, but I would have none of it. I fought back.

"Storm!"

"We can't wait," Wren said, moving in front of me. Kudos to her, there was a touch of sympathy in her voice. "We need to get somewhere safe."

"We are somewhere safe," I said, brushing her out of my way. "They can't touch us here."

Wren's gaze whipped from me, back to the brawl going on not nearly far enough away, and back to me. "Can't touch us here? Are you crazy? We're only like a hundred feet away!"

"Feet mean nothing to me. We are safe." Wow. Maybe all that TV wasn't helping Starren as much as I'd thought.

"There's a border here at the city limit. They can't hurt us once we're inside. All good."

Wren pursed her lips, looking decidedly unconvinced.

Ignoring her, I tiptoed as close to the line as I could without crossing it. "Storm, come back, we're safe!" The shrieking and screeching continued. "I'm going back for him."

I barely made it over the line before two very different hands dragged me back.

"Don't make me knock you unconscious," Starren said. The threat was real. She sounded bored. Whenever that happened, watch out.

I gestured helplessly toward the puffs of fire. "I can't do anything this side of the line. If something happens to him, I'll never forgive myself."

The words were barely out of my mouth when everything around us went silent. Completely silent. If any animals had been stupid enough to stick around, they at least were smart enough to not announce their presence now.

"Storm?" I whisper-yelled. "Storm?" My voice was starting to go up. I couldn't lose him too. I couldn't live through that.

And then, movement to the left, in the dark. Starren's sword went up and Wren tensed. She must have lost her gun.

Storm trotted toward us in his normal dog form. Actually, which would be considered normal? I didn't know. I didn't care. I dropped to my knees and clutched him tight to my body, even with him being more mangy than normal.

"You're such a brave boy!" I shoved him away and glared into his eyes. "Don't you ever do that again. You could have gotten hurt." How much could he understand? I didn't know, but he definitely knew I wasn't happy. "Thank you."

"It really was her dog," Wren said to no one, sounding a little out of it. She had taken a lot in over the last twenty minutes. Who could blame her?

"Let's go. We have a long walk," Starren said.

All three of us looked towards the remains of Wren's car. There wasn't much left. Sirens sounded in the distance.

"Even more reason to go," Starren added. "Let's get out of here."

"I could call…" I thought about Wren being here and changed my mind. She didn't need to know about Jaden. Not yet, anyway, not until we figured out if she could be trusted or not. "Never mind."

Yep, super sneaky. No way she caught that. Okay, I was really bad at this stuff.

"Never mind it is," Wren said briskly. She brushed her hands off on her pants. "Girls. Let's get back to your apartment. We have a lot to talk about, and I want to do it somewhere a little more comfortable."

"A little?" I asked, insulted.

She gave a firm nod. "A little."

CHAPTER FOUR

The walk back to the apartment was quiet. And cold. None of us had taken the time to grab winter clothing when we'd left the apartment earlier. We had been in a bit of a hurry.

Storm escorted us all of the way to the apartment building. But, per usual, he stopped outside and wouldn't enter.

Wren eyed him warily, and kept me between us. She'd shown her protective side, so apparently she just thought he wouldn't hurt me. She was right.

"You're such a good boy," I crooned at him. "Don't you want to come in? Come on, you can do it. No way Starren can say no after what you just did for us."

She rolled her eyes and crossed her arms, but didn't say no.

He walked with a slight limp, and had patches of singed hair, but seemed in over all good health. More than I could say we would have been if he hadn't shown up. I shivered, remembering how the tree branches had jumped to my aid, but hadn't been able to do a thing. Starren and Wren would have died tonight if he hadn't gotten there just in time. And I would be on the way to Faerie right now, about to visit my super villain father.

I scratched him under his chin in one of his favorite spots, and he nearly groaned in joy.

"Why haven't you shown me that side of you before?" I asked.

He cocked his head, but of course, no answer. Looked like dragons couldn't speak any more than dogs could. Had he come through a portal? He had to have right? How had he gotten through? Could he change back and forth from a dog to a dragon on a whim, or did it just happen when he crossed out of Sanctuary? I wished I could ask him.

"Let's get in where it's warm," Wren said.

Storm let his tongue hang out for a second, then tore off into the night, like there was something out there only he could hear.

Maybe there was.

I watched until he was gone. Partially because I always worried about him, and the other part because I really, really didn't want to have this whole conversation with Wren.

She hadn't run screaming yet, that was something.

But would she put up with the weird as well as Nina did? She'd seen a whole lot of weird tonight. And a good chunk of that weird had been me. Twinges of old fears hit me right in the gut. What if she wouldn't accept me for who I was? What if she thought I was a freak?

To humans, I was a freak. Something so different from them, it could hardly be understood.

But so far, the humans that had found out had still looked at me as me first, not fae. Trish me. Stupid, mouthy teen, Trisha. Not heal quick, command plants Mareena, or whatever my dad had called me.

Rebecca, Dan, Nina. They hadn't cared that I was fae. Would Wren?

My shoulders slumped as I moved to the front door and paused. I couldn't be lucky this many times. Wren hadn't called the cops on us, or shot us or anything. Well, hadn't shot us because she found out, the shooting had really been unrelated.

I hoped. I mean, I had said 'we're fae,' right before she shot at us, but I was going to choose to believe it had been Starren running at her with a sword that had caused her aggression, not what I'd told her.

She's Nina's sister. She's cool. My pep talk didn't help my mood much. What if she'd hit some secret button on her watch like in Supergirl, and now all her military buddies were on the way to grab us and drag us off somewhere? There was no going back to her not knowing with everything she'd just seen.

She'd kept it together surprisingly well. Definitely better than Nina had. But then, Nina was a lot more attached to me than Wren was, so watching me get hit by an arrow had probably been more traumatic.

What was worse than this? At the moment I'd almost throw myself out of a window to get away. Might not work out so well in Sanctuary though, I'd just get carted back over the border, putting Starren at risk again.

We got into the apartment. Starren was last, closed the door behind us and leaned on it. "Okay, human. Spill. What are your plans for us?"

I was tired enough at the moment that the addition of spill almost made me giggle. It sounded so foreign coming from Starren's mouth.

Wren held her hands up. "I don't have enough information to have a plan at the moment. How about we sit and talk about all this?"

Starren glowered from the doorway. Talking wasn't her strong suit, by a long shot.

"Sure." I gestured toward the old, smelly couch. "Have a seat."

She did, watching us out of the corner of her eye the whole time.

I followed, but sat on the floor in front of the TV. Starren came and stood beside me, leaving Wren with the entire couch to herself.

"So, how about we switch off who asks questions?" Wren asked, her tone so bright it sounded fake. Not a good plan. Starren didn't like fake.

"Okay," I answered. "How did you know about the lying thing?"

"I didn't, not for sure." She settled into the couch, grimaced, and sat back forward. "Nina slipped up once and said something about it being nice her teen couldn't lie to her. She brushed it off really well and I didn't think anything of it at the time, but once they started acting weird I went back through all of our conversations in my mind and wrote down anything strange that had come up. Around you, it's a lot of quiet, or a lot of weird. Like why they suddenly wanted to move to Fort Wayne. I have the answer to that question now. How exactly does all this work with you being safe inside the city limits? You're sure we're safe here? Nina and Dan are safe? Who was that guy, and why was he trying to kill you?"

"Too many questions," Starren grumbled. But her voice sounded better, a little more at ease. The fact that Wren was handling safety issues first probably made Starren feel like maybe the human wasn't so bad.

"Okay, then," Wren said. "Are we totally safe here?"

"Yes," I answered. "It's called Sanctuary, and there's no violence allowed."

"Our turn," Starren butted in. "Do you intend to tell anyone what you saw tonight?"

"What would you do if I said yes?"

Starren leaned forward, eyes slits. "You have to answer my question before you get another question."

"At this moment I don't intend to tell anyone. I wouldn't put my niece at risk." Her eyebrow went up. "But if I find out that you did something to Dan and Nina, or that you don't care about them and have been using them this whole time, you're going to wish I hadn't seen all that." She relaxed a little and smiled. "I trust Nina's judgement, even though sometimes she is a little too forgiving. I just wanted to get that out there."

Starren relaxed against the wall a little. Apparently Wren's honesty even when she didn't have to be honest meant something to her. The fae were a very deceitful people. Every time I thought about the days we'd spent in Faerie, I disliked my kind more.

"How does Sanctuary work?"

"There are Sanctuary cities scattered around the earth, where fae powers do not work and fae aren't allowed to harm each other," Starren answered when I didn't. "This is one of them."

Wren cocked her head. "How many cities?"

Starren started to answer.

"Wait, nope, I'll circle back to that, I don't want to waste my question," Wren said. "But you hurry up and ask yours, I have a lot more I want to know about this whole situation."

"Dan and Nina are safe," I interrupted. "You shouldn't have to use a question for that."

Starren sent me a withering look.

"They are perfectly fine, they just forgot everything in their life that has anything to do with Faerie." I teared up, the hot tears warming my still chilled face. "Including me."

"Oh, honey," Wren jumped forward and pulled me into a tight hug. It felt so much like Nina's, the strength, the warmth, that it just made the tears start to flow.

Starren stepped away, looking incredibly uncomfortable.

Wren held me close until I got myself together, even pretending not to see the snot stain on her still-perfect-after-a-car-accident-and-terrified-getaway jacket. Well, used to be perfect, until a minute ago.

She leaned back, squatting close enough to pull me back in if needed.

"How did it happen?"

"They ate food. In Faerie. It affects humans to differing degrees," Starren said.

"In Faerie?" Wren looked shook. More shook than when we'd been running for our lives from demon dogs who spit acid.

"Wait, the food affects humans to differing degrees?" I asked. "How do you know that? You didn't know that before." All my attention was on Starren now. She wouldn't meet my eyes, kicking backward at the wall a little. "Starren?"

"Well, I told you I might have someone who can help. I've been looking into things. For you."

I jumped off the floor and got all up in her space. "And?"

"Can we talk about this later?" She did a little head boop toward Wren. Yeah, good excuse, but it wasn't going to fly.

"No."

She still avoided my gaze.

"And?"

"I couldn't find out much, because it hasn't been used much. But I'm sure that the guy I told you about will be able to point us in the right direction. I talked about the whole thing with a friend and was assured that our trip wouldn't be for nothing. If, and this is a big if, he knows anything, we wouldn't have to go back into Faerie."

I whooped and jumped at her, grappling her into a hug that she would pretend she didn't want, but was getting anyway. And ignoring the fact that she hadn't mentioned any of this earlier when we were talking. We had been interrupted.

"How do we get a hold of him? Is he near? Does he have a phone? Please tell me he has a phone."

"No such luck. We'd have to travel. Outside of Sanctuary."

Ouch. I stepped back and plopped onto the couch, back in the pit of despair. I would do anything for Dan and Nina. But tonight had quickly proven that leaving Sanctuary was a really, really bad idea. Nina would kill me if I died. And if she knew who I was.

"What are we going to do, Star," I whispered.

"Hey," she came over and sat down beside me. "At least he isn't in Faerie. He's somewhere you know." She smiled. "The Fae Distribution Center."

The Fae Distribution Center? I hadn't even known she'd heard me call it that. "So we just have to make it to D.C.?"

"Yes, not nearly as bad as trying to get back into Faerie."

The wild swing of emotions was on its way back up. D.C. We could do D.C. We just needed a plan.

"As in Washington D.C.?" Wren asked.

Starren just fluttered a hand at her like she wasn't worth answering.

"Yes," I said. "We used to live there."

Wren rolled her eyes. "Yes, I know. But there's all this fae weirdness going on, I wanted to make sure that D.C. didn't stand for Distribution Center."

Oh. Well that did make sense.

"No. There's an access point to a tunnel in D.C."

Starren kicked me and glared.

I shrugged at her. There was no point in keeping things from Wren now. It was extremely unlikely, but maybe she could help in some way. In for a penny, in for a pound as Dan would say. He liked all that weird old stuff.

"Nina went to Faerie?" Wren asked. Oops. I hadn't really answered her when she asked basically the same thing a minute ago. "Nina, my big sister, Faerie."

"Yes." I flapped a hand toward Starren. "She was in trouble and I tried to sneak away to go and help her. That didn't go over well."

"I bet not."

I waited for her to connect the dots that it was my fault Dan and Nina had gone to Faerie in the first place, and therefore my fault that they'd forgotten me. But either she didn't think that or she was too nice to say it. She seemed pretty smart, so I was going to go with too nice.

"I'm in. We have to do something. Nina's giving all your stuff away right now."

Tears instantly refilled my eyes, but I smashed down the feelings trying to ride in my chest.

"She knows she had a foster daughter, and a foster son, but she doesn't remember any specifics," Wren said. "It was very disconcerting. Where is Cray, anyway? The way Nina talked he was practically adopted too."

"Staying with friends." I didn't tell her the Martan's. I didn't know if she knew who they were or not.

Wren's leg jiggled a little. "I'm going to head back to Nina's. She's going to think I died. My cell phone was in the car, I'm sure it didn't make it. I need to make a few calls, but I also need to know you girls aren't going anywhere." She gave me a pointed look, and then Starren. "Promise you aren't leaving for D.C. without me."

I crossed my arms in front of my chest. "That's not fair. You don't understand what you're asking. What if you get hit by a car tonight? Or your appendix bursts? Or your job calls you back to wherever you live, and you can't come with us? We just wouldn't be able to go."

She considered that for a moment. "Okay. Promise me you won't leave until nine a.m. tomorrow. That should give me plenty of time to set things up with work and Nina."

Starren laughed. It wasn't a nasty laugh, like normal, so be thankful for small blessings. "We have no reason to promise you this. We can leave whenever we want."

"Oh, but you do. I can get you to D.C. safely. Trisha said back at the 'accident,'" she threw in air quotes, "that you weren't supposed to be attacked with a human around. I'll go with you, make sure everyone actually knows I'm a human this time, and voila."

Oh, she was good. "We don't need you, but thanks," I said. Nina would hate me if I got her sister killed.

Starren studied her. How was she not shooting this down right away? "Do you have access to another vehicle?"

Well. This was not what I'd been expecting, but should have been. Starren was very practical, and didn't mind using others to get what she needed.

"No," I said. "She doesn't."

"Yes," Wren corrected. "I do. I'm going to see this through. I hate seeing my sister how she is right now, and I want it fixed. Asap."

I mean, yeah, me too. But hadn't she seen enough weird tonight to be done?

"I can rent a car, or borrow one from a friend in the area. Are we doing this? Leaving in the morning? Is there a way we can make sure they know I'm human?"

"They won't care about killing one human, so we need to be around many. Leaving in the morning would be safer," Starren said.

"Morning it is, then. We'll stay on super populated roads, and hide you two for the first hour of driving, just to be safe."

I groaned into a pillow. "Are you kidding me?" I glared at Starren. "You're just going to let her come?"

"Yeah, and about all that earlier," Wren said. "Nice you can heal like that." She nodded toward Starren. "Can you too?"

Starren lifted an eyebrow but didn't answer.

"Oh come on, I haven't run freaking out yet, you can't just answer my questions now?"

Starren took two precise steps forward, bending down, very much in Wren's space. "I'm allowing you to come because we need your vehicle. We don't need you. Remember that." She straightened up. "I could 'borrow' a car or truck, but then we'd have to deal with the human law enforcement, and it would waste our time. We need to be around humans as much as we can, not avoiding them. You're allowed to come, but I do not trust you. Will never trust you."

Wren shrugged. "I don't need you to trust me. Just work with me."

She bumped me. "You, on the other hand, are family, so we're going to work on this trust thing." She stood and stretched, then headed for the door with a slight limp. I'd forgotten she'd been injured. Hopefully it wasn't too bad. "I'll be back in the morning, eight o'clock. You'll still be here?"

Man, she was good. I could convince Starren to take Jaden's truck and go without Wren if she left without a promise, but I didn't want her knowing about the Martan's for some reason so I'd have to wait.

Starren nodded before I had a chance to stop her, and that was as binding as an oath. Shoot.

"Be ready," Wren said, and left.

"Ughhh." I dropped onto the couch. This was going to end badly. There was no other option. That was the only one that made sense. The last time we'd taken humans to Faerie, it had ended in disaster. Nina pretty much dying, me getting injured, and of course, Dan and Nina not even knowing who I was anymore. The only thing that could go worse was if someone did die. Permanently. I eyed my sister sideways, hoping she wouldn't notice. She was too lost in thought. How could I function without her? What if I lost her too? Was the risk/reward ratio good enough to go on this trip again? That's what Dan would ask me, if he knew what was going on.

I took a breath, fighting internally. I needed to calm down. We weren't going all the way into Faerie. Just the Fae Distribution Center, just a tunnel that led to Faerie from Earth. It wasn't nearly as bad as Faerie, I'd spent a lot of time there back in the fall learning about being fae from Cumat, and nothing had gone wrong.

How was Cumat anyway? Never thought I'd miss the dwarf, with all his rules and rituals. But it would be good to see him again.

Did that mean I was going? Sounded like it. How could I, when all I had left in this world would be at risk? How could I not, when I might be able to get my parents back?

I looked at Starren again. She was willing to do this for me. She didn't have anything to gain by helping. If she was willing to take the risk, then so was I. D.C., ready or not, here we come.

CHAPTER FIVE

Ugh, traveling was borinnnggg. I'd forgotten how boring. Sure, the first hour, passing through the city limits and getting away from Fort Wayne had been as far from boring as possible with how tense the entire car was, but the hours after? Ugh.

Apparently big, feathery, black, death hounds couldn't be out during the day without humans seeing them. Who knew.

The trip to D.C. was going to take even longer than it normally would, because we were sticking to only extremely large highways, and stopping only at huge truck stops.

I impatiently banged my leg against the seat in front of me, causing Star to throw a glare over her shoulder.

I glanced at my phone screen to check the time. Two minutes later than the last time I'd checked. Five hours down, a little more than five to go. We were far enough away at this point that I felt safe letting Jaden and Cray know I was going to be gone for a couple days.

Not telling them had been my first thought, but Cray would notice I wasn't at school, and the first thing he'd do was call Jaden. I'd be so dead. I would probably still be dead for leaving without them, but hopefully less dead.

Wren had called the school pretending to be Nina earlier and told them I was sick. She'd been very convincing. Good thing humans could lie. We didn't need the school calling Nina to tell her that her daughter was skipping and her saying what daughter. That might not turn out well.

We pulled into a gas station. It was one of those huge ones, with semis blowing past, cars flowing all around us. I jumped out of the car Wren had borrowed from 'someone' and dodged a couple other vehicles as they went past, making my way into the convenience store.

Getting away from Wren and all her questions for a couple minutes would be nice. No, I hadn't known Storm was a dragon. No, I didn't know where he'd went, he did this often. No, he wasn't going to eat anyone. I assumed.

The shelves of snack food practically called to me as I went by them. Now that we were out of Sanctuary, my natural need for extra food was back in full force. I pushed it down though. Starren and I were on a strict budget. Things like chips and candy bars definitely weren't on it.

I used the restroom real quick and took an extra second to stretch before heading back to the car. My muscles healed instantly, so I didn't really get sore sitting around, but my brain kept telling me I should be. Look at that. I'd been human long enough to develop new thought patterns.

Wren gave a little wave as she passed me, headed for the bathroom.

A man watched our short interaction intently, then went back to studying the back of a Hershey bar when he noticed me noticing him. Weirdo.

A woman checking out at the counter studiously avoided looking at me, even when I said excuse me to get around her. Okay, maybe the guy wasn't just a weirdo. Something was up.

I paused, panicking a little. Did I go grab Wren, or did I run to Star?

It would be pretty obvious I'd caught on to them if I went back to the bathroom. I continued to the door, ducking my head a little. Stupid. They already knew it was me, why was I doing that?

I jogged back to the car. Starren was doing stretches outside the passenger side door, oblivious to the fact she was almost causing accidents as cars passed.

I grabbed her by the shoulder and nodded toward the woman who'd followed me out of the gas station. The man wasn't far behind.

"Two more, watching from the blue car two pumps over," Starren answered. "Get in the driver's side. You have your permit, it won't look out of place."

I did as she said, she was the tactical one. We could pull up to the door and be waiting when Wren came out.

She jumped in beside me and shut her door a little harder than was necessary in this nicer vehicle. "Get us out on the road."

"Uh, what?" I asked, starting the car. "How will Wren be able to find us?"

"She won't. This solves two problems at once. We don't want her knowing where the tunnel access point is, and we don't want to wait on her. Go."

Both very good points. Plus, I didn't want her getting hurt. "What if they do something to her?"

"They won't. She doesn't know enough to matter to them. She's far safer without us than with. They can't just take her from a place like this without anyone noticing, and they don't have a solid reason to anyway."

It made sense. My stomach ached at the thought of leaving Wren behind, but what Starren had said about her being safer without us? Yeah, I totally believed that. Humans and fae did not mix well. With a few very important exceptions.

I started the car and put it in drive, easing out into the parking lot. We were to the stop sign that went out onto the road before I saw Wren come out of the store in the rear-view mirror.

She looked to where our car had been, glanced around the parking lot, and then got angry. She yelled something and ran toward us.

"Go, go!" Starren said. "Get us out of here before she draws too much attention."

I floored it and the car lurched forward. Nice car, yes, sports car, no, which was probably a good thing.

We made it the short distance up the road to the highway on ramp in record time. I panicked. "I don't know about this, Starren."

"You drove on the way to Colorado when you were coming to Faerie to save me, Jaden told me."

I couldn't take my eyes off the road even for a second to check her expression. Was she trying to be encouraging?

"Yeah, that was a whole lot different than this. No traffic where I was driving. No traffic, Starren!"

"Breathe. You got this. You've done far greater things."

She *was* trying to be encouraging. What was happening to the world? But I did as she said, prying each finger from the steering wheel and putting it right back, just with less of a death grip.

"You're going to have to go, Trish!" Starren said, looking out the back window. "They won't be far behind."

"Since when do fae have cars?" I asked, strangling the steering wheel again.

"Stupid question. Jaden has a truck, Wade had a truck, all the fae you've known on Earth have had vehicles."

True, but those weren't normal circumstances. I floored the pedal and cut around one of those big fancy cars. *Sorry*, I mouthed to the old lady driving it as we went by. She glared, then went back to concentrating on the road.

"Take this exit." Starren grabbed my arm and we swerved toward an off ramp.

"Why? We're getting away!"

"They'll expect us to be on this road, especially if Wren talks. We can't let them drive us into an area that has few humans, but we need to try something."

"And what if they have a Cray?" Cray could sense fae energy, and if he knew someone, could track them down pretty well. His ability was rare, but there had to be more of him out there somewhere.

"We'll deal with that if it happens. As of last month, Father had been desperately trying to replace Cray, with no luck. We're going to assume that's where we're at now. Prioritize threats we know are active."

I blew out a breath. That made sense. We were doing fine.

Until a dark SUV swerved across traffic and went up the ramp after us.

I gunned the little car until it was whining, flew over the road and right back down onto the highway using the on ramp.

The SUV followed.

"Crap, crap, crap." I swerved around a pickup, and then a semi, nearly jumping out of my seat when the semi laid on his horn.

"I think that means he's angry," Starren said.

How did she sound so calm? "Yeah, good guess."

The SUV was out of sight for the moment, so I streaked across the lanes again and took another off ramp. Me staying on the highway was going to get someone killed. And that someone would probably be Starren, considering I'd be fine.

There the SUV was. But it couldn't get around the poor semi in time, and missed the exit.

I didn't even take the time to think right or left, just instinctively went right since I didn't need to check for traffic as carefully.

"We need to switch vehicles," Starren said. She stared out the window like one would just appear.

"It's not that easy, Starren. And if we do steal someone's car, then we'll have the humans looking for us too. We should just get to D.C. as fast as we can."

"Better the humans catch us than the fae," Starren said.

I shivered. True. I'd lose my sister, and who knew what Father's plans were for me. "If we see one easy to grab, we'll go for it. Until then, I'm just going to drive. We should have enough fuel to get there." Well I didn't know much about fuel, actually. "I think."

"Give me your phone. I need to look at roads."

Wren had been navigating, so I didn't even know what area we were in. I'd just been calculating time, not miles or whatever.

I handed Starren my phone and she pulled up the map, studying it for a minute. "There's another highway we can take for a bit, before getting back on the other one. It's the best way to get to D.C., so I hate to waste much time and take a huge detour. We're still far enough away that they hopefully haven't been able to guess where we're headed."

I didn't like hopefully. Hopefully scared me.

"Wait, does this mean you're expecting me to drive in D.C.?"

Starren looked at me like I was crazy. "Yes. Who else?"

She had a point. She didn't drive.

Maybe it was a good thing Nina didn't know me at the moment. She'd want to whack me upside the head because I was being an idiot. Not that she ever did, but I had to believe she wanted to sometimes.

I clenched and unclenched my fingers. Habit. They couldn't get sore really, not when I wasn't in Sanctuary. But it did remind me of Dan trying to teach me to drive, and cracking stupid jokes to get me to relax. I smiled a little, then forced myself to stop. Was that the first time I'd smiled thinking about one of them since all this had happened? Was this how people felt after a loved one died, and they didn't know how long had to pass before they were allowed to be happy again?

Starren said something in the fae language that I didn't understand.

"What?" I asked.

"They found us again."

I'd slowed down to the speed limit, hoping not to attract any extra attention, but those four words sent the accelerator to the floor again.

The poor engine revved as we barreled down a small two lane highway.

The SUV behind us gained ground with very little effort. It pulled up alongside us in the left lane.

"Ram them," Starren growled.

"Uh no, have you seen the size of their vehicle compared to ours?"

The window on the back passenger side started down, and Wren's angry face came slowly into view.

"Uh, what?" I asked no one in particular.

She yelled something, but with the straining engine, wind rushing everywhere, and my heart beating in my ears, I couldn't hear a word she said.

She mimed rolling the window down.

"Ignore her," Starren said. "She's been taken over by the enemy."

I rolled my eyes. That seemed a little far-fetched. I rolled down my window and let off the gas, just a little. It wasn't like we were getting away.

"Stop! We need to talk!" Wren was still hard to understand, but I could at least make out what she was saying.

Starren leaned across me. "No!"

I slowed even more, almost to the speed limit.

The SUV swerved behind me to let a couple cars pass from the other direction, then swung back around beside us.

"Yeah, those guys at the gas station? My guys. I didn't tell them what was up, just that my niece and I needed some protection. These are my friends!" Wren shouted over the rushing winter wind. "I asked them to watch out for us on the trip to D.C., that's it. They're on our side."

I glanced at Starren, then jerked the wheel when I almost went off the road on that side. Maybe I should slow down a bit more. "Is it possible someone is controlling her mind, could make her think that she's telling the truth?"

Starren shrugged. "I'm sure it's possible. There are many fae, and not all of them like others to know what they're capable of."

"So, what are the chances then?"

Starren settled back in her seat, her face all pouty. "Not good."

I slowed the car way down, coasting forward while I looked for a safe place to pull off. Well, how was that for looking like an idiot. Talk about an over-reaction. But she had known we were both paranoid. She should have told us. I almost didn't feel bad about leaving her behind. Almost.

Wren walked up to the car. She tugged on the handle, but neither of the two of us inside had hit the unlock button.

"Come on, guys, let me in."

Stony faced, Starren just stared ahead.

I sighed. She probably felt bad about leaving Wren behind. Or she was plotting how to get around her word not to hurt any humans without my permission. It could go either way, who knew when it was Starren we were talking about.

Being the bigger person, or at least telling myself that, I reached forward and hit the unlock button. Out of the corner of my eye, I saw

Starren's hand flex around the hilt of her sword, that sat comfortably in one of those weird pockets that led to Faerie. No chance of a human seeing it by accident there.

"You should have told us." I might have to be the bigger person at the moment, but that didn't make me happy. "You freaked us out, bad."

"I know, I'm so sorry." She looked sorry as she climbed into the back seat. Genuinely sorry.

I softened a little. I'd made a lot of mistakes, been forgiven a lot. She deserved it too.

"It won't happen again?"

She held out her pinky. "Never again."

Starren finally looked over, her normal haughty Starren face on. "Pinky promises don't just make things better."

I literally had to stop myself from rolling my eyes. No more TV for her.

"You can go," I yelled out to the SUV. Them sticking around just meant that it would take Starren longer to let Wren settle back in. I studied her in the back seat. "How did you find us again?"

She cringed for a second, looking like she was deciding if to lie or not. "The car has a tracker. I put it in last night when I borrowed it." She must have seen the steam start to roll off Starren, and put her hands up in a placating gesture. "No one can track us but that SUV." She pointed over her shoulder. The SUV hadn't moved.

Of course they hadn't. What military types were going to listen to a sixteen-year-old girl.

She stuck her arm out the window and waved, and the SUV started to move, cruising slowly by.

"You have nothing to worry about from them. They're only here because I asked them to be. What if that guy from last night shows up? Or those dog things? That was so crazy."

She had a point.

"There is nothing your friends could do about Vilan or about the death hounds." Starren acted like she was stating the obvious. "They would only die also. Do you care so little for your friends?" She shook her head. "This is a very bad sign." She turned to me. "We should throw her out. Her friends can pick her up, after she shows us how to disable the tracker."

Oh Starren, always straight to the violence.

"I think we need her. You can't drive, and I'm so done with this," I said. "Besides. You know you would have done the exact same thing if you were in her position and had her resources."

Starren stared me down like she could force me to be stronger with just her mind, but then gave in. "If we see any sign that you are doing anything behind our backs, you're gone," she told Wren.

"Agreed." Wren stuck out her hand and they shook on it.

I just rolled my eyes again and got out of the driver's seat. My legs wobbled a bit, making me grab at the car. Yep, good thing I wouldn't be driving for awhile.

Wren very deliberately left both doors open when she got out, and then flew into the driver's seat like I was going to jump right in there and take off. Valid fear, maybe.

Starren just snorted.

I slipped into the back and laid flat out.

Wren pointedly put on her seatbelt, which was smart in her case. But she'd seen how I could heal, she couldn't complain if I wanted a nap. After all that adrenaline, sleep would be tough, but at this point, it seemed like a good idea. I didn't want to have to sit here in awkward silence, or try and make conversation, either one. Starren wouldn't be trying, that was for sure.

So whether I actually fell asleep or not didn't matter. As far as everyone in here was concerned, I was out.

CHAPTER SIX

It took an hour of pretending, but I did eventually fall asleep.

And thankfully, made it almost there before Starren reached back and poked me. That was one way to pass a boring car ride.

I sat up and stretched.

Wren glanced back, waited a moment for me to wake up, then went into the lecture I'd been trying to avoid.

"You totally embarrassed me, you know. I'm never going to live down how I lost two kids on a road trip."

Starren glared.

"Yes, kids. Both of you."

Ha. If only she knew half of Starren's history. She'd be much less likely to make her mad by calling her a kid if she knew how easily Starren had taken out the fae council, some of the most powerful fae ever born.

Sure, Father had been there to help, but he hadn't done much. Starren's immunity to magic and deadliness with a sword made her dangerous to the fae.

"If you were adults you would have made more effort to find out what was going on before panicking and running," Wren continued.

"We weren't pan-"

Wren held up a hand. "If that's true, that's even worse. You don't leave members of your team behind." She glared at Starren and then at me in the rearview mirror. I sank back in my seat. "I'm not talking just me. A team has to know that they can trust each other. I've got both of your backs, and I'm not leaving you anywhere. Can I trust you to do the same for me?"

I nodded. Starren gave a non-committal grunt. She was still learning how to work on a team. Fae didn't team up much, and when Starren had, she'd always been the leader thanks to our father. It made it hard for her to just be a teammate.

Wren relaxed a little. "Good. And good work being on your toes. Jason and Brenda are two of the best. I can't believe you noticed them. The other two are in training, but they weren't even close to us. Jason sent them home now anyway, he was pretty mad."

"Maybe they weren't doing their best since they were following kids." Starren slumped in her seat like a grumpy teen. Now that I thought about it, I didn't actually know how old she was. She probably wasn't much older than me, just seemed like it.

"No, they don't work in half ways. You caught on fair and square. Impressive."

"You won't be pulling anything like that again, right? No more 'friends.'" As if Starren hadn't asked a variation of that question several times now.

"No, not unless I see a need to call in the cavalry."

What exactly did Wren do? Nina had always been all vague about how she was in the military, but even she didn't seem to know what she did. Right now it would be nice to have a bit more information.

My phone buzzed.

Oh shoot, in all the mess of leaving Wren behind, I'd forgotten to text Cray. I checked my phone. Two missed calls from Jaden, four from Cray, and seven texts. All the texts were variations of where are you, and you're in so much trouble.

Probably should have handled that before I took a four hour nap. To be fair, I had been shot yesterday, and that type of healing took a lot out of me. At least Cray wasn't the type to risk leaving Sanctuary to use his ability and try to pinpoint where we were.

Somehow we'd managed to avoid the fae so far. For what I'd been expecting, this trip had been pretty uneventful. Fingers crossed.

Now. How to answer my kind-of brother and my almost-boyfriend. We didn't date or anything. I was just really growing to like him. And I knew he liked me, even though he didn't really bring it up. He could see pieces of the future, and while he'd never flat-out said we would end up together, he'd definitely dropped a few hints.

Which made me freak out, and yet have a sense of peace at the same time. That's how most things affected me, like I was two people in one.

I started a group text so I could just get it over with in one move. 'had to a take a road trip. star's with me don't worry.'

Ha. Like adding don't worry at the end would actually make them not worry.

Even with him being able to see parts of what would happen in his life, and therefore mine, Jaden still worried all the time.

It was kind of sweet.

My phone buzzed twice in quick succession.

why? where?-Jaden.

you had better not be doing anything stupid. —Cray.

So now I had to decide how much of the truth to tell them. 'trying to help dan and nina, had a lead.'

All exclamation points from Cray. 'why am I not in on this? they're my parents too.'

Well that made me a bit defensive. They were my parents first, he wouldn't even know them if it wasn't for me.

'didn't want anyone getting hurt'

My phone rang and Jaden's smiling face popped up. Bet he wasn't smiling right now. I hit the decline button.

'can't talk. in the car.'

'why does that matter'

Uh, good question. Did I want to tell him about Wren? Not really. But he was too smart to fall for me saying I didn't want to talk in front of Starren. Starren literally knew all my secrets. It was kind of sad.

'that's all I can say right now. miss you guys, talk to you later' I hit send before I realized I'd just told them both I missed them. What was wrong with me? Nina cracked the emotional wall, and now everyone was breaking through.

Cray sent me a grumpy face emoji, but Jaden didn't answer.

How far could you push a good guy before he gave up on you? I didn't know, and I didn't really want to find out. But I wanted even less for his family to be put in danger. I didn't want Wren to know about him either. Not that I didn't trust her... but she might let something slip to someone she shouldn't.

If Starren and I got hauled away by the government, that would be bad enough. But we didn't even have anyone that would miss us. Cray and Jaden some, yeah, but they'd get over it. Jaden had two sisters and a mom who would be absolutely devastated if they lost him again.

No, I'd made the right decision. He was just going to have to forgive me. He always did.

"We can park here," Starren told Wren in the front seat.

I looked out the window. Wade's old apartment. A wave of both good and bad feelings overwhelmed me, nearly suffocating. Wade had helped show me that even if my family didn't want me, I still deserved love. I truly believed that had helped me open up to Nina. But then everything he'd done since... I'd never forgive him for shooting Nina. Never.

My blood boiled and my jaw started to ache from how hard I clenched my teeth. A real feat with how quickly I heal. The trees dotting the sidewalks around the parking lot began to whip and sway.

A hand grabbed my knee and my attention snapped to the front seat. The trees leaned in toward the car, ready to tear apart my target. It was Starren, giving me something else to think about, no doubt knowing what was going through my mind.

"You okay?" Wren asked.

I forcefully unclenched my hands, feeling the little cuts from my nails heal.

"Yes," I ground out. Okay.

The trees around us slowly went back to normal, but I could feel their anger still. *Thank you, but he isn't here. These are my friends.* I didn't know how much the trees could understand, so friends just seemed easier.

I took a moment to close my eyes while Starren and Wren unhooked their seatbelts and opened their doors.

Hopefully Wren had been so focused on me that she hadn't noticed the angry foliage. A couple people on the sidewalk had. They were walking past on the asphalt now, instead of the sidewalk, eyeing the trees.

It was winter, weird things like that happened with the weather. They'd forget about it by the time they got to wherever they were going.

I didn't know what to do with this anger hanging around just under the surface. It popped up far too easily lately. I balled my fists and relaxed, then repeated, releasing some of that energy. Wade had better stay out of my way. Nina had been there last time, and I'd been able to control myself because I cared what she thought of me.

Controlling myself would be a whole lot harder now.

"You're going to have to pretend to be fae," Starren was telling Wren. "The penalty for a human crossing into the tunnel is imprisonment, we can't allow humans to go around telling each other about us."

"Got it. But won't anyone be able to tell?"

"Not Cumat, or the friend we are going to speak to. And everyone else will be avoiding me. With the Council destroyed, they will be scrambling to figure out their place in this new life. I don't expect that they took well to Father's coup."

Wren looked confused. "I have no idea what you're talking about."

Starren sighed, then walked off, not taking the time to explain. Shocker. It wasn't Wren's fault she didn't understand the inner working of fae politics. She hadn't even known about the fae until last night. I still didn't know what was going on half the time, and my mom had drilled all that stuff into me since before I could talk.

I jumped out of the car and headed after Starren. If I waited too long she'd just head in without me, and then I'd be running up and down those super white halls knocking on doors until I found her.

The chirp of the car locking followed, and Wren jogged after me.

I got around the corner just in time to see Starren disappear into the wall. Good thing too, I hadn't used the portal much, and it had been awhile. How embarrassing to run right into the wall in front of Wren. I stepped up and put my hand through while I waited a second for Wren.

"You're going to have to hold my hand," I told her when she caught up, sticking my hand out. I shrugged. "It's the way it works."

She shrugged back and took my hand.

I pulled her through the wall.

Inside smelled weird. Like something burnt, but not quite. And the normal lighting along the walls was gone.

Something was wrong.

"What the heck?" Wren said loudly when she got through the portal. I clamped a hand over her mouth.

"Shhh. Something isn't right." I kept hold of her hand, I could see in the dark pretty well, but she probably couldn't. "Starren?" I said quietly. "Star?"

A hand grabbed me out of a really dark spot on the left, and I slammed backward into Wren, hardly able to keep myself from shrieking.

I glared at Starren, my heart thundering out of control. "What was that for?" So much for being able to see pretty well in the dark.

She just put a finger to her lips, and headed up the tunnel, sword out. Good plan.

I slid my sword from its invisible sheath. Wren's grip on my arm tightened, and I didn't complain even though she would have left bruises on a human. She pulled a gun from a hidden holster.

"You can't use that here," Starren whispered.

"What?" Wren asked.

"Firearms are unpredictable around the fae. You can't use that." Then she moved on, like the issue was resolved. She was way too used to people just listening to her.

Wren put the gun back. That wasn't to say she wouldn't have it ready later.

We inched forward, the smell getting worse.

The chiseled rock walls, normally pristine, were covered in a black tarry goop that slowly ran down toward the floor. The same goo trailed on the floor in the sand.

I crouched close to the wall and moved forward, being super careful not to touch the junk. Starren was avoiding it like the plague, so I figured I'd better too. A closer look didn't help me figure out what it was. Maybe it was just some weird fae thing, but I didn't think so.

The stuff got worse as we moved out of the entranceway and into the real hall. I hopped over streaks of it smeared across the tile as the hall started whitening out. Once I made it to where the doors started, I slid to a stop, gripping my sword tight enough to make my fingers tingle.

The usually spotless hall bled tar everywhere. It went on into infinity in front of us like normal, but that was the only normal thing in the whole place.

Doors all down the hallway were blasted off their hinges as if someone had checked each room looking for someone.

If I was in a movie, this was the part where I'd start calling for Cumat in a hushed voice. No way I was going to do that for real. The characters that did never ended up making it out of the warehouse/forest/jungle whatever.

Was he okay? Was he even here? As far as I knew, he didn't have any fighting skills whatsoever. Would we find his lifeless body here somewhere? We'd never gotten along, but I surely didn't want him dead.

I held my breath and took a small step forward, sticking to Starren like a shadow. It would be totally awesome if there was someone we could go to for help right now. Father would be glad to hear from me for sure, but there was a good chance he was the one responsible for this.

The first door was shattered, white slivers all over the floor. It wasn't wood, at least not Earth wood, too glowy. Must have been brought from Faerie. I peeked around the frame. The room was empty, still white inside. I moved on to the next one on the left, while Starren took the one on the right. This room was covered in black, the tar dripping down the walls. I noticed a lump on the floor. I waved my arm at Wren, who seemed to be guarding the hall, then went back. A body. I rushed forward and bent over a guy probably in his twenties. He was on his back, eyes staring blankly at the ceiling, mouth open like he'd been screaming. I reached a trembling hand forward and felt for a pulse, trying not to get any of the goo layered across his chest on my hand. Nothing.

I backed away, sick. Pausing at the doorway to get my trembling muscles under control, I took a deep breath and waited for Starren. What could have done this? Afraid to go back into the hallway, I held my position in the doorway for a moment, watching.

Starren came out of her room and sprinted over to mine. She saw the body and bolted straight for it, putting out a hand to check for life. None, of course.

I watched the hallway, probably not able to hear an enemy coming with the pounding of my pulse in my ears. Nothing moved. I slipped out, keeping as close to the wall as I could while still avoiding the icky goo slathered on it in places. I took the lead and Star let me, falling back into the pattern of me being the shield or bait because I would heal and she wouldn't.

Each door we came to looked like the first. Most of the rooms were empty, and all of the empty rooms were still pristine white. Seven rooms had bodies in them, all covered in black tar.

There was the girl I'd passed in the hallway all the time last year. I didn't recognize the guy in the next room at all. After that was the boy who'd stuck his head out of his office to watch me walk by the first day I'd shown up, here to kill Wade. I choked back a sob as I stumbled out of that last room. He didn't look very old. I checked every body, nearly praying that each one wasn't someone I knew.

None were and none were alive.

The next body we stopped at, Starren flipped over and jerked, her face spasming before going into its regular mask.

"Did you know him?" I asked quietly.

"He's the one we were here to meet."

No, no, no, it couldn't be. Dan and Nina.

I shoved all that down. First we had to find out about Cumat.

Still hearing nothing, I gave up trying to be quiet and rushed forward, dread rising to even greater heights as I got closer and closer to Starren's old room. Would Cumat go there? I didn't know. I didn't know anything about protocol.

The door was still shut, but covered in goop like something had been working hard to get in. I tried the handle. It didn't move. Now what? What was on the other side? Did I want to risk getting the attention of whatever had done this? Was it still here? I took a deep breath and looked over my shoulder. Starren was coming in hot. She knocked on the door lightly, in a pattern.

I watched the hallway, a hundred terrible scenarios with different things coming to kill us going through my head. Maybe we should have stayed quiet. How long ago had this happened? I tried the door handle again, nothing. The only sound in here was my crazy breathing, somehow the other two seemed to be holding it together just fine.

I reined it in a bit, working to get control. This was the only door that was closed. There were survivors inside, there had to be. We'd have to risk making some extra noise. I nodded at the door, and Starren did her knock again, quietly at first, then hitting it harder when there was no answer.

"Who is it?" a muffled voice came through the door.

I nearly collapsed from relief. It sounded like Cumat.

"Open up," Starren said.

"Starren?"

"Yes, it's me."

Some mumbling went on behind the door.

"Open it, you can't leave her standing out there."

I started to lean on the door, relief making me a little weak, then noticed the tar and thought better of it.

The door swung open. A hand reached out, grabbed the front of my shirt and jerked me inside, waited a second for Starren and Wren to slide in, then slammed the door after us.

"What are you doing out there? Did you see anyone else?"

I looked around the room and nearly cried. Cumat and a few fae I'd seen around but didn't really know were all there staring at me like I was a ghost. Like they weren't the ones to just have witnessed a massacre.

Cumat came forward and almost pulled Starren into a hug, then seemed to think better of it. "We're saved!" Even though his words were hopeful, his voice was hushed. The other fae huddled back in the corner. What they must have seen...

Waving all three of us down closer, Cumat continued to whisper. "Did you see anything out there?"

I couldn't look him in the eyes. "Nothing dangerous. Just black goo on everything. And... bodies. Eight. They're all dead." When he didn't answer, I looked. His face was totally blank. My gaze swung to the other three. They all wore similar expressions. "But those are just bodies, right? The people are back in Faerie?"

"No," Cumat answered, tears shining in his eyes. "We're not on Earth here. Death is the same as it would be in Faerie."

"What did this?" I whispered.

"A monster." Cumat's voice shook. "I didn't get a good look at it, but it was like nothing I've seen before."

"We tried to fight back. We tried to get to the others..." One of the other fae spoke for the first time, his voice cracking in the middle of what he was trying to say. He looked away from me, no doubt trying to hide what he was feeling.

"How did it get in? Isn't the portal supposed to keep this kind of thing out?"

"It was Father," Starren said, sheathing her sword with a loud thawk. "It had to be."

I stared at her for a second. "I don't follow."

"Think about it, Trisha," she said. "This hall has the protection of the Council. Nothing is supposed to be strong enough to break in."

"Does that still work? Now that there is no Council?"

"Yes. Just because the caster dies, does not automatically make all spells inert," Cumat answered, apparently unable to hold himself back from teaching me something.

"But Cumat would have seen him. He would know if Father had been here, right?" I knew what our father was. Selfish and dangerous. He'd had Starren kill the entire Council so he could rule Faerie. But I wanted to believe he wouldn't just kill young fae like this, ones that weren't even old enough to have moved to better positions in Faerie.

"He may not be directly responsible. He wouldn't have to be here if someone was helping him," Starren said. "No, he didn't do this in person. I think he can control things we don't understand. I thought I'd seen everything to do with Faerie. I guess I was wrong." Starren admitting she was wrong? I blinked a couple times, trying to hold back my surprise. Today must have really shaken her.

"What happened to the monster?"

"Azmieal warded this room. The thing gave up attacking the door after..." Cumat said. "Forever."

Starren grabbed the hilt of her sword. "How long ago did it leave?"

Cumat just looked at her, a slightly dazed expression on his face.

"Cumat, how long? Is it still here?"

"Just before you arrived. I was afraid you were it, trying a different tactic, though it didn't seem intelligent enough to have such a thought."

"We can wait a bit, let it move down the hall, then head for the portal," I said.

"I'm not leaving until it's dead," Starren answered.

Oh no. That was her bullheaded tone. Nothing changed her mind when she got that tone.

"Starren. There are only two of us, and we don't know what this thing is capable of. We don't even know what it is. We should get out, let Cumat bring in some people more equipped to deal with this."

She set her jaw. "We are the best. We are extremely equipped to deal with this." She waved her sword. "If I have to go after it alone, I will."

I crossed my arms. "What about these people?" I gestured toward Cumat and the others. "Are you just going to leave them unprotected? Leave them here, with no one to defend them if we don't make it back?" Wow, was I being the logical one? Something was seriously wrong.

"It killed fae, Trish. It killed my-" she interrupted herself. "People I worked with. It might be killing more now. The tunnel is long, if it just left, it may still be looking for someone." She grimaced. "Or someones. It may be looking for us. And if so, we brought this down on our people. How many doors will it break through? How many bodies will we find? Do you remember right before we fought the trolls all the way back in California? How I wanted to leave, but you wanted to attack?"

I nodded grudgingly, not liking where this was going.

"This is even more serious. We have to save our people."

I didn't consider the fae my people. But I did consider Starren to be my people.

"We can take a look. If we find it and it isn't hurting anyone, we leave it alone. Our first priority is to make sure the others get out safely."

"Um, can I chime in on this?" Wren asked, raising her hand. When no one answered, she just continued. "Are you both crazy?" she shouted. "You want to go after a monster? Nina would kill me if she found out! Let me get some backup in here."

"No humans," Starren said. "We've done this many times, we don't need help."

"Usually with Wade," Cumat said.

Starren glared.

Wren's gaze zeroed in on me. "You've fought monsters before?"

I shrugged. Were trolls monsters? Probably to Wren. The hyran was for sure, but we never really 'fought' it. Everyone said we would have died if we'd tried, so no, that didn't count. Goblins counted. And Father.

"We've fought many battles together," Starren said. "Trisha is a competent fighter."

My face heated up with all the beaming it was doing. That was the highest praise I'd ever heard leave her mouth.

"She still has much to learn, but even though it has been some time since we last fought, I have been training her and she's improved."

Maybe unwise of her to tell Wren that, just in case Nina ever did get her memory back. She would not be happy with the kind of training we'd been doing.

"I'm with you, Starren," I said. She hadn't been happy about it, the times I'd dragged her into trouble, but she'd always been there, and always fought ferociously. The least I could do was the same.

Wren didn't need to know about the time we'd tried to kill each other over Jaime, Jaden's little sister. Best keep that little tidbit to myself.

Starren went to the door, took a deep breath and opened it a crack. After she was satisfied nothing was waiting on the other side, she motioned to us and took off out the door.

The three of us slunk down the hallway. Cumat and the others watched for a second, then swung the door closed behind us. Starren stopped at every body to check for signs of life. I couldn't blame her. I knew more about injuries, fatal or otherwise, than most people and could tell they were all dead before we even got close. But if they were my friends I'd have to check for myself too.

"I should just grab you and hold you down until you actually consider what we're doing," Wren mumbled behind us. "At least let me go ahead of you."

"Hey," I said. "What you saw yesterday wasn't a fluke. I can heal. I'll be fine."

"There's no way possible you can die? You know, like some kind of monster goo shoved down your throat all the way to your toes? Are you sure about this?"

Well that was an interesting thought. One I rather wished she hadn't brought up. I could take the tiny particles of oxygen in water and breathe them somehow, but what happened if there was no oxygen at all?

Ignoring her question, I moved up closer to Starren. "How far does this tunnel go, anyway?"

"To Faerie," Starren grunted.

"Uh, yes, I know, but how far is that?"

"However far it wants to be."

That made perfect sense. Not. She always got all cryptic when she was upset.

"I just don't want to accidentally go there." Or purposefully go there, or go there in any way, shape or form. All those years wondering about my dad, wasted.

Starren ignored me, stopped, and squinted ahead. "Do you see something dark?"

Now that she mentioned it, yes. A dark blob, much bigger than anything coating the walls stood out against the stark white.

"Do you think…"

"Yes." Her voice was grim. She hefted her sword and took off at a controlled jog. Everything she did was controlled. Except when she watched TV. Sometimes that got a bit wild.

I tightened my grip on my sword and followed her.

CHAPTER SEVEN

We moved forward far faster than we should have, the tunnel leaping ahead of us, doors flying by on either side, all smashed, no signs of life.

I'd never gone this far into the tunnel when I'd been working here with Starren, Wade, and Cray. The portal room had been as far as I'd gone, and that we'd left behind awhile ago. I switched my sword to my other hand, giving my palm a chance to dry. I was not a fan of fighting. Wade had always seemed to enjoy it. Starren seemed impartial, but she was good at it. Really, really good.

We were moving far quicker than a jog like this would have normally done.

"What's going on?" Wren sounded out of breath. She seemed like she was in good shape, so it was probably the fear talking. "Who's doing this?"

"No one," Starren answered. "Faerie has a mind of its own. It does not like this beast, and wishes us to dispose of it."

That seemed like a lot of assuming to me, but I couldn't argue, because I didn't know how things worked.

The doors sped by even faster.

And then we were close enough for our first look.

The creature, or fae, or whatever it was, was the black goop itself.

It dripped and re-formed, body sloughing off like a volcano, but then melding back into a somewhat humanoid form.

"What is that?" Wren whispered behind me.

I didn't have an answer.

We were too close too fast.

Its head snapped sideways at an unnatural angle, body still sloughing toward the next door. This thing was slow as molasses.

It cocked its head, and the goo dripped away in a circle.

"Name," it said, the small circle a mouth. Its voice was smooth, like melted chocolate, but deep.

"Starren. That mean anything to you?"

Its head continued to tip until it slipped into the rest of its body, and then re-formed. It looked at me. "Name."

I didn't answer. Because I didn't want to, of course, not because I couldn't or anything.

"Name," it said again, its body puddling and flowing into position so all of it was aimed at us.

"Wren," she said, pushing around me. "My name is Wren."

The goop monster lifted an arm, pointing a quickly dissolving finger at me. "Name."

"Who wants to know?" Okay, yes, rude, but I get really mouthy when I'm nervous.

"Name." It moved forward, flowing across the floor.

"Sorry, sorry, Trish! It's Trish."

It stopped, I assumed staring at me, but it didn't have any visible eyes.

"Come with me."

Okay, it hadn't said that for the other two.

"Why?" I squeaked out, not sounding nearly as confident as a few seconds ago.

"Come with me."

I dropped the point of my sword to the ground and looked to Wren, then Starren and back to Wren. "Is this thing pre-programed with only a few answers?"

"Uh, I don't think that's the question you should be worried about right now," Wren said, gun pointed at the blob thing.

"What's your name?" I asked it.

No answer as it advanced.

"Look, I just want you to know before you get over here that my sister and I can totally take you. If you have any brains at all in there, you'd better use them and head back to wherever you came from. And yeah, you found me, so stop hurting people, okay?"

"Come with me."

Like I'd really thought that would work. Worth a try. But this thing was giving me the heebie-jeebies, and I got the bad feeling that we weren't going to be able to take it.

"You aren't touching her," Starren gritted out.

The thing contemplated her for a second, then swung its arm, the whole thing elongating as it came at her, the creature's body shrinking, its arm growing until it was long enough to take a swing at Star.

Oh no it wasn't. I jumped in front of the arm and got whacked into the wall. My skin sizzled, every centimeter that it'd touched.

"It's hot!" I yelled, smacking at my smoldering shoulder. The skin beneath had already almost healed, but it still didn't feel great hitting my burned flesh.

Starren rolled her eyes. "I could have gotten out of the way." The thing swung at her again, and she proved she was right by ducking sideways at the last second, giving herself plenty of space.

Maybe I was getting a little too zealous about this whole not let anyone get hurt thing, but she was the only family I had at the moment. Father didn't count, and who knew where Mother was, if she was even alive. After seeing Nina dead on the ground... She'd come back, but nope. No one else was getting hurt on my watch.

She took a swing at the thing. The blade sliced right through it like it was butter, but the beast didn't seem to notice. It took another swing at her and she nearly fell over backward to get out of the way.

Not great.

Wren got her gun up and had two shots fired before I even noticed her aiming.

The creature didn't acknowledge the hits. It absorbed the bullets on one side, and they clinked out the other.

Wren sucked in a breath, and tried again, with the same results.

Well this really didn't look great.

"What now?" I asked Starren quietly.

"You run."

It started sliding toward us, no legs, but molten goo rippling it forward. "Trisha. Please come with me."

I looked to Starren, my eyes no doubt a little wild.

"Run," Starren said again.

"Not without you!"

"It's not going after us without you here. Be bait, Trish."

She didn't call me Trish often. Bait was something I could be.

I took off down the hallway toward the portal at a dead run, going past several doors before looking over my shoulder.

It was coming after me, and it wasn't so slow anymore. It flowed past Starren and Wren without a glance.

Starren hit it from behind, paring pieces off as it slid by.

The thing didn't care. It just kept coming. What was wrong with that thing? Did it not feel pain?

Running the other way had pushed us faster and faster. Running this way was like running through a swamp, every step trapped in the air.

It caught up, fast, reaching out to grab me as Starren hacked and chopped at it, trying to help.

This wasn't doing any good. I wasn't going to get away. And where was I going to go anyway? Would it follow me out the portal into D.C.? I turned to face it, throwing up a hand. "Stop!"

It slipped to a stop, but I couldn't tell what was going on since it didn't seem to have a face.

"What do you want?"

"I have been sent to find you," it said.

"By who?"

Whatever it was thought for a second. "I have no answer to that question. You will come with me."

"I will not come with you, not without more information. Why did you hurt all these people?"

"I was sent to find you."

"Are you supposed to hurt me?"

Its head tipped forward, and it looked at the ground. I could practically see a repentant expression even with no face.

"No, you are not to be injured. Please come with me."

"Let's go," I told Starren and Wren. "No way it can force me to go with it, its touch causes me harm." I stuck my finger out to lecture the thing. "Do you hear me? You burned me when you touched me, you can't do anything."

My hand shook a little, and I put it back down quickly.

"Please come with me."

"Ugh, so annoying." Maybe if I could view him as an annoyance, I wouldn't be as freaked out as I was at the moment.

Wren inched around it until she stood right beside me. "Why do you want Trish?"

It cocked its head to the side, looking inquisitive, like Storm when he was waiting to see what I was going to give him out of my backpack. Where was that dragon when you needed him.

Wren stepped in front of me. "Why. Do. You. Want. Trish." Wren's voice so strongly sounded like Nina's that it almost brought tears to my eyes. She was just in my corner, just like that, just because we were family.

I hoped.

"Name?" it asked.

"Wren. I already told you that."

"Affiliation?"

Wren looked at me like I would have an answer for that. I shrugged.

"United States Air Force."

The tar flowing down the thing's sides froze.

"Human?" it asked.

"Uh, yes?" Wren's answer sounded more like a question. But either way, she had to be human. If she was fae, she wouldn't be able to lie.

With a squelching groan, the thing melted into a huge puddle of goo.

Wren jumped backward, knocking into me, but just getting out of the way of the goo coating the floor in waves before it melted her skin off.

After a couple deep breaths, Wren asked, "What just happened?"

We were all still frozen in place, staring down at the pool of black on the ground.

"Apparently he has orders about humans, just like the golem you told me about," Starren said.

I scooted in for a closer look. Was it still alive?

"Golem? What's a golem?" Wren asked. "What's that thing? What's going on?"

I didn't have any good answers for her. "Golems are these creatures made out of mud and stuff, they're basically formed to fill a need for the person who makes them, and they follow orders to the letter. There's a stone golem that guards a tunnel we took to Faerie. It had orders to not let any humans see it, we were in the middle of a fight and when Dan and Nina showed up, it just stopped moving."

Starren tipped her sword down and let the goo it had accumulated drip off into the puddle. "We need to check on Cumat, and then we need to get out of here. Everyone should evacuate. We can get Cumat on it. You," she pointed her sword at Wren. "Stay here until we have everyone out. You need to keep it in this form."

"Excuse me?" Wren asked. "You expect me to stay here while you and Trisha go and do something else? We all know what happened last time I wasn't around the two of you."

"Fair point," I said.

"Doesn't matter," Starren answered. "We have to keep this thing down, and we have to get everyone out of here. We can't do both those things with you along. As soon as we're done getting everyone out, we'll be back for you."

Wren crossed her arms. "Nuh uh. I don't think so."

"We'll have to bring them back this way anyway," I said. "They're going to want to go to Faerie, not Earth."

She eyed the floor. "It's not coming back?"

"Not with you around," Starren said.

"We'll only be ten minutes, at the most," I interjected. "Trust us, please. This is the best chance we have at keeping everyone safe." Hopefully it wouldn't come back, hopefully it didn't re-congeal or whatever while we were gone. I tapped my fingers against my thigh, internally screaming at the thought that I could be leaving her here in a lot of trouble, on only a hopefully.

She grimaced, but nodded, not taking her eyes off the ground.

"Let's go," I told Starren, turned and sprinted up the hallway. The faster we got Cumat and the others out, the faster we got back here.

I beat Starren to the door and pounded on it. "Cumat, it's us. Get out here, it's safe. Ish."

Nothing happened.

Starren caught up and did her weird little knock. Of course the door opened then, though only a crack.

"Ms. Starren?" Cumat whispered out the crack.

"Yes," Starren said. "You can open. We're safe for the moment."

Even as terrified as he was, the door popped right open. His trust in Starren must have been even deeper than I'd thought.

"Did you kill the beast?" he asked.

"No." Even with only one word, Starren could announce how perturbed she was by that fact. "But it has orders to avoid being seen by humans, and the other one with us is human, so it isn't going anywhere as long as she's standing there."

Cumat's eyes widened. "You brought a human here?"

"Yes," Starren said. "And I'm only telling you this so you know that I trust you. Don't pass it on to anyone."

Cumat's eyes teared up. Poor guy, his emotions were being yanked all over today.

"Let's go. I don't want to stand around just in case it decides it's more important to grab Trish than to stay hidden from humans."

We moved out into the hall as a group, Starren automatically going to the front, and me falling in beside her. Wren had better be okay. I hardly knew her, had just met her, but Nina loved her and so I had to keep her safe.

We turned to go toward the beast.

"Wait," Cumat hissed. "We don't want to go that way."

Starren paused. "I'm going to return you to Faerie."

"Why would we want to go to Faerie? It's a hundred times more dangerous for us there than on Earth right now. With no Council to serve under, we've been flailing around, terrified of who would decide to become our new master." He studiously looked away from both Starren and me. "The current... leader, wouldn't be a good match for many of us."

Current leader. Quintin. My Father. The evil dude that had taken over Faerie by force, not long ago.

"Understandable," I got out. The soft fae were sent to work places like this, the ones that didn't want to hurt anyone. These fae weren't normal fae, cold and heartless. "Will you be okay out in the world?"

"All of the operatives here have studied humans, all of them are experts on human culture."

"Uh huh," I said. "But will they be able to pass for human?"

Cumat's shoulders slumped. "I don't know. They have the knowledge, but it's much different attempting to follow through with it."

I sighed. We couldn't just let them go into the world. What if the humans figured something out? What would happen to them if the government knew they weren't from Earth? Nothing good, I was sure. And if the fae found out that one of their own might accidentally give away their secret...

I motioned Starren over to the wall. "We need to get them to Sanctuary."

She looked at me like I was crazy. "They aren't our responsibility."

"No, not really. But look at them."

She did.

They were pitiful at the moment, worn down by terror and adrenaline.

"You would give up your chance to find a cure for your humans? Because we aren't going to have a chance like this again."

A bad feeling squirmed through my gut. "What do you mean? The guy we came to see is dead."

Starren scratched her head. "About that... I did want to see him. I really thought he could help. But there is another option. Someone I didn't want to see. He's in Faerie."

"Are you kidding me?" That came out a little louder than I'd meant it to. "I'm not going back to Faerie! No way!"

Starren shrugged. "Okay. Better for me. I really don't want to run into Father anyway. And the guy who can help us... I'd rather not see him either. I just thought you were willing to do anything to make your humans remember, that's it."

I wilted against the wall. Anything for Dan and Nina. That's what I'd been saying. Anything. But Faerie. Father. The father I'd always wanted turned out to not be my biological dad, but Dan.

"Fine. Anything. How far into Faerie are we talking?"

"Not far. One of the portals can drop us close to where we need to go. In and out, that's it."

In and out, that was it. In and out. Sure.

"Wait a minute. How do you know this guy?"

Starren wouldn't look me in the eye.

"Star?"

"I'm not going to talk about this now." She nodded toward the other fae. "Ask me about it later if you want."

"Why?"

"Not. Now." Starren took off again.

It only took us a moment to get to the portal outside with the pace Starren sent. It was better that way. The fae following us didn't have time to get good looks at their fallen co-workers.

"Wait here," Starren told Cumat. "We're going to have the human take you to Sanctuary."

"What?" I asked. "I don't think she's going to agree with that."

"Leave us with a human?" Cumat asked.

"Yeah, you have a problem with that? If we let you just go out into the world, you're going to be around humans anyway."

Cumat blanched, but didn't have an answer.

"We're going back for the human. Wait here." And then she just left. Like usual.

I ran after her. As soon as we were out of hearing distance I grabbed her arm. "Wren is not going to be happy about this."

Starren pulled me to the side. "Here's our chance. We can leave her, for good this time."

I hated the thought of leaving her again. But it would be safer for her, for sure. Faerie could be a terrible place. And we hadn't brought food for her. We'd found out what happened in that situation the last time we'd gone there.

"Why did you tell Cumat about bringing a human here? You could get yourself in so much trouble."

Starren lifted an eyebrow. "How much more trouble could I possibly get in? Father is already enraged with me. I doubt I could do anything to make him hate me more at this point, other than kill you."

"Hey! He doesn't even know me, you're the one he should care about."

"Whoever has the girl wins the war. That's all he cares about."

Ugh, I hoped whoever had said that crap got what was coming to them. It had literally changed the trajectory of my life.

"We can give not getting in more trouble a try."

Starren barked out a laugh. "I got this. Don't worry about it."

The hallway helped us along again, and it was only a few seconds before we were back to Wren. The poor woman didn't take her eyes off the goo on the floor even as we got closer.

"Finally! I was worried. Did you get everyone out okay?"

"Yes, all clear."

She frisked us both with her eyes, doing the same check for injuries Nina always did. It would be good to get away from her, and the fact that everything she did reminded me of Nina.

It was too painful.

"We have something we need you to do..." I trailed off, trying to think of something that would actually make her want to run the fae back to Fort Wayne. That was a long road trip to do in twenty-four hours.

"You must take the survivors to Sanctuary," Starren interjected.

So tactful.

"What? No. What are you two doing?"

"We're going on. Into Faerie." My stomach rolled as the words left my mouth. I was going back to Faerie. Was I nuts? Forget about all the dangerous creatures, about having enemies, just the fact that my Father would do anything to grab me and lock me up again was enough to keep me far away. But I had to.

Oh now she stopped looking at the goop, when I wanted her to not be looking at me.

"It isn't safe there for you. And those people need help. And Nina's going to worry about you," I said. "Plus, we don't have food for you, and we don't know how long we'll be gone." That last one would be hard to argue with.

"We don't want what happened to the other humans to happen to you," Starren said. "Plus, we'd just leave you outside the portal. You can't pass without being in direct contact with one of the fae."

Anger crossed Wren's face. I'd be mad too. No one liked to be backed into a corner. We weren't leaving her much of a choice. The only thing she could decide for herself right now was if to take the carload of fae with her on her way back or not.

"Sorry, Wren. It's what's best."

She still looked mad, but maybe a little less so. Hopefully it wasn't just my imagination.

"Can you get them to Sanctuary, where they'll be safe?" Starren asked.

Her posture softened. "Yes. I'll get them back safely." She looked Starren straight in the eyes. "You have my word that I'll do my very best."

"No one should be after them at this point. Whoever sent the monster thinks they're dead. And no one else cares about them. It should be a perfectly safe babysitting job. Just drop them at our apartment." She fished the key out of her pocket and handed it to Wren.

She really did have a soft spot for Cumat. I couldn't see her doing that for anyone else.

Wren sighed and took the key. She came over and pulled me into a tight hug. "Nothing I can say will make you come back with me, will it?"

I held her at arms length. "Nope."

She moved like she was going to hug Star, but Starren just slid under her arm. "Better get going."

Wren backed down the hall a few steps. "Actually, I think you'd better go first." She nodded toward the glob.

Oh, good plan. I gave her a thumbs up, and Starren and I headed for the portal room.

We hadn't gotten far when Starren turned back to Wren. "Don't let them out of the car if you can help it. They don't know how to act around humans."

"Wonderful," Wren muttered, loud enough for me to hear. "Four days," she yelled after us.

"What?" I asked.

"Four days, and then I'm coming after you. I'll force one of these guys to get me through the portal, with some backup, and we're coming after you."

I paused. Coming after me, or coming after the discovery of a lifetime? It didn't matter. Either way spelled disaster. I hadn't known her long, but long enough to know that she meant what she said. Four days. We'd just have to be back to cell phone service by then. Anything more...

We stepped into the portal room and a wave of nostalgia hit me. Oh for the days when we were a team, and I didn't know about my father, even if I hadn't known what I had with Dan and Nina. But, no Jaden, so that was something that had improved. Even just thinking about him now made me miss him. I checked my phone again, but there wasn't any signal. If he'd finally answered me, I wasn't getting it until we stepped back on Earth. I turned it off to save the battery.

Starren stopped in front of the portal, messing with something on the side of it for a second. "You ready for this?"

I closed my eyes for a second, took a breath, and then opened them. "Yes. I'm ready." This was it. No going back. For Dan, and Nina. I stepped through the portal.

CHAPTER EIGHT

The cool, slithery feeling of going through a portal felt strange. It had been a bit. But not long enough. Long enough wasn't possible.

We stepped out into a clear glade, the strange sunshine flowing down around us, the trees as beautiful as ever, all the shades of purple and blue there were. I sucked in a breath as the world spun. No, no, why was I back here. This was stupid. Last time I was here, Nina had died. No, I didn't want to be here, couldn't be here.

But I was.

I sucked in another deep breath, reaching for something to balance myself with.

Starren clapped her hands in front of my face. "Get it together. I'm not happy being here either."

She was right. She'd dealt with so much more here. Father had been horrible to her. But surely she had some good memories here too. I didn't have any of those. At all.

"How long have you known about this?" I asked.

She looked at me blankly. It was a pretty abrupt question, but I needed to get my mind off of where we were.

"About this person who can help us?"

She started walking without answering my question, setting a pretty determined pace. Good. That should mean she knew where we were going.

But bad, because she wouldn't answer me.

"Starren?"

She whirled to face me. "You aren't going to let it go, are you? Just can't let anything go."

I shrunk back a little. It'd been awhile since she'd showed such real anger toward me.

"I didn't want to tell you about him, because you'd want to go to him. I thought maybe, if you didn't have Dan and Nina, you'd need me. And that maybe, if we did go back, you'd realize that if you'd never come to rescue me, you'd have your other family, and not want me anymore. I thought that we could be a family. Plus, he's my ex. And it didn't end well."

"We're a family anyway, Starren! It isn't like that, where you have a limit on how many people are in your family!" How could I have known how she was feeling? She barely showed that she could feel. But I did feel bad. It should have been obvious, if I'd been paying attention. Then the rest of her words hit me. "And hold up, your ex? You dated?"

She dropped her head. "I know that now. But I didn't then. I had nowhere to go, no one to have my back. As much as people like to put on a front that they don't need those things, I don't know anyone that actually doesn't. Except maybe Father. I sat in prison, thinking about you and what you'd been willing to do for your family, and asked myself, who would I be willing to do that for? Who would be willing to do it for me? No one. But then, you showed up. Wade went and got you, and you came. Then I started to understand."

I was still mad, but I could understand her motivations. I'd been pretty awkward when I was learning to be part of a family too. And she'd grown up with Father. Father! Such a horrid person. Wait, ex? "Why didn't you tell me you have feelings for someone? That's something sisters talk about."

"Had," she corrected. "Had feelings. Father didn't care for it."

And that explained everything. Father had completely run her life.

I tried to imagine what Nina would do in this situation, and awkwardly patted her hand.

She smiled at the effort, but pulled it away.

Maybe she was over this guy, maybe not. She thought she was though, or she wouldn't be able to say that.

"So you broke up with him because of Father?"

"No. He broke up with me because of Father."

Okay, this guy was going to tell us how to fix Dan and Nina, and then I was going to kill him. He'd hurt my sister, and that was a big no no.

"He won't be able to do anything for them directly, but he'll be able to tell us who can. After that, we just have to find whoever it is, make them tell us, and do whatever they say. Easy."

Her positivity freaked me out. She was never positive. Was this fake positive, or see the boy she liked positive?

Did she still like him? Chickening out was lame of course, but it was Quintin who had made him do it, and Father made that goop monster back there look like a puppy.

Still, she deserved better. Now that I knew she could actually have feelings for another person, I was totally going to set her up when we got back. My friend Rosie would know someone her age. I didn't have my own love life figured out of course, but figuring out someone else's was always easier.

Jaden's face popped into my head. What was he doing right now? Was he still mad at me? I'd be mad at me if I was him, but I still knew I'd made the right choice.

We'd been much closer since our Faerie excursion, but I still wasn't ready for any kind of relationship. Wade had screwed that up for me for awhile. Something about your boyfriend shooting you and manipulating you made it hard to trust anyone else when he was done.

Flowers bloomed in the bushes around us, filling the air with different scents. I would have appreciated it at a different time, but right now I was just too distracted to really care.

Jaden wasn't that kind of guy, in any way whatsoever, but still. I was happy for now, being friends. I knew he was there for me, no matter what, even if he didn't owe me for saving his family anymore. He didn't owe me a thing after coming along on that disastrous trip to Faerie.

"So how far is this guy?" I asked Starren.

"Carver," Starren said. "Only a couple hours of walking."

Ughhh. Why was there always so much walking? The fae didn't like mechanical stuff, but surely they had horses or something. Scratch that. I didn't know how to ride a horse.

This part of Faerie felt much younger than the area we'd been in last time. The trees were smaller, and felt... different. They were more exuberant? One reached out and caressed my cheek as I walked, startling me.

I jumped sideways. Okay, that had never really happened before. I gave the tree a weak smile, not wanting to offend it.

The grass rustled as we went by, wiggling in happiness.

Starren pulled her sword and turned toward the brush. It wilted. Starren puffed out a breath. "I thought something was in there. What are you doing?" Starren's voice was hushed, like maybe the plants wouldn't hear her.

"Me? I'm not doing anything, ask them what they're doing!"

Starren batted at a patch of grass with the flat of her blade. It shrank to the ground. The whole atmosphere seemed to shrink.

"Hey, be nice," I said. "It didn't do anything to you." And just like that, the happy came back to the forest.

"There is something seriously wrong with you." Starren sheathed her sword and marched off.

"Not as much as is wrong with you," I mumbled. She was out-voted too, because I was sure the plants would agree with me, and there weren't any other living things around. I hoped. Living things in Faerie were scary. Like mermaids. Beautiful things of legend on Earth. Terrifying creatures of murder in Faerie. That's just how it worked here.

I trudged along after Starren for what seemed like forever. How did such a city girl get the ability to communicate with plants? I hated being out in nature. At least I used to. A friendly little bush reached out for me to smell its flowers.

It didn't seem so bad anymore.

But it would make walking around on Earth awkward, if the plants were behaving like this. I didn't know if they would do that at this point or not, I'd only been out of Sanctuary to head to D.C., and hadn't been out of the car long enough to notice.

Oh, fire fruit. I plucked one off a tree, careful to only take a tiny bite. This was the one thing I did like about Faerie. The food was luscious.

But thinking about food in Faerie made me lose my appetite. Eating the food had been what led to Dan and Nina losing their memories.

I dropped it, the taste good and yet horrible in my mouth.

A branch snatched the fruit out of midair, and held it out to me.

"Thanks." I took it back half-heartedly.

I slowly munched on it as we walked, forever and ever. I finished it and dropped the pit. Before it even hit the ground, a branch put another in my hand.

Starren eyed me.

"What?" I asked defensively.

"That's getting kind of ridiculous."

"Yeah, I know, but what do I do about it? I don't know how this works." I held the fruit up. "I'm full, want one?"

She took it and took a giant bite.

"Wait, no!" I was too late. I waited for her to collapse in pain. Fire fruit was spicy in small quantities, and an inferno in large. I waited for her to start crying and spit it out. How did she not know about fire fruit? She grew up here. But nothing happened.

Starren just stared at me while she chewed for a moment, then turned and walked away.

Um, what?

Something tapped me on the shoulder, and I had another piece of fruit placed in my hand. "Thanks."

We walked and walked. I carried the fruit like an idiot, because I didn't want to hurt the trees' feelings.

Eventually we came upon a brook.

"Oh, nice." I trotted forward and went to let the water run through my fingers. Starren slapped my hand away before it even got wet.

"What are you doing? Do you regrow body parts?"

"Star. It's water."

"Trisha. It's Faerie." She took the bruised piece of fruit I'd been carrying around for the last hour from my hand and tossed it into the water.

Sliver flashes devoured the fruit before it had even sunk below the surface, pit and all.

"What's wrong with this place?" I yelped, taking a big step back. "I was going to drink that!"

"Why would you drink silverbiters?" Starren asked. And she was completely serious.

"I thought it was just water."

Starren looked confused for a second, like she'd forgotten that I didn't have much experience here. She took my arm and tugged me closer. "See the little ripples under the water? That's the only give-away." She looked up and down the small stream. "Well, that and the fact that there's nothing edible along this section of water. We need to cross, but we'll have to travel a fair distance to do that. That's where the length of this trip comes from."

I glanced up at the tall trees lining the stream. "There is another way."

Starren looked up where I was looking. "Oh no. Nuh uh. Not after last time we were here, not after you swung us all the way down from the Council platforms. I thought we were going to die."

I smirked. That was the first time she'd ever admitted to me that she was worried about anything. I didn't even have to ask the trees. Branches reached out and wrapped around both of us, looped gently around us several times, and then snapped across the wide but shallow water and deposited us on the other side.

Starren bent over. "Ohhh, I hate that so much."

I flat out laughed this time. I knew that rolling feeling well, but I had pretty much adjusted to it at this point.

With a pat to the closest tree, I went over and squatted down by Starren. "Ready? Take your time if you need it."

She glared at me, but for once it didn't feel like an angry glare, more of a playful one. Even being back in Faerie with all the bad memories, she was a different person than she'd been before, and that was a pretty awesome thing.

She waved her hand in the direction she wanted us to go and straightened. "It should be less than an hour's walk with that shortcut." She stretched her neck. "Remind me to never get on your bad side. Again."

I wrinkled my nose at her and started off in the direction she'd pointed. This having a sister thing wasn't so bad. I was definitely adjusting to it.

A nice bounce in my step lagged after the first fifteen minutes. Walking was so boring. My mind wandered. What was this dude Starren had been with like? What was his name again? I opened my mouth to ask her, but snapped it closed when I saw her face. Tense. She'd gotten more and more tense as we walked, and I hadn't noticed.

Maybe she disliked this guy as much as I disliked Wade. Hopefully not, because I didn't know if I'd be able to hold her back if she tried to do anything. Not that I wouldn't be able to physically hold her back, at least with a tree's help, more of the I wasn't sure if I'd want to kind of thing.

Carver, that was his name. Hopefully that was his given name and not some nickname he got for being a terrible person. What kind of guy could attract an awesome person like Starren? She was a self-contained unit, I wouldn't have thought she'd willingly let anyone in. I'd had to force it. Hard.

Was there a time in Starren's life when she hadn't been this... Starren? I stared at her, trying to see past all the layers.

She noticed and her face went grumpy.

Nope. She'd been raised by Quintin. She probably was like this since she was a baby. Except she'd had mom for awhile. How old had she been when mom snatched me and ran? And why hadn't she taken her with us?

Bringing it up would probably be suicide, so I kept my thoughts to myself, for once. That was one topic both of us stayed far away from.

I'd lost track of time when Starren slowed. "We're almost there." The tension building in her body was nearly palpable. By now she was a wound wire, waiting to snap. "I don't want to do this," she admitted, bouncing on the balls of her feet in an uncharacteristic show of nerves.

"Well, thank you."

She gave me a withering look.

"No, I'm serious. You wouldn't be here if it wasn't for me. I appreciate it."

"You're right, I wouldn't be here if it wasn't for you." She caught my eye. "I'd still be in prison, or worse, with Father. Thank you. I don't think I ever said it. Thank you."

Okay, I had no words for that. I just shrugged it off, looking away, but she just kept staring.

"You're welcome?" I said, but it sounded more like a question.

And that was it. She straightened her shoulders and marched off.

I quickened my pace. Time to wish for the boredom of walking. I was about to meet the man that was strong enough to make Starren give him the time of day. Hopefully he wasn't any scarier than she was. Ha.

CHAPTER NINE

Moving into a clearing, a small hut came into view, trained out of living tree branches and limbs.

Was this guy some fearsome warrior tired of the carnage like in so many movies and books? Someone hiding from society? Pfft. If it was fae society he was hiding from, more power to him.

The place was really nice. Somewhere I could imagine Nina retiring, with a pretty garden and a little creek in the back. Hopefully it wasn't a deadly creek, like the last one we'd seen.

Starren paused, took a deep breath, set her face into her usual mask, and marched up to the door. She aggressively rapped three times, and then joined her hands behind her back in an at ease military position.

"Chill, Starren, it'll be okay," I said.

She gave me a withering look, and didn't even have to speak for me to know what she was thinking. I had no way of knowing if it was going to be okay or not. But I sure couldn't wait to find out.

I bounced, unable to contain my excitement. Not only would it be cool to meet this guy, but he might be able to tell us how to fix Nina and Dan.

Starren glared at me again, and I dialed the excitement down a notch. At least on the outside.

After a few more seconds of no one answering the door, Starren rapped again. It wasn't like the place was big enough for the guy to not have heard her the first time, but considering I was ready to rip the door off its hinges, I felt she was justified.

"Carver, I know you're in there, open the door."

"How do you know he's in there?" I asked.

"He's not out here, and he no longer leaves the property." She pounded on the door with her fist this time. "Carver!"

The sound of locks clicking rang through the door. It opened a little, but not enough for me to see much. Starren's restraint in not kicking down the door was impressive. She wasn't great at waiting. Whoever, hopefully Carver, was on the other side must have been satisfied, because the door swung open wide.

A cute guy about an inch taller than Starren's not that tall frame stood on the other side. He was in a robe, his hair all mussed. He blinked at us.

"Carver." Starren's normally chill tone was completely frigid. A shiver went down my spine, and it wasn't even directed at me.

Wait a second. This was Carver? This was who I built up to be some undefeatable warrior? He was more like Cray than Wade.

"Starren!" His face lit up for a second, but then the fae mask went on. "What are you doing here?"

"I need to ask that you pay the debt you owe me."

I kicked her.

She looked at me like 'what.'

"How about we start this over, shall we?" I asked. I was more eager to have him answer her question than she could ever be, but not like this. I stuck my hand out. "Hey. I'm Trish."

He stared blankly at my hand. Oh yeah. Fae didn't do that. I awkwardly pulled my hand back and rubbed it on my jeans.

"I'm Starren's-" Starren kicked me. "Friend."

No comment. He was just checking Starren out.

"We've traveled a long way to see you."

Still no comment, from either of them.

I threw my hands up in the air. "Nothing? From either of you?"

Carver attempted a causal lean on the door frame, missed and almost fell. He stumbled for a second, then regained his balance. "Hello, Trish." He spoke to me, but he watched Star. "I am ready and willing to pay my debt, what must be done?"

So formal. Fae and all their stupid.

"I don't need anything done," Starren said. "Just information." She looked around him into his hut. "Somewhat sensitive information. Are you alone? Does anyone live here with you?"

Ha. Not very subtle. This was painful to watch.

"No one else is here. Do you... travel with anyone other than Trish?"

I would have laughed out loud if this wasn't taking up valuable time. I needed Nina back.

"Are we going in or what?" I asked. "I don't care if we ask him out here, let's just get it done."

Carver scooted Starren over so he could see out behind her, suddenly looking very worried. "Come in, come in. We shouldn't be out in the open like this."

Starren had her *he's crazy* look on, but I ignored it and pushed past her. If he wanted to talk inside, great, whatever, we just needed to get this talking over. I nearly buzzed, practically hearing Nina say my name.

"Since when can we not be out in the open?" Starren asked as I pulled her inside. "This is a perfectly safe part of Faerie."

Ha, if this was the perfectly safe part, I didn't want to see any more. The water had tried to eat us. What happened in the dangerous parts, the ground wanted a meal too?

Turning from Starren, I got my first good look at the inside of the hut. But here it wasn't a hut. I felt my mouth fall open and stopped hard enough that Starren ran into me from behind.

Inside, it was a full blown house, sprawling out in front of us. The floors were a beautiful polished wood, still alive. It was more like a loft, actually, with everything in one room. A kitchen, dining area, bedroom, and a beautiful library. Fae had books? I drifted closer to get a better look. Nope. They were human books. Lord of the Rings. Chronicles of Narnia. Alice in Wonderland.

"Where did you get these?" I asked, whirling around to face him. "Do you travel to Earth?"

"No." He sent a grin toward Starren. "Starren picked them all up for me."

All of them? There had to be a hundred. This said a lot about how much she must have felt for him, to do something that she would find nonsense for him like this.

I waved my hand around. "How did you do all this?"

"Carver is very talented," Starren said. "He creates all of our pockets for us."

It took me a minute to get what she meant. The pockets that led to Faerie, that had way more space than they were supposed to. Like the one she kept her sword in.

Carver's grin turned kind of sappy and Starren instantly hardened back up. He drooped a little, making me feel bad for him. What exactly had happened between the two of them?

"What information do you need, Starren?" He sounded defeated now, like some hope had been dashed.

"I'm sure that even here in the middle of nowhere you've heard about how some humans came into Faerie."

He nodded. "I also heard that you brought them here to kill the Council. And that your Father had to take over the government of Faerie because of the slaughter."

"No," Starren barked. She closed her eyes and took a deep breath through her nose. "That's not how it happened."

"So you didn't kill the Council?" he asked, his gaze swinging back and forth between Starren and me.

"The humans ate fae food while they were here," I interrupted. "And now they don't remember anything about the fae. How can we fix it?"

"You expect me to help the humans who came here to kill the Council?" He crossed his arms in front of his chest. "You should know me better than that, Starren. I didn't like a lot of things the Council did, but to just kill them in cold blood? How could you?"

Starren looked away.

"She was tricked into doing it. And it wasn't by the humans, it was Quintin," I said.

"And you must be the sister." He nodded toward me, but then spoke to Starren. "I thought you'd kidnapped her."

"You should know not to believe the things you hear around here," Starren got out from behind gritted teeth. "Do you know of a cure?"

Carver studied us, one at a time, for what felt like forever. "I know someone that should be able to help. Her abilities with the mind are extraordinary. She can wipe memory, and it follows that she should be able to restore it. But with the way things are right now, you'd have a difficult time getting to her."

"What do you mean, with the way things are right now?" Starren asked.

"It's dangerous out there. Someone has been attacking your father's men. And Faerie is wild far beyond its normal. Strange creatures have been coming out of the dark forests, devouring everything they can get their hands on."

"We can take care of ourselves, Carver. Just tell us who can help." The words had barely left Starren's mouth when pounding started on the door.

Carver stiffened, horror on his face. He put his finger to his lips and gestured us over frantically, stuffing us in a small closest and closing the door carefully.

I held my breath, trying to ask Starren with my face who it was. She seemed to get the message, but shook her head no. She didn't know what was going on either.

The front door creaked open. "Hello." Carver's muffled voice came through the closet door. "What can I do for you?"

Starren's hand slid to her sword hilt. She better not try to pull that thing out in here, she'd get either me or herself, and I knew which one it would be.

A woman's voice barely made it through to the closet. "Your Lord and Master, Quintin, King of all the Fae, requires your presence at the new palace."

"Palace?" Starren mouthed to me.

I nodded.

I could practically feel the anger radiating off her.

"There is no palace," she mouthed again.

That made sense. The fae didn't do almost anything like the humans did. And they didn't let one person have power for sure, so a palace didn't really make sense. Even the Council didn't live in one place, they just met for special occasions. In general, the fae government just lived and let live, unless something they saw as a problem cropped up, then they were all in your business. So had Father built this palace?

"Can I change and grab my things?" Carver asked.

"That is acceptable."

The door shut, a little harder than necessary, and I heard his lock click into place.

Footsteps shuffled over to the closet. Carver opened the door and put his head in. "Stay here until we're long gone. I don't know what's going on, but I don't want you mixed up in it."

He was about to be dragged away and he was looking out for us? No wonder Starren liked him.

"The person you're looking for is called Nara. Last I heard of her, the Council had her imprisoned in Fairbent."

"Nara? Girl about my age, Nara?" I asked.

He nodded. "You know her?"

"We met." Under terrible circumstances, in the prison. Wade and Jaden had freed her after we'd run from Father, but she'd taken off after that and I had no idea what had happened to her.

I leaned weakly against the wall. "How are we supposed to find her?"

Banging started on the front door. "Hurry up. We want to be through Firten Forest before nightfall," a different guard shouted through the door.

"Coming," Carver yelled, taking off to a wardrobe in the bedroom section of his home. He grabbed a knapsack out of a cupboard. "For emergencies." He held it up so I could see, but it didn't mean anything to me.

Starren pushed past me and followed him. She grabbed Carver's arm and jerked him to a stop. "You're not going with those guards."

He smiled. "It's okay. He probably just wants someone to play with a bit. Or some information, though I don't know why he couldn't just have his goons ask. No big deal. And plus, you'll have someone on the inside. Never a bad thing."

"I don't like this, Carver. It's too dangerous."

"What are our options, Star?"

Aww, he called her Star too. I'd never meet anyone else who dared to do that.

"Either they take me, or we, mostly you, fight them. And if we fight them, your father is going to know I had help," Carver said. "And who would help me, but you? He'd know you're in Faerie. And then the guards won't be asking so nicely if I'd go with them."

Her face went mutinous.

"There's no back door to this place?" I asked.

"No. I felt safer with just the one," he said.

I wandered toward the back. "Is this the farthest point from the guards?" I asked. "I'm all mixed up with the dimensions being different inside and out. Would the hut hide us here?"

"Theoretically." Carver walked over to stand by me. "But you saw the house from the outside, there isn't a whole lot of space behind. Plus, it would take us quite awhile to saw through the wood. My grandfather started these trees growing into place hundreds of years ago, they're much thicker than you'd think."

Starren bounded over to stand on my other side, eyes bright. "The trees are living."

It came out as a statement, but Carver answered. "Ah, yes?"

"Do it," Starren told me.

I laid my palm against the wood and closed my eyes, concentrating. These trees were old. Their essence flowed through me, whizzing me through season after season. Slowly they took notice of me, like they were waking from a deep sleep.

It took a moment, the guards pounding on the door and yelling, Starren and Carver breathing, everything fading away. But then, ponderously, a small hole, only about the size of my pinkie, began to open.

I kept at the trees, quietly urging them to give us more room. As they woke, they started to get angry.

They had loved Carver's family for centuries, and now the only one they had left was under attack.

I wrestled the thoughts of tearing through the guards out of their minds, focusing on giving us a way out. They fought back, thinking that Carver was in the safest place he could be. I showed them images of the guards bursting through the door, and of the fae that would follow if something happened to them.

They relented, opening up the hole just enough for us to squeeze through.

I motioned Starren through first, staying to make sure the hole remained open. She grabbed Carver's hand and pulled him after her, his mouth hanging open.

As I moved into the opening, I rubbed my hand against the wood, thanking the tree for helping us, and for its restraint.

The wall took longer than I'd expected to pass through. Carver was right, we would never have been able to cut through there in time, even if we'd had a chainsaw.

Starren and Carver carefully stood on the outside of the hut, out of sight of the guards, but not touching any of the wood. It wasn't like the tree was going to hurt them at this point, it had just helped them.

I started to speak, but Starren chopped the air with her hand, stopping me. She pointed to the trees forming the back of the clearing.

So far. Could we really make it that far without anyone seeing us?

The grasses in front of us slowly stretched up, adding several inches to their height. Starren grimaced, but went down on her elbows and knees and started to army crawl toward freedom.

Everywhere she crushed the grass, it flowed back up around her, making it impossible to see or track her.

Thank you, I told whatever or whoever was listening.

Carver followed Starren, and I followed Carver.

The pounding behind us turned into a splintering sound. The fae had decided not to wait.

Oh crap, the hole! I turned around to go back and close it, but the tree was wise enough to have the gap already filled. Whew.

Footsteps pounded around the outside of the hut in our direction. I dropped to the ground, eyes held tightly closed, like that would help. I had no doubt that Starren and I could take a few guards, it would be simple.

But then Father would know we were here. And so far I'd managed to avoid killing anyone by accident. I'd really rather not do it on purpose.

The guard didn't linger. The hole had disappeared, and there weren't any doors. As far as the guards could tell, Carver was still inside, hiding somewhere.

As soon as the guard jogged by, I started crawling again, at double speed. What happened if they caught us and got rough with Carver? Or Starren? I'd nearly killed Starren after Nina had been shot on our last visit, assuming it had been her that had done it. I shivered. I'd almost killed my sister without even thinking.

And if Nina hadn't been back to stop me, I would have killed Wade. I hadn't told the trees to hurt him, but they had felt my rage, my hate, and had taken it upon themselves to stop the source.

Would I be able to control them if something happened again? Control myself? The thought of finding out sent my arms trembling, and my stomach clenched.

I just needed to make sure I was never in that position again. Then I'd never have to find out if I had the self-control necessary or not.

I still crawled when I reached the trees, until I almost bumped into Starren's legs. She reached down and hauled me up, putting a finger to her lips.

We moved as quietly as possible, the grass fluffing back up behind us so that we didn't leave any kind of trail.

Starren made us walk a good fifteen minutes before she let us talk.

"What was that?" Carver yelled in my face. "I've never seen anything like that!"

Starren shoved him away from me. "None of your business," she said. "You don't even know it was her."

He glared at her. "Are you trying to tell me it was you?"

She lifted an eyebrow.

"Because last I knew, you didn't have any powers."

"Keep it down," Starren growled. "We don't know what powers the fae that were sent after you have. One of them may be able to hear this distance. We should be whispering if talking at all."

His face went chagrined. "Sorry. I should have thought of that."

"I only stopped us so we could come up with a plan, and we don't travel farther in the wrong way if we want to choose another direction. I didn't even check when we left, because it didn't matter at that moment."

Carver looked around, eyes wide. "Are we lost?"

I kicked him in the ankle. "This is your home area, are we?"

He looked around again, taking his time. "All the trees look the same to me. I wasn't paying attention." He turned in a circle. "If we hit the stream, I'll know where we are."

"We might as well come up with a plan first," Starren said.

"No, we should get somewhere safer first."

I let them argue, closing my eyes, feeling through the tree roots for a water source. There. Ahead and to the right, not very far.

"That way." I pointed.

The two of them stopped arguing and looked at me.

"The water is that way." I pointed again.

"Then we need to choose now. What are we doing?" Starren asked.

Carver studied me. "How do you know that?"

I shrugged.

"What are our options?" Starren asked, pacing a little. "One, go to the prison and try to pick up where Nara went. Two, go back to Earth and get," she paused, eyeing Carver, "help from someone who will be able to find her, or three, go back to Earth and stay there. Leave the humans as they are."

"What?" I balked. "No!"

"I was just presenting all our options," Starren said.

"Number three is not an option. And I'm not a fan of number two, either." Cray would be able to find Nara. But at what cost? He wasn't much of a warrior. And he was so sweet and kind that this type of thing bothered him enough to make him sick. I wouldn't involve him unless we had no other choice, at all.

Carver cocked his head. "These humans mean a lot to you?"

I nodded. There was no getting around that.

Carver hefted his pack on his back. "Alright then. Fairbent Prison, here we come."

CHAPTER TEN

For once, travelling wasn't boring me. I pushed the others. Harder than I should. In my mind I knew that they could drop from exhaustion before I even felt truly tired, but my heart didn't care.

As we got closer and closer to this forest the guards had been so worried about, the presence of the trees and plants faded. I didn't notice at first, lost in my head, but once I did it was obvious. They were there physically. In fact, there were brambles here, unlike anywhere else I'd been in Faerie. But the plants here felt gloomy.

"We should find somewhere to stop for the night." Even Carver's hushed voice sounded wrong here. Loud, and yet muffled. Harsh. "Before we get deeper into the wood. Even fae who live here have been going missing lately."

I shivered. As if this place wasn't terrifying enough, now something was preying on the top dogs of the area. But Dan and Nina. "We should see how far we can get."

"Here. This is how far we can get," Carver answered. "Or there's a good chance we wind up dead."

I wanted to argue. But I knew it wouldn't do any good. I couldn't get anywhere without them.

We walked a short distance farther before we found a spot Starren deemed suitable, in some reeds near a small brook.

Even the brook was wise enough to not make any sound here.

None of us were going to get much sleep tonight.

"I'll take first watch," Starren said. She stepped into the darkness before I could protest. Suddenly all of this just shot to the top of the creepy factor.

Carver sat on the ground, and I followed suit, putting us back to back. I didn't know him well enough to trust him, but having him at my back was sure better than it being open to whatever prowled in the trees. Neither of us tried to lie down.

"So," I said.

"So?"

"What happened between you and Starren?" Odd time to be asking about this? You betcha. But we both needed a distraction, and I might not get another time to ask this stuff. Might as well use my time wisely.

"We were incompatible."

I snorted. "Who says? Sure, I was a little surprised when I met you that you were her type, but I can see it now. I think you'd be great together."

"Well good for you. And that's kind of insulting."

"I didn't mean it to be, sorry." We sat in uncomfortable silence. These conversations were hard to have when you couldn't read the other person's facial expression. "Seriously though." Tough conversation to have, but that didn't mean I was just going to let it go. "What happened?"

"Her father wasn't happy with us being in a relationship." His voice was guarded, his back warm but stiff against mine.

"And that was it? You just gave up on her?" My back was about to be more than warm. He didn't deserve Starren if that's as little as she meant to him. "She sure was important to you, huh."

He twisted so he could look me in the face. "Don't say that. It was for her that I ended things. Her father thought it was too human. Fae have more alliances than marriages, and the fact that we had feelings for each other upset him." He settled back, hunching into himself.

"And I'm not exactly the ambitious type that her father would want for her."

That checked out. "But maybe that's one of the things Starren loves about you."

He turned back and beamed. "You think she loves some things about me?"

"She wouldn't have been with you if she didn't. If she wasn't looking to use you, then she must have cared about you. Those are your two options."

"True. And she wasn't using me, I know that much."

"So are you going to try again?"

He hunched back over. "I wish I could. But it isn't that simple."

Now it was my turn to flop sideways, so I could just barely make out his face in the shadows. "She's worth it, isn't she? She'll take you back, I can tell. She seemed confused why you wanted to leave her in the first place."

"I didn't want to!" The words burst out of his mouth. "I didn't want to at all." Okay, much more appropriate voice level there. "Her father made me, you already know that."

"Yeah, he isn't a good guy, but I don't think he'd actually hurt you, Starren would know and then she'd be mad and all that. Plus, at this point they're fighting anyway, it's not like you're going to put a rift in their relationship."

"It wasn't me he was going to hurt," Carver whispered, checking the trees like he was afraid Starren was eavesdropping. "He said he'd make her life horrible if I didn't listen, send her on terrible assignments, force her to hate me by making it look like I'd done something terrible toward her, who knows. That man is crazy."

Couldn't argue with him there.

"I didn't want to leave, but he didn't even let me stay in the city." He motioned back toward his home. "That's why I was back there, where I grew up. I love the place, but it's lonely."

Yet another person Quintin had ruined. How did someone get to the point that they only cared about themselves like that? I winced, glad it was dark. I'd been there. I'd only cared about myself before Dan and Nina had showed me what unconditional love felt like. Pretty good, that's how. But now that I knew, I'd never go back. I'd never let myself.

"He's out of the picture now," I said. "Maybe you're safe to try again."

"He'll never be out of the picture." Carver sounded bitter. "But maybe that doesn't matter so much anymore, now that Starren has seen him for who he really is."

I kept quiet there. Starren had always seen him for who he was. She just hadn't known what to do with that. Now Dan and Nina's kindness was leaking through me to her, and she was changing, whether she liked it or not.

"We should get some sleep." I shut down the conversation like I hadn't been the one to insist on having it. Starren wasn't much of one for talking, and really didn't like to share her feelings, but I needed to see if I could get a hint before I pushed Carver toward something impossible. If his heart got broke because I made him feel like being with Starren was an option when it actually wasn't, I'd never forgive myself.

"True," Carver said. "We're going to have to take our turns on guard duty." He went quiet for a moment. "But sleeping is going to be pretty difficult."

"True," I answered, but didn't add anything. No use the two of us making each other more nervous. We sat in silence, pretending everything was okay. I liked the talking much more. My mind wanted to wander to how Nina was doing, but that was something I refused to think about at the moment. The quiet unnerved me, worse than I'd expected.

Did I ever say I was good outside of the city? Nope. City girl through and through.

And at least at home there were comforting sounds in the dark, even in nature. Frogs. Those big bugs that lived in the trees. Whatever else nature wanted to do at that moment. But here? Total silence.

I hated silence.

Fort Wayne wasn't a big city, but it was decent sized and there was usually something going on.

This was plain weird, even for Faerie.

It took me at least twenty minutes to get drowsy. I didn't want to check the time on my phone though, both to save power and because it just seemed downright stupid to flash an artificial light around right now.

Eventually I did doze off. The only way I knew was because something startled me awake.

I jerked up straight from where I'd slumped against Carver, sending him sprawling on the ground.

He didn't seem to notice.

What had woke me?

Ha. Probably just paranoia.

But then I shivered. The entire time I spent in Faerie a couple months ago, the temperature had been super steady. Another shiver went through me, this one not because of the cold.

Something was off.

A dense, chilly fog drifted at us from the trees, getting thicker by the second.

This fog. This weird, cold, unnatural fog. I knew this fog.

"Starren," I half yelled, half hissed, my heart kicking it into high gear. "Star, where are you?"

I shook Carver, admittedly a little wildly.

He mumbled something, but seemed to be waking up. I jumped to my feet, but stayed crouching down. Hopefully it didn't know we were here. I reached down and shook Carver again.

"Wass going on?" Carver asked.

"We need to find Starren, right now," I told him. But he wasn't moving quick enough.

I kicked him.

"Hey!" he yelped.

"Shhh. We need to get out of here."

A hissing laugh sounded out in the darkness. "Child. I thought you were going to avoid this place."

I wildly looked to Carver whose eyes had gone huge. He was very awake now. And then my eyes went straight to the snakelike beast sliding between the trees, and stuck there like glue.

How did she get here?

I scrambled back, dragging Carver with me.

A blur jumped out of the trees and grabbed Carver from the other side, pulling us both along with the force. I barely held in a shriek, dropping Carver's arm, my mind registering Starren's form at the last second.

"What do you want?" I asked the hyran, my voice breaking in the middle.

She stopped, her stillness somehow more intimidating than her slithering. "Now child, is that any way to talk to an old friend?"

"What are you doing here?" Maybe I could keep her talking, and at least Starren and Carver could get away.

"Isn't that what I just asked of you?"

She was right. But fae were so annoying. They never wanted to give a straight answer. My mind whirled with different crazy ideas of what to tell her that would somehow slip in as truth. I had to think like the fae, come up with something close enough to the truth to get by, but far enough from the truth that it didn't cause any problems. Problems, like, you know, death.

But then, I didn't care much for how the fae did things. Yes, I was fae. I couldn't change that. But it didn't mean I had to act like them.

"You're right." What a proud moment, my voice only quivered a little. "I didn't ever want to come here. But I came to help a friend, and then that spiraled into another problem, and so here I am, not here once, but twice."

She started laughing, hard. The hissing gurgle made me want to throw up, but at least that meant she was happy. Maybe.

While she was distracted, I checked over my shoulder to see how far Carver and Starren had gotten. Nowhere. Literally nowhere.

I shooed them.

Starren sent me her typical glare, though it did look a little less intense than normal, which I took to mean she was freaking out too. Then she shook her head at my shooing.

Ugh, why didn't anyone ever listen to me. It was for their own good. For some reason this thing seemed to like me.

"Refreshing," the hyran hissed out. I didn't think she meant it as a bad hiss, but I didn't know how to tell for sure. I'd only met her once before, and only for about five minutes. She'd kindly decided not to eat us when Wade, Starren, Cray and I had disturbed her on Alcatraz Island.

"I see you have your blade happy friend with you."

I glanced over my shoulder again and made a face at Starren. There wasn't a thing we could do against a hyran, and Starren had been the one to tell me that, so having her sword out was just antagonizing. She'd said she'd killed one once, but hadn't elaborated, so I was a little doubtful she could do it right now.

She let the tip drop to the ground, but kept it tightly in her hand.

The hyran squinted at Carver. "But I don't think that one is one of them you had before."

"Nope," I said. "That's a different one."

The hyran grinned, moonlight bouncing off her rather pointed teeth. She slapped her side and kept smiling. "I knew it. After four hundred years, I'm getting better at this recognizing fae thing."

"Four hundred years?" I whispered to myself. Just how old was this thing?

She settled back, using her tail to prop herself up. "I find you very entertaining. What is this problem you mentioned?"

I didn't actually know how she felt about humans. I did know that she didn't much care for the Council, she'd told us as much back at Alcatraz. But how would she feel about the fact that I'd brought humans to Faerie?

"A question for a question," I said, taking my lead from the whole thing with Wren. "Why are you back here? I thought you liked Earth, and being around the humans. You didn't sound like you much cared for Faerie either, last time we talked."

Her face went dark, and she looked angry.

"All fae registered to be on Earth had to return to be counted when the Usurper took the throne from the Council. We were told we were to report in and then be allowed to return, but now the portals are locked and the tunnels guarded." She smiled a little. "I think they'll come to regret that."

Okay, probably better to not mention the fact that 'the Usurper' most likely referred to my father, who'd made Starren help him kill the entire Council. And this also explained why Firten Forest had become so dangerous.

"Now my turn. Why have you returned to Faerie?"

Oh crap, I should have been thinking this through. "I have a ...friend." I paused, carefully weighing each word. "That's having some problems, that I thought someone here may be able to help with."

She perked up a little. "Is this friend human?"

I nodded, not even arguing with her about the fact that it was her turn to answer a question.

"Two humans were here with the Usurper's daughters when they slaughtered the Council."

Abort, abort, this was getting into very dangerous territory.

"Might you know these daughters?" she leaned in, like my answer was important to her.

There was no not answering this, and there was no lying. "Maybe?"

She laughed. "You don't know if you know them? Is that because," she pointed a bony finger at Starren, "you are them?"

I choked, my brain blank enough I probably wouldn't have been able to tell her my own name if she'd asked. This was it. We were about to die. Right here, right now. Dan and Nina were better off not remembering me, they wouldn't have anyone to grieve if they didn't know I existed. Poor Wren would always wonder what happened, but too late to do anything about that now.

"I'd known the fae of the Council for hundreds of years," she said.

Oh no. I squeezed my eyes closed, waiting for the first blow. How would she kill us? Did she have poison? Crush us? Would I heal, over and over, only to be turned to pulp again and again?

Then she laughed. "And I've hated them since the day we met. I knew I liked you. You don't know how much you helped the fae that day. Now we only need to be rid of your father, and all will be well." She paused, looking around. "The woods are no longer safe even during the day. No one should be out after dark. Even one such as you. Come." And then she turned and left, just expecting absolute obedience.

She was going to get it.

I started to follow her, checking to see if Starren was coming.

She just stood there, looking torn.

I motioned for her to come. She'd told me back when we'd first met the hyran that she was extremely dangerous, and even the most powerful of the fae would not be able to stand against her.

But she fed on human fear, not fae, so she had no reason to wish us harm.

I hoped.

Plus, there was that age old adage, if she'd wanted to hurt us, she'd have done it by now, right? Unless she just wanted us to walk to her lair so she didn't have to do the work of dragging us.

That would be about right with how things had been going lately. She'd probably lock me up to be her court jester or whatever. They didn't have TV here, they had to find their entertainment somewhere.

Hopefully that entertainment didn't involve her figuring out how hard I was to kill and having fun with that. I might not die easily, but I still felt everything.

Reluctantly, I moved after her. It didn't feel like a choice, as if it was inevitable. What would she do if we said no?

"Someone is targeting those loyal to your father," the hyran said as she moved forward, way faster than I would have expected. "If they find out who you are, you would be in danger."

Was she really protecting us? She was fae enough that she couldn't lie, right? She was from Faerie. Still, like I'd found out way too much the hard way, lying and not telling the truth weren't exactly the same thing.

"I would throw my full support behind these rebels, if I could find them." She didn't seem to wonder if we were listening. Must be nice to be so high up on the food chain that she automatically knew that we'd be hanging onto every word, trying not to die. "But they hit hard, hit fast, and then are gone."

She looked back at us, head turned completely around but body not even slowing as it moved forward. "Maybe you will come into contact with someone from this group. Maybe you will be able to tell me more about them."

I shrugged. It wasn't impossible, but hopefully we didn't run into another fae this whole trip, except for Nara of course. A pipe dream, but I could cling to it.

"You will be safe with me for the night, and then you can leave in the morning, on whatever your secret mission is. If your last mission was to clean out the Council, I can only dream about what you're here for this time."

Whew, she wasn't going to keep insisting I tell her what we were up to. Apparently she wouldn't care, but I'd still rather not get into it, just in case. I didn't correct her about what our mission had been last time.

"So, ah, how far is your, lair?"

And there was that snorting laugh again. "I prefer it be called my home. And it's only a few minutes walk away."

It got quiet.

Uncomfortable quiet. I looked back at Starren and Carver. Shouldn't someone else think of something to say for once?

But now that it was quiet, I began to hear other things. Things I kind of wished I hadn't heard.

Something snuffled in the brush, way too close for comfort. I tried to use the trees and feel out what it was, but none wanted to help. None even really responded. I shrunk a little closer to the monster I knew, hoping I didn't have to meet the monster I didn't.

A beat of massive wings above had me practically crawling on the hyran's back, Starren and Carter crowding in close.

The hyran looked back at us, then looked up. She had to be able to feel our fear, it was, after all, her food of choice, even if she preferred human.

The wingbeats got louder. Whatever that thing was, it was huge, and heading our way.

I clung to the hilt of my sword, ready to pull it as soon as needed.

The hyran cocked her head and let out a strange keening call. The wingbeats went frantic, bursting away from us.

I let out a pent up breath. But at the same time, that just made things even more scary. Whatever had been up there was scared of our host. And if whatever it was feared her, I did too.

Not encouraging considering the amount of fear I'd already had for her before.

The forest all around us had gone completely silent again, after the hyran's display.

Starren and Carver had fallen a little behind, leading me to believe that Starren had come to the same conclusion I had about the level of scary going up so high it broke the bar, not even just raising it.

"So, uh, what do you like to do for fun?" I asked the hyran. Silence wasn't my forte.

Even the snicker from in front of us sounded sinister.

"What makes you think I do anything for fun?"

Well my question hadn't been very well thought out, had it. "You just seem like a person who likes fun."

Starren choked behind me.

The hyran's head whipped around behind her again, while her body kept traveling forward.

"What?" I asked after a few moments of her staring at me.

"You just called me a person." She lifted her neck, getting quite a bit taller than me. "I don't think a fae has ever done that before." She slid forward a little faster. "One of the reasons I left Faerie. I prefer humans."

"And that's something I've never heard a member of the fae say before," I answered.

The laughing started back up. Maybe I should be worried about her mental health instead of being worried that she was luring us back to her lair to kill us. Or maybe I should be worried about both things.

"You are different, little fae. Very different." I could practically see her pointy teeth, the grin in her voice was so strong.

I stepped over a fallen branch, studying it as I went by. I'd never seen a dead branch in Faerie before. Everything here seemed to thrive. "Is that good or bad?" I asked. "The different thing."

I knew, of course, why I was different. I'd grown up with humans instead of fae. Mostly decent humans, though some didn't really know how to handle a bratty teen.

"In most cases, different is good. But especially so in this case." She stopped in front of a craggy rock face. "Here we are."

Squinting in either direction didn't reveal anything, so I craned my neck up. That didn't help much either. I tipped back until I almost toppled over, but didn't see anything.

"Up we go."

And then she grabbed me, hauling both of us up the rock face.

I bit down on my tongue, hard enough to make it bleed, while trying not to scream.

"Hey!" Starren yelled from the base, but we were already far out of range of her and her sword.

I closed my eyes and shrank into the hyran. Should I be more afraid of getting eaten or dropped? I cracked an eyelid, looking down at Starren and Carver shrinking below. Eaten. I'd probably heal from a drop like that.

Much to my surprise, the hyran actually let off quite a bit of heat. If I'd thought about it, I would have expected her skin to be cool, like the snake three quarters of her body looked like. But no, it was almost soothing.

"What should I call you?" I asked, mostly to break the silence.

She tipped her head around, looking me deep in the eyes to the point I almost wiggled free and let myself drop the three or so stories to the ground.

"There is great power in names," she said, uncharacteristically solemn. "But I will give you mine. Ratheothen."

Okay, no way that was going to come out of my mouth correctly. "Can I call you Wraith?" It just seemed appropriate, with the fog and all.

And there was the laughing again. "Yes, you may. And what am I to call you? Your friend back on Earth called you both Trisha and Trish."

"I answer to either," I told her. "Whatever you like better."

She heaved me over a ledge, her pale, corpse-like face level with mine. Her smile was much more intimidating at this angle, and I hadn't thought that possible. I consciously kept my body still, stopping the automatic reaction to flinch back from those three inch needles.

"As you wish, Trisha. I will be right back with your friends." And then she fell.

I jumped forward to peer over the edge, heart racing, but the dark crowded in enough that I couldn't see to the forest floor.

If she'd just died, how in the world was I going to get down from here? Same way probably, but that was going to hurt like heck for far longer than I'd like.

It took too long, giving my anxiety enough time to ratchet up so high that I'd convinced myself she'd landed on Starren and Carver and all three of them were dead, leaving me alone in the world. But then, the slight scratching of scales on stone drifted up. Apparently Starren and Carver didn't have much to say.

Carver came flying over the ledge first, thunking on the floor to my right.

Less than a second later, Starren got tossed up, rolling once and landing on her feet, of course.

"She brought both of you at the same time?" I asked incredulously.

Starren nodded, her face pale in the strong moonlight. The rocks blocked it below, but up here everything was bathed in a glittering silver glow.

Then Wraith was there, living up to her name really well. She didn't even use her arms, just slithered up the wall like it was no big deal.

Yeah, glad she liked me for some reason. And I needed to keep it that way somehow.

"So, introductions," I said. I pointed at Starren. "Do you want to go first?"

"Oh, I remember her," Wraith interrupted. "In fact, I distinctly remember telling you, Trisha, that I would enjoy seeing you again, but not to bring her."

"Oh, snap," Carver said.

"What?" I asked. "How in the world do you know that phrase?"

He shrugged. "Starren doesn't always bring me the classics."

"Sorry, Wraith, I didn't know you'd be here." I intentionally left out that Starren would have come either way, and she definitely noticed. Not much got by someone who had seen so much.

Carver bowed politely. "I'm Carver."

Nice and simple. Nothing that the monster who was our host could be offended by. I liked it.

Starren played with the hilt of her sword, her face that stony look, completely without emotion. "Starren."

Wraith's long neck whipped back, making her tower over us. "Starren? The Starren that killed the Council?" She dropped her head back down, her golden eyes zeroing in on Starren's face, impatiently awaiting an answer.

The playing with went to a full on grip of her sword handle. "Yes."

A creepy smile burst across Wraith's face. "Why didn't you say so! We will make the best of friends."

I whooshed out a breath I hadn't noticed I was holding, and Starren blinked really fast, slowly releasing her death grip on her sword hilt.

"As long as you don't use your pheromones on me again," Starren muttered.

"Is that how that works?" I whispered. "I couldn't figure out how she was controlling you back in Frisco when magic doesn't work on you."

Wraith laughed. "As you wish, Starren. Come, come, I don't have much, but what I do is yours."

She led the way down a small tunnel, surprisingly quiet for all her bulk.

We turned a corner, and in front of us the tunnel opened up into a cavern. Completely opposite of what I would have expected, it was dry and warm, with some type of crystal lighting the walls.

An ornate table took up the center, and a massive hammock took up the far wall.

A hammock? An interesting sleeping choice for an eight foot tall snake monster. But then, what did I know.

"I don't have actual beds," Wraith said. "I don't get many visitors. But you can use those," she nodded toward some cushions. "Things are much safer during the day right now. Not safe, oh no, but safer. You can leave in the morning."

Hearing her say that dropped my anxiety level a little. She was fae, so if she said we could leave in the morning, she had to mean it.

Starren moved over to a cushion and sat gingerly down, legs crossed but still obviously able to get into a fighting stance within a second. "What's going on that's so dangerous? I've travelled these forests at night all my life."

"Things are waking," Wraith answered. "Things that haven't been seen in centuries. Things I wouldn't want to tangle with." She smiled, her pointy teeth not quite as scary any more. "Definitely things you don't want to meet. There is even talk of a dragon." She threw her hands up. "A dragon! Who would have thought. I've never even seen one of those."

I carefully avoided looking at Starren. Wraith was very good at reading things, and I didn't really want her to know I accidentally had a pet dragon. Or did he have a pet fae? I didn't know.

Starren settled back a little, no doubt trying for the illusion that she trusted Wraith. I went over to join her, and Carver shuffled over behind me.

"What's causing all this unrest?" Carver asked. Though I had stereotyped him as one who would be nervous in this type of situation, he seemed perfectly calm. Either he was great at pretending, or he really was chill at the moment.

"The infighting among the fae."

Starren snorted. "There's always infighting among the fae, no one can get along with anyone."

Wraith's golden eyes blinked slowly, staring Starren down.

Starren held up her hands.

"This is different. There is always petty squabbling, bids for power, attacks on a small scale. But it seems that Quintin has a nemesis, one who no one knows. His attacks are escalating, and he has a strong following. No one has ever seen him, or even the fae that do his dirty work. But many fae lives have been lost." She grinned. "What a tragedy."

She'd made it very clear back in California when I'd first met her how she felt about the high fae. I couldn't really say I blamed her. I hadn't had much luck with them either. But that didn't mean I just wanted them to die.

"Good," Starren said. "Let them all kill each other."

Ouch. That was more bitter than I knew she had floating down under the surface. Her hate for our father had come out very strongly multiple times, but I hadn't heard that sentiment against the entire fae population before.

"Let them weed themselves out." Wraith reared back, a somewhat evil, satisfied smirk on her face. "High fae reproduce very slowly, preferring not to have children until they are over a hundred. This is the chance for the rest of us to come out of the shadows."

Oh boy. We needed to be careful here or we'd be accidentally joining some revolution.

"I can see how that would appeal to you," Carver said soothingly. "The high fae haven't treated the low fae very well throughout history."

She cocked her head, like she was trying to figure out the meaning behind his words. Carver definitely did a better job of being fae than either Starren or I did.

Carver gestured toward Starren and me. "I would just like to help my friends at the moment."

"Of course, of course," Wraith said, coming back down to a more chill level. "And what are you helping them with?"

"They need to find another friend."

"Her name is Nara," I interjected. "Last we saw her was outside Fairbent Prison."

"I like this fae already too, if she was an enemy of Quintin," Wraith said with a smile. "I'm meeting more decent fae today than I even knew existed."

"Do you know where she is?" I asked. How weird would it be if the monster I'd connected with in California could help me find a girl I connected with in prison in Faerie.

"I don't."

I drooped into the cushions, which were surprisingly soft. Of course she didn't. That would have been too much to ask.

"But I know someone who would. You aren't going to enjoy speaking with him though. Ferid."

"Ferid?" Starren asked. "Ogre Ferid?"

Wraith smirked at her.

"That's not good."

"Why is that not good?" I looked to Starren, to Carver, Wraith, anyone to give me an explanation. "What's not good about that?"

"Ferid and I... we don't exactly get along. Well. Or any of his friends, for that matter."

I could totally read between the lines. Not getting along meant they'd tried to kill each other at some point. "Are you kidding me? They hate you too? What did you do to them?"

She looked embarrassed. "You remember how Wade told you my sword was forged from ore out of the HighCrest mines?"

"Yes?"

"And that the mines are owned by the ogres?"

A sinking feeling started in the pit of my stomach. "Yes?"

"They don't really like to give up their ore. I don't know what they use it for, but they don't share."

Oh great. Another group of fae that hated my sister.

"What are our chances of finding Nara without help?"

Starren winced. "Not good."

"Maybe you should just stay here, and I'll go ask," I said. "He doesn't have any reason to hate me."

The whole room erupted in laughter.

"What?" I asked everyone. "What's so funny?"

"Even if you made it to the Mines, which is very unlikely, you wouldn't make it close enough to Ferid to get a word out. A morsel like you would be considered very tasty," Wraith said.

I sucked it up and did my best to keep the fear off my face. "Ogres aren't considered fae?"

"Yes, but lower fae."

"Lower fae have different standards than the high fae," Starren adds. She sounded just a little more smug than usual, which was impressive considering a minute ago we were talking about the fact that this ogre hated her, and she hadn't seemed too pleased about it.

"We have to try something! Every minute we're away is another minute that Dan and Nina could get in trouble because I'm gone! What if someone starts poking around and I'm nowhere to be found? What if the cops think I ran away and they didn't report it, or worse, they murdered me or something? What if they leave Sanctuary and get grabbed by someone after me?"

"We are going to help them. But if we go and try to pick up Nara's trail, we have a much better chance of surviving," Carver said.

"Who are Dan and Nina?" Wraith asked the room.

"Her human parents." Starren settled back into the cushions. "They ate the food."

"Oh." Wraith went quiet for a second. "You don't know how to help them, do you?"

"No." I deflated a little. I hadn't let my hopes get up far, but that was something I couldn't completely control. Hope was all I had left. Hope, Starren, and Jaden.

"Why did you take them food from here? That was very foolish."

"I didn't. They were here. Father forced them to eat." The thought turned my stomach. Wade I could just hate. My father I shut all thoughts of off as they came up. I didn't want to think of him. Couldn't think of him without the anger leaking out, without causing all kinds of accidental damage now that I was outside of Sanctuary and the plants felt what I felt.

Quintin had better hope he never saw me again. His powers of manipulation couldn't control my brain, and so couldn't stop me if I wanted to do something. Or even if I didn't consciously want to. The plants would have killed Wade if Nina hadn't stopped me last time.

This time, there was no Nina.

"You brought humans into Faerie?" Wraith started her wheezing coughing fit. "And here I thought I couldn't like you any more than I already did. Burning down the whole fae way of doing things, eh."

Okay, yes, I was, but not intentionally. I just wanted my family. And to be left alone. In that order.

"Not that it matters much. There may not be any fae left before long." Wraith said.

"What does that mean?" Carver interjected. "Things have been bad, but not extinction of the fae level bad."

"And where have you been? Tucked in some tiny hole somewhere, reading your life away? It's gone past bad." Wraith settled in against the wall. "Fae are going to be the end of the fae. And I'm going to be here to watch."

I looked to Starren, to Carver and back. "Aren't you fae?"

Wraith laughed, but this wasn't a laugh I'd heard before. Dark. Oh yeah, we were back to me wondering why in the world we'd followed her back to her lair.

"Don't you know. I'm a monster."

The cavern went silent. Okay, very stupid question. How did I always manage to mess things up?

"Rest. I'll help you down in the morning." And then she jumped and grabbed the wall, climbing up into the dark. She wasn't going to use her hammock?

We all craned our necks trying to follow where she went, but it was far too dark.

"I didn't even know that wasn't a ceiling," I whispered.

"Me either," Carver answered. "Do you think she has another room up there?"

"Shut up, both of you. She can probably still hear you," Starren said, far quieter than the level at which Carver and I had been speaking.

Well that was a creepy thought. And now I wasn't going to sleep. At all.

Unfortunately, I was mostly right about the not sleeping thing. Even more unfortunately, I was a little bit wrong. Whatever time I slept was plagued by the faces of the fae back at the Distribution Center. I wanted to say that I would find whoever had done that to them, but I couldn't. I had to fix Dan and Nina. Had to.

Grit in my eyes, I blinked a few times. The small amount of sleep I did have made it pretty tough to keep my eyes open. Why was I up again?

"Trish. Trish!" Carver's annoying whisper. That was why. What in the world did he want?

"Go away. I just got to sleep."

"Starren is gone!"

Okay, that got me up. I bolted into a sitting position from the floor, wildly looking around and grabbing at my sword.

"What do you mean, gone? Wraith didn't..."

Carver's face was barely visible in the dim lighting. "No, I don't think it was anything like that. We were talking, after you went to sleep. She said she had something she needed to fix, and that she should just go to the Mines by herself since having us along wouldn't help her case any and that we'd be in trouble because of her. I thought I had her talked out of it when we went to sleep!"

The thing she needed to fix was that I was in this mess because of her. I'd thought she'd gotten past that, but in typical Starren fashion, she'd just not being showing me what she was thinking.

I jumped up, mostly awake now.

"We need to get going if we're going to catch up."

Carver scrambled to his feet. "But your... friend needs to take us down the cliff face. I don't know how Starren managed to get down. What if she fell? What if..."

"It's Starren. But hopefully managing all that did slow her down."

We took off for the cave entrance. Faerie didn't seem to have a sun like at home, but the light was just starting to brighten our surroundings as we burst out of the cave.

I made my way straight to the edge, peering over, hoping for a glimpse of Starren. No such luck.

"Either she didn't take that way, or she's already gone."

"Oh, she's long gone."

Wraith's voice nearly sent me following Starren over the edge, but no doubt in a far less dignified and far more splat on landing way. Had she been listening to Carver and me this whole time?

"How long?" I ask.

"Since right after the two of you fell asleep. Four human hours? But she spent most of it trying to get to the ground."

"Ah!" I stomped my foot. Petty, but it did make me feel better. "We need to get down there!"

"And leave me? Just like that?" Wraith had that weird dreamy tone of voice, the dangerous one from back at Alcatraz.

I blinked excessively, gritting my teeth and trying to keep it from affecting me.

Then she laughed. "Just kidding, dear. It was fun having you here, but I do prefer being on my own."

She swooped forward, grabbing me like Nina and a sack of cat food she was donating to the shelter, and went right over the edge.

Clamping my teeth shut was the only thing that kept the scream inside. We landed, softly somehow, and she dropped me to the ground, slithered up the side of the mountain, falling again with Carver only a moment later without giving me any time to recover.

"Thanks," I muttered.

"You're most welcome. And as long as you are at war with the fae, you're welcome here. Stop in if you need anything." She smiled, her pointed teeth making it look extremely sinister. "Don't go letting that father of yours change your mind about anything. Anything. You hear?"

I nodded, smiling back, but the smile was fake enough I was pretty sure she could see right through it.

She took off, straight up the cliff face again, without another word.

"You have very odd friends," Carver said. He was still slightly bent over, looking a little queasy too.

"Don't I know it."

"How are we going to find Starren? We can just head for the mines, but there are so many different ways to get there, and so many entrances."

I scooted over to a small flower, bright purple with black edges, and leaned down. "Have you seen a fae woman walk through here recently?" I asked.

The little plant sluggishly thought for a second. None of them seemed healthy in this section of the woods, but they did feel more alive than they had last night. Once it was moving, it wiggled for a second, then bent over to the side, pointing.

"Thanks."

I took off in that direction, Carver trailing behind.

"Strange friends, indeed."

I didn't have to ask again. The plants waved us along, dodging back and forth, making sudden turns that didn't make sense like Starren really thought that could throw us off the scent.

Well. Without help we'd be so lost, so I had to give her that.

A small yelp ahead made me pause, then jog forward. Starren hung there from a tree, fuming.

"Really? You're playing dirty. I thought the trees were weird here."

"Me? You're the one that ran out on me when I was sleeping. Again. I'm never going to be able to sleep when you're around, I'm always going to be waiting for you to run away!" I crossed my arms, Starren no longer being the only one to fume. "Why'd you leave me? You know Father is after me here, and you didn't even try to make sure he doesn't find me?"

"Taking you with me meant certain death. Leaving you behind meant a chance of death. I went with only a chance."

"Finding Nara shouldn't be certain death."

"Finding Ferid probably is."

Hard to argue with that, even though I wanted to slap her. Poor Jaden. And Cray. No doubt this was how they felt when I'd left them behind. And if Father got to us? They would never know where we'd gone, what had happened to us. But no one else would miss us. Maybe Wren would think about her weirdo niece every once in awhile, but that was it. Neither of us had anyone else.

"Are you going to let me go now?"

"Oh yeah, sorry."

Starren dropped lightly to the ground, rubbing her wrist and glaring hard enough to make anyone quake. Anyone but me. That glare lost its effectiveness when used too much. And I'd been on the receiving end at least a hundred times. Maybe a hundred just in the last week. Sad when you considered how long we'd known each other. Not long.

"So. Where are we going?"

"The mines, where else?"

"No need to snap," I snapped back at her. Oops. I was going to blame it on the lack of sleep, but really it probably stemmed from the fact that she'd tried to ditch me. Again. She was a great warrior and all that, but hadn't I proven to her repeatedly that I could take care of myself? "Why aren't we just going after Nara? As much as I want Dan and Nina back as soon as possible, I also don't want to die."

Starren marched off, back rigid. But she didn't say a thing.

"You can't just leave me behind!" I rushed to catch up with her. "I'm more prepared for anything here than even you are, at least I have powers!"

She spun around to face me and I jerked to a stop.

"Just because you have powers makes you think you're prepared for Faerie? You should know better than that after what you did to your parents."

A slap couldn't have done more damage.

"I didn't mean to..."

"Of course you didn't. But you didn't know. There's a lot you don't know, so stop acting like you do." She about faced and started power-walking again.

"I'd know if you told me stuff!"

She just kept marching.

"It's not like you tell me anything!"

She whirled around. "You don't want to know. I've tried talking to you about stuff before, and you shut down. You don't want to know about Father, or about my life, or anything fae, you just want to be wrapped up in your little human world."

I swung my eyes away so I didn't have to meet hers. Carver was looking at the ground, apparently smart enough not to get in the middle of whatever this was.

"Now leave it be. I didn't want you to die, leave it at that."

I gritted my teeth, nearly literally biting my tongue. She actually thought she'd been open and honest about her past? About our father? That just showed how screwed up she really was.

This whole thing was her fault. If she'd just come to me in the beginning and told me she was my sister, warned me about our father, we wouldn't be here right now. Dan and Nina...

I blew out a breath, squeezing my eyes closed and attempting to get things under control. Dan and Nina wouldn't want me being like this all the time. Always ready for a fight right now.

Fighting felt better than actually feeling.

I squashed that thought right down.

Carver gave me a sympathetic look and followed Starren, who'd marched off again.

It wasn't really her fault. And she felt guilty enough already. I had to keep this rage tamped down. Had to. My family depended on it.

CHAPTER ELEVEN

Stupid Mines. Stupid walking. Stupid Faerie.

Nothing but Dan and Nina could have gotten me back to this place.

We'd tromped on in silence for what seemed like hours.

Well. I tromped, the other two lightly glided. Apparently that was something all fae but me had in common.

Are we there yet kept almost slipping from my mouth, but I'd held it in so far. Not likely I could much longer. Starren was probably glad I was still miffed at her, it kept me from complaining out loud. Kind of a coping mechanism. Starren wouldn't explain to me why all of the sudden we'd switched plans, and I'd given up asking her.

The woods had taken an even darker turn. I hadn't thought it was possible, but the feelings from the trees had been getting more and more fearful, angry, as we went along. That didn't help my mood.

What I couldn't tell was if they were just mad in general, or if something specific had them riled up. Hopefully it wasn't us.

This was the first place I'd been in Faerie that didn't look perfect. The trees had branches shattered and hanging lifelessly, the bushes were missing whole chunks. Something weird had happened here. Something bad.

I stopped at a particularly hostile thicket. It whipped around, even with no wind. Starren stopped to watch, raising an eyebrow but still not ready to talk after our spat.

Lifting a hand, I stepped forward, lightly laying it against the thin bark of whatever kind of tree this was.

My whole body jolted, my hand stuck to the tree like I'd touched a hot electrical wire. Visions popped across my view, visions of several of Father's soldiers. They were attacked by a dark flash in the trees, slashed to pieces as it ran back and forth past them, their screams curdling my blood.

I tried to pull my hand away, but couldn't.

Woodland creatures paraded by my eyes, slaughtered by something I couldn't even see. Innocent fae, traveling through the wood, murdered.

Starren jumped forward and grabbed me, jerking at my frozen arm. I barely felt it.

Suddenly a branch lashed forward and snapped across my cheek. Instinctively I covered the wound, my hand free.

Starren jerked me back from the tree and pulled my hand down. The welt had mostly healed at this point, but probably still looked a little angry.

"What just happened?" Starren yelled.

The trees around us groaned.

"Shhh, Star." Carver's gaze whipped around. "I don't think they like that."

"There's something in the trees," I whispered.

"Yeah, I got that, it attacked you," Starren said.

"No, the trees are reacting to the violence they've seen here, they hate it. There's something killing things, something hiding in the trees."

The words had barely left my mouth when a branch whipped forward and gently touched my face. My view of the real world shrank again, and I could see us through something's eyes. Something big. And angry.

"Run!"

Neither Carver nor Starren questioned my somewhat panicked order.

Carver took off first, which was great since I didn't know where we were going. Starren followed him, and I was right on Starren's heels.

The forest went deathly quiet, the trees deadly still, everything hushed and waiting to see what happened.

Everything still except for us, bulldozing a path right through the foliage.

We ran until I was about ready to start panting, and I had perfect lungs.

Starren slowed, looking around us. "Why did you yell?" She didn't look at me as she spoke, keeping her eyes on the trees.

"I don't know what it was, but we're being tracked. Hunted. The trees are scared of whatever it is."

"The trees are scared?" Starren asked. "So it's a lumber jack or something?"

I was so impressed with her human knowledge I almost missed the insult.

"No, I can't explain it exactly. The trees are... in pain? Because of this thing. It's killing anything that moves."

A slight crackle in the trees sent all of us looking to the left.

And while we were all looking to the left, something streaked through on the right, slashing as it went by.

A shriek ripped free as I took several slices up my thighs, dropping me to the ground. The trees around us whipped into a frenzy.

Starren moved to cover me, sword ready.

"Is it gone?" Carver asked.

"No." I grabbed onto Starren, pulling myself up. "This is what it does. We need to get out of here."

A whoosh of air went by, part of a black shadow, and Carver yelped, grabbing his bicep. Blood dripped from between his fingers.

"Run!" Starren said.

The trees whipped around us as we ran. The plants were wild, like they didn't know what to do. Their hopelessness sank down into my soul.

The shadow ripped by again, far faster than we were.

I was last in line, and got the brunt of it. I gasped as something tore through the skin over my ribs.

Blood ran down Starren's neck and Carver's ear dribbled.

The trees moaned around us. Their anger, fear, and... guilt? Made me dizzy. I stumbled.

Starren slowed. "Come on!"

"Go without me!"

She grunted and turned to grab me.

The thing barreled toward us out of the corner of my eye. No, no, not Starren. I shoved Starren to the side, doing my best to follow her but not getting completely out of the way in time.

Thankfully the other wound had healed, or I'd have crisscrossing ones right now.

Starren jerked my arm and I took off after her, trying to guard her back, trying to crush down the terror ripping its way through my body.

It came at us again, from another direction, its trajectory never making sense compared to the pass that had come before.

I tripped nearly faceplanting, my heart banging in my ears. Scrambling to catch up to Starren, I tripped again, a tree root sliding back into the ground after I'd regained my balance.

"What are you doing?" I screamed at the forest, still running forward at breakneck speed.

Disgust. More fear. And the guilt. Why the guilt?

A vine wrapped around my wrist as I ran, not slowing me, not even trying, but my vision glossed over again.

The forest. Happy, joyful.

And then a person, who looked vaguely familiar, but I couldn't recognize walked through, touching the trees, sending them into fits of anger, destruction. They even tore into each other as they mindlessly destroyed anything they could touch. What could make them do something like that?

Tears spilled down my cheeks at the rage the trees were showing each other. Who could make them do something like that?

Then the shadow monster appeared. The trees were happy, relieved, just for a second. Before it took out its first victim.

Someone had caused this pain. Why had the trees been happy to see the shadow?

The vision stopped, and I came back to myself, standing like an idiot with a monster after me. Starren yelled something, looked like she'd been yelling for a second, but my ears still hadn't engaged.

"Go on." I shooed her forward, and turned back to the way we'd come without waiting to see if she listened or not.

My heart got three stuttering beats in before the shadow hit me, leaving a bloody gash on my thigh and then was gone. I stumbled sideways, spinning to follow it. It hit me again, this time from the right, laying open my cheek as my thigh healed.

But this time I guessed its direction correctly.

The thing was of the forest. It was causing damage to protect the trees. I could feel it. But we weren't here to hurt the trees, and it was going to kill us.

Did the trees control it? Did it control the trees? Did any of that mean... worth a try. I turned and faced it.

It came at me, head on. I dug around inside for any bit of bravery left over after all the crap from the last few days. *Stand your ground, Trisha. Stand your ground.*

When I could feel the coolness of moving air, I held up my hand. "Stop!"

It did.

I bit my lip to stop myself from crying in relief. That had worked? Really?

The creature swirled around, obviously fighting itself, fighting my control of it.

Sweat broke out all over my body and I stared it down, pushing every inch of my very strong will into it.

The angry swirling lessened. The deep black of shadow lightened to a grey smoke, and then the white of a wispy cloud, before gently evaporating.

I stood, frozen in place, not able to move a muscle.

Starren's familiar footsteps came up behind me.

"Is it gone?" My voice wobbled way too much for my pride's sake.

"I think it is." Starren's voice was hushed, like she was afraid just her saying that it had left could bring the thing back.

"What was that?" I asked, finally letting myself blink, my eyes grainy and dry from not letting them close.

"A forest spirit, I'd say." I hadn't even heard Carver walk up.

"Do you think it's gone?"

"I don't know."

I really didn't like either of their answers. But I let myself drop to the ground anyway. There was no stopping that at this point.

The grass around me wept. I forced my head up. More guilt, but this time less. It was cut with relief, making it a little easier to handle.

I put my hand down, and where I touched, the grass reached up and brightened.

"What are you doing now?" Starren asked. She meant it to sound sarcastic, of course. But it came across weirded out. Weirded out was what I'd always worried my human family would be, not my fae family.

"I don't know."

One of the angry looking tree branches reached forward, and I put my hand out to meet it. It wrapped around my wrist.

The anger still burned inside it. I pushed back with feelings of light and joy, sky and sun, and the anger faded. The gnarled branches smoothed, and the limb retracted, the tree slowly releasing its tension.

Another tree lashed forward, not as gentle with its grip. I gritted my teeth and fought for it. Finally, it let go.

I looked around at the rest of the trees. They definitely looked better off than they were before, but they were going to need some help.

Moving slowly I stood, putting my hands up in a placating gesture, doing my best to be non-threatening. How did you look non-threatening to a tree? I stepped forward.

They weren't very happy about it. Branches tangled and untangled in angry dances, blocking out whatever light source Faerie had.

"Let's just go, Trish," Starren said quietly from somewhere behind me. "That thing might come back."

"It's not coming back." I put all the confidence that I didn't have into that statement, praying it was true.

"Do you know how troubled this section of the wood must be to have drawn out a forest spirit?" Carver asked. "We shouldn't be standing around."

"Just a minute." I kept my attention on the closest tree, watching it like someone trying to help a trapped and injured lion. "You're okay," I crooned. "It's all about to get better." I channeled every time I'd been about to lose it and had Nina's calming presence there to help me. I definitely didn't know what I was doing without that.

The trees kept up their angry thrashing, but it didn't feel like it did before. Not nearly as scary.

Close enough to place my hand on another trunk, I closed my eyes, forcing in the good vibes. This one was easier than the other two. The whole forest interconnected, roots wrapped around each other, branches intertwined. The job got easier with each tree I helped.

Slowly, the light came back to the forest floor. The creaking and groaning of trees waiting to cause pain diminished, until it disappeared altogether.

I'd helped about twenty trees. It was enough. The joy at being freed from an anger that wasn't theirs spread like a wildfire would, making the leaves reach toward the light. A bird twittered somewhere off in the distance.

"Well that's pretty brave," Starren said.

I beamed at her. "Thank you."

"No. The bird, dummy. To come back here already."

"Oh."

She slid her sword back into its sheath. "Leave it to my sister to fix an angry forest."

"Hey. That should sound like more of a compliment. Like, 'wow, my sister fixed an angry forest. I wonder how many lives she's saved?'"

"Nice work, Trish," Carver said. "How did you learn to do that?"

That was a great question. With no answer. "They told me they were in pain, I just tried to help."

A vine stroked my check where the monster had sliced it open. It had healed, but the skin was still sensitive and the touch tickled.

That made me think about the other slices, which made me look down at my clothes. I stuck a hand all the way through my shirt. "Seriously? Now I have to go tromping around Faerie with my skin hanging out?"

Carver raised his eyebrows incredulously. "That's what you're worried about?"

Starren looked me over. "She has strange priorities sometimes. You get used to it."

I glared at her for a second. The trees around us writhed.

"Sorry, sorry, I'm not really mad."

Whoever had done this was terrible. Trees and plants in general were very peaceful. This had been intentional. An act of war.

"Someone caused this. Someone came through here and turned these trees crazy." I started walking in the same direction we'd been desperately running for our lives thirty minutes ago.

Starren caught up and grabbed me. "Someone with your ability?"

I shrugged. "I didn't see that much. I just know that they went through and did the opposite of what I just did until the shadow monster appeared and started killing things."

"Forest spirit," Carver corrected.

I flapped my hand at him. "Yeah, yeah, forest spirit. I think it thought it was protecting the trees, but I'm not sure why."

"Great," Starren grumped. "And I thought one of you was bad enough."

We walked a couple steps.

"Anyone got anything to eat?"

The rest of the day went by uneventfully. Which was nice, for once. The forest we walked through felt wary, but had none of the anger of the trees earlier.

Thankfully. All that emotion stuff was exhausting.

And I didn't want to think about how my emotions affected the plants, because that meant I needed to get better at controlling them. Bottling them up. I needed to figure out how to be more like Star.

And I'd thought she was so cold when I met her. To be fair to myself, she had been cold. But now I knew why. It was just easier that way. So much easier, if you didn't care.

Then I saw Nina's face, grinning at me with a tray of cookies, and I knew. I could never not care again. Not caring was terrible.

"We're getting close," Starren said.

My head snapped up. Finally!

But... what?

There wasn't anything around us that looked like a mine of any kind. The forest went on around us, just like it had since we'd left Carver's.

"Don't ogres live in smelly holes in the mountains or something? How is this..." I gestured around us. "A mine?"

"Humans dig into mountains because it's easier," Starren said. "Ogres don't care much about easy."

That wasn't intimidating at all.

"Okay. We should probably have been talking about what to expect those last however many miles."

"Death," Starren said grimly. "Just expect death. If it isn't death, then I'll consider us lucky."

"How optimistic," I muttered under my breath.

"Then maybe we should be coming up with another plan," Carver said. "What about going back to following Nara's path? That plan was much safer."

"Can we get them to come above ground somehow?" I nodded toward the trees. "Then we'd have some help."

"We can try." More optimism from Starren. But really, what could be worse than the monster we'd just encountered? I shivered, the fear from the trees back near the spirit resonating through my brain.

"Ferid will send others after you," Carver said. "He isn't going to come up here himself. That's not a great plan, it announces our presence with no helpful results."

"I don't know that he won't come," Starren answered. "He likes to take care of things himself. We didn't leave things in a good place the last time we saw each other."

"After you stole his ore?"

She winced. "And maybe a jewel or two."

I groaned. "We're doomed."

"That's what I've been trying to tell you."

I straightened. "We've been doomed before. I'm sure we'll live through this to be doomed again, until the final time when we don't survive our doom."

"Easy for you to say." Starren shrugged. "What? I'm serious. You come back from the dead."

Carver squinted at me. "Back from the dead?"

That showed how much Starren trusted him, to speak in front of him like that. Starren didn't make mistakes. It was annoying.

"How about I ask to meet him first, and if he says no, we try something different? How does he feel about Quintin?" I asked.

"Hates him." Starren's voice had gone monotone, like it always did when our father was mentioned.

"Figures. I haven't met anyone that doesn't. I guess I won't mention who I am then, just that I need his help with something."

Starren snorted. "He's as likely to eat you as help you."

I really should have listened to my mom better when she'd been trying to teach me this stuff. "I still don't get that. I thought ogres were intelligent."

"They are. That doesn't mean they won't eat you. Aren't there humans that eat each other? I saw it on TV. Unless that was one of the fake shows?"

"Not fake." When she'd first moved in she'd thought all TV was human history. That had taken some interesting explaining and a lot of behind the scenes videos to finally change. I still had to clarify for her sometimes.

"Well then, I'm not sure why you expected any less from ogres."

Good point. Basically I'd never really thought about it. And though it didn't change my determination to do anything to get Dan and Nina back, it did put a damper on my enthusiasm. "Point me in the right direction."

She did. Literally, she just pointed, right at a boulder I hadn't even noticed.

"That rock?"

It didn't look like anything but your average boulder, just like the seventy-two others we'd passed today. Mossy stuff, check. Cracks and stuff, check. "Are you sure? How do I move it?"

Carver stepped forward and felt around for a second. "It's here somewhere."

"Wait, you mean you've been here?" I glared at Starren. "She brought you here when she came to steal ore from the ogres?"

Carver stared at me, then looked at Starren, his hand flapping around on the rock. "Yes?"

"Star! You try to leave me behind all the time, and I can come back from the dead, but then you take Carver with you on some stupid death mission?"

She shrugged.

"To be fair, she did suggest I stay behind. But I had maps of the tunnels that she needed, so I got to come along." He beamed at her. "That's when we officially became a couple."

I crossed my arms. "How romantic."

A latch clicked. "Ha!" Carver fist pumped the air. In a very weird way, like he was trying to imitate something he'd read.

The stone began to lift. It tilted backward, until it looked like it should tumble over, but didn't. Beneath where it had been, a tunnel went down, curling off underground until I couldn't see where it went. It had been carved out of the rock, smoothly cut, with the same type of lighting as at the Fae Distribution Center.

Starren smirked at Trish's face. "Ogres are very mechanically minded."

"I guess so."

We all waited. I wasn't sure what the other two were expecting, but I figured a watchogre of some type would be coming to figure out what was going on.

Nothing.

Impatient, Starren grabbed a small stone and chucked it down the tunnel. It didn't make a sound. Nothing to even start the echo I would have thought would follow.

We all tensed, hands on weapons.

Still nothing.

"I guess they trust their door," Carver said.

"I guess so." Starren let go of her sword and blew out a breath. "And I guess that means we're going in."

Without waiting to see if Carver or I had anything to say about that, she took off down the tunnel.

"Seriously?" I asked Carver.

He shrugged. "It's Starren."

I snorted in a pretty fair imitation of her snorts. "And that's all that needs to be said."

I moved to the edge of the tunnel where the stairs started winding down. Just looking, I probably wouldn't have been able to guess that it was underground. Too bad I already knew.

There were some very bad things about not being able to die. Being trapped underground seemed like it ranked pretty high on that list. I hadn't given it any thought before, but now...

Now it was too late. My sister had been dumb enough to go down. And I'd be dead before I let her do something like this without me.

CHAPTER TWELVE

Somehow the fact that this wasn't some drippy, creepy cavern out of the movies almost made it worse. At least in the movies, you knew what to expect. 'Don't go in there,' made a lot of sense when you were watching someone do something stupid on screen.

Yeah. If someone were watching us right now, that's probably what they'd be saying.

The steps were perfectly even. The wall, perfectly sculpted. Maybe these ogres were Egyptians or something. Seriously, how did they make it look like this?

Catching up with Starren had been easy. She wouldn't admit it if I asked but now that we were this far, I was pretty sure she was glad we were along.

I wasn't sure I was.

Yeah, the whole not letting my sister die alone thing was important. But the thick dread creeping through me felt pretty important at the moment too.

Neither of the other two spoke, at all, leading me to believe we were in the same boat. Or cave, as it were.

We continued down for some time. The only indication that we were still descending being the stairs, and the air temperature.

Somehow the walls stayed exactly the same. Weren't there supposed to be layers or something?

In through the nose, out through the mouth. In through the nose, out through the mouth. Nina's advice. Which had me thinking about Nina, which wasn't good at the moment. My emotions were all out of whack.

Tears pricked my eyes. I would not cry in front of Starren and Carver. It wouldn't happen, I wouldn't let it.

I'd been saying that a lot lately, like I had any control.

The thought made the stupid tears worse. I swiped them away. Now was not the time for a breakdown.

There. The end of the stairs. Something different to think about.

And at the bottom of the stairs, the tunnel veered off in two directions. Something to think about way too much.

Starren stopped, staring ahead. Not looking down either tunnel, just staring.

I moved past her and looked down the left tunnel. Nothing looked any different than the tunnel we'd been following. The right tunnel proved to be the same.

"Now what?" I whispered.

"I'm thinking," she whispered back. Somehow she made even her whisper sound angry. I needed to start practicing this stuff.

After all this, I was only going to care about the people I could protect. No more. I couldn't give up caring completely, Nina had accidentally seen to that with all her stupid kindness and stuff, but I couldn't just leave my heart out here waiting to get pummeled.

Nina. Dan. Starren. Jaden. Cray. No way I could leave Jaime off this list. And if Jaime and Jaden were on there, Rebecca and Lucy had to be too, even if I didn't like Lucy. Jaime would be devastated if something happened to her mom or sister.

Wren should be on the list. And maybe Rosie.

Ugh. Why was this list getting so long? But that was it. I was never adding anyone else. If Starren left me here thinking about this crap much longer, I was just going to pick a direction and go with it.

"Left," Carver said.

"What?" Starren came out of her thought coma. "Last time we

came through here, we were moving too fast to pay any attention to directions. How do you know that?"

"I was going back through the maps in my head. We want to go left."

"Just like that?" I pointed at my own head.

"Ugh," Starren said. "It's always just like that with him." She left us standing there and started down the left tunnel.

At least one of us knew Carver well enough to be confident he knew what he was talking about.

More shiny tunnel. We walked until we came to a section that veered off in four directions. Carver pointed right instantly. Was he some kind of genius or something? Maybe this was part of his ability, which I hadn't asked the details about but probably should know. So many abilities out there, and I had barely scratched the surface, meeting fae. Yeah, it could stay that way.

We hadn't made it far down the next tunnel when something made the hairs on my neck stand up. I spun around to see two giant creatures with some kind of pointy staves behind us, not even moving like they were waiting for us to notice them.

Starren didn't even need me to say anything. She felt my tension or something, because she spun around to face them also.

The butterflies in my stomach began batting around.

Ogres were even more huge than I'd expected. Tall, yes, I'd guessed that part, but I could probably lie sideways across their chests and not touch both sides.

Maybe it was the armor. Yeah, had to be. They weren't that big under the armor. A dull grey that should have been ugly, but somehow wasn't. If that stuff was made out of the same ore Starren had stolen for her sword, there was no way we were getting through it.

Full face masks on their helmets. Full armor down their legs. The only skin showing was on their arms, covering huge muscles.

Well shoot.

"Uh, hi," I said brilliantly.

No answer. Bright eyes shown from the helmets that hid the rest of their faces.

Starren moved up in front of me. "We're here to see Ferid."

No answer.

Starren backed up, slightly, herding me and Carver down the tunnel.

A grinding sound behind us made me flip around. The wall had lifted, and two more ogre moved into position, trapping us. Shoot, shoot, this was why I hated being underground.

The guards took a step in unison, keeping pace with us.

No plants. No help. Just the regenerating. And all of Starren's training she'd attempted to beat into me. Even with that, this would hardly be a fair fight. I'd seen Starren do some crazy things, but four ogres? That seemed like a bit too much to hope for.

"Just take us to Ferid," Carver said.

"Why should we bother Ferid with you?" one of the ogre asked, his voice smooth and deep. Carver spoke first in English, and the ogre answered in English. "Everyone knows the consequences of entering Hiath Homed. Our path is clear."

"How'd you know about us anyway?" It didn't come out as sassy as I'd have liked. Not nearly as sassy as I'd intended. But it would have to do, since internally I was about to flip out.

"The tunnel was created in such a way that it brings all sounds straight to the guard chamber. We've known of your presence since one of you threw a rock down our tunnel, littering our home ground."

Littering their home ground? As in, they cared that there was a rock out of place? Oops. Wait, these were ogres right? That didn't follow. It was the mermaids all over again. That had been quite the learning experience.

The ogres in the direction we'd come from tipped their spear things at us, moving forward without giving any orders. The ones in the direction we'd been trying to go started backing up, keeping us in their sights.

"Where are you taking us?" Carver asked. He sounded so calm. How did he sound that calm? I'd been a bunch of almost die situations, and this one was bugging me the worst. Other than when Nina had been involved, of course.

I'd come to rely on the plants far too much. And there weren't any plants down here.

"To the kitchens."

"Oh, that's okay, I'm not hungry." Which was weird. I was always hungry. Apparently terror took even my appetite.

"That's good. You won't be the one eating."

Crap. Double crap.

I squeezed my eyes closed as I stumbled along. Would they be able to chop me up? I didn't know how that worked since thankfully I'd never been in that situation before.

Time for a new tactic.

"Do you know who you have here?" I planted myself.

The ogres just kept walking.

When I got poked I glared and jumped back out of reach.

"I asked you a question!"

"It doesn't matter. You all taste the same."

Well that was insulting. I pointed at Starren. "Your boss has a bone to pick with her." Oops. Poor choice of words. "That's Starren. He hates her."

One of the guards cocked his head, considering Starren, but our pace never slowed. Stupid tunnel, exactly the same as when we entered, long and ugly. Just what I wanted to be the last thing I saw.

"This information doesn't change anything," an ogre said.

"Won't Ferid want to kill her himself? I think you'd better keep her alive." It was a good try Carver. Really.

"Everyone's orders on this matter are clear. She's slippery, and must not be allowed to escape. Ferid will appreciate the meal he is given, without having to go on the hunt himself."

With that, the guard moved his spear back to get some momentum, and shoved it forward, right at Starren. She jumped out of the way before I had a chance to intervene.

The first guard's strike seemed to have given the others permission. In unison, they all came at us.

Carver dropped to the ground, knocking Starren down to join him.

This was it. They would die. I'd be left here alone, to regenerate for who knew how long, until an ogre got tired of me and took off my head or something.

I dropped on top of Starren and Carver, shielding them with my body. Maybe I'd lose my head or something. Anything would be better than watching the last of my family die. *Please, no.*

The spears came down together, hard.

A weird scratching noise started up and down the tunnel on the other side of the wall, loud enough to be nearly deafening. The guards froze as the sound reverberated. They seemed as confused by it as I was. We had to wait a moment before it faded away.

"I thought you were only supposed to be able to hear stuff at the guard station?" I asked one of the ogres.

He looked to his friend, but then the spears went right back up.

Ah, if only my stalling tactics were better.

Again the spears came at us, but just as one was about to make contact with my shoulder, roots burst through the tunnel walls. Dirt clods pelted around us. A root grabbed the spear closest to me and began to thrash, beating the ogres back. Whether that part was intentional or not, I had no idea.

"Stay down!" I shouted to Starren and Carver, doing my best to shield them with my body. Hopefully this was a rescue mission, or we were so dead.

The roots twisted around the ogre closest to me, jerking it back and slamming it against the wall, dangling it in the air. It grunted and went for a sword hanging from its belt, but didn't scream like I would have.

Another branch broke through the wall, lashing the ogre's gauntlet firmly to its body, making its hand immobile.

"Let's go." Starren took off without waiting, taking advantage of the opening the trees had given us by taking out the ogre. The other ogres were busy, hacking at roots and trying not to get captured like their comrade.

We stopped a short distance down the tunnel to watch the carnage. Three ogres were down for the count now, the fourth losing any advantage it might have had as smaller roots came through the floor, trapping it in place.

"I almost feel sorry for them," Starren said. She turned and kicked me. "Being in that position is terrible."

"You've done that to Starren?" Carver asked, his tone disbelieving. Aww, and here I thought he didn't get protective. Apparently he did.

"She deserved it."

He looked to Star.

She shrugged.

"Let's go," I said.

"We need a plan." Carver jogged after me, Star behind him.

"Agreed, but let's go as we make a plan." I wasn't the brightest, but standing around waiting for more of those guys to show up didn't seem like a great idea. "How do we get out of here?"

"Not until we see Ferid," Starren said from behind Carver.

"I'm not going to risk both of your lives this foolishly, we'll figure something else out when we get free."

"Not without seeing Ferid," Starren stubbornly repeated.

I threw my hands up. What was with my family? Everyone always knew what was best, and it never matched what I thought. Especially when it was stuff about me. I of all people wanted this to be over, but if we died, I'd never forgive myself.

We didn't get a chance to truly argue. Four more ogres burst around a curve in the tunnel. Starren didn't even get her sword up before the trees crushed them to the walls.

"That's getting more and more creepy," Carver said.

"Agreed," Starren answered.

Agreed.

We ran forward together, Carver calling the shots when we got to sections where we had to choose a direction.

A few more turns and I lost track of the amount of ogres lining the walls, like flies in a spider's web.

Something grew in the distance ahead of us. The tunnel opened up into a room, lit by an orb in the ceiling, droplets of cool blue light floating down around us.

I screeched to a stop.

Here there were eight ogres crushed into unnatural positions against the room's walls. In front of us, massive doors stretched up in an intimidating barrier.

Starren stopped. "Trish?"

Trish this, Trish that. What was I supposed to do about giant doors? I walked forward and placed a hand against one, feeling it pulse. The door was bare, no carvings, no symbols. No handle.

I pushed. The door didn't even notice.

"What do you expect me to do about this?" I asked Starren. "I'm not Supergirl or Wonder Woman, I don't have any strength."

The irritation I'd kept under the surface bubbled up again. I tried to shove it back down. It didn't help much. Nothing helped much. Even with all the things I could do, I still couldn't help Dan and Nina.

Roots broke out of the floor around us, snaking their way to the door, finding any tiny crack, any dimple, and forcing their way in. The door creaked and groaned as it fought back.

But it was no match.

The door shattered into millions of pieces, dusting the room around us, tinkling to the floor. I coughed, and waved my hand, trying to see past the cloud in the air.

"I just wanted you to do something like that," Starren said.

"Yeah, yeah."

The debris settled a little, allowing me to see past the length of my arm. Ogres. A whole lot of ogres.

They formed a line in front of us, at least fifteen wide, and longer than the dust would allow me to see.

"Oh crap," Carver whispered behind me. It echoed in the huge chamber, the first time anything had acted natural since we'd stepped underground.

As one, the ogre in the front row lifted their spears.

Oh crap didn't quite convey how I was feeling at the moment.

A rumbling started, and tree roots wormed their way through the beautiful ceiling, working their way down.

Somehow the ogre held the line. I was internally freaking out, and I was the reason they were here.

"Stop!" The authoritative voice rang through the hall. It was deep and strong, sounding exactly like the other ogres who had spoken so far in this stupid mad dash underground.

The haze cleared enough that I could make out a throne, with an ogre on it. It looked exactly like the rest. Didn't even have a crown, no robe, nothing but the same exact armor as the rest of them.

"Stop before you cause any more destruction. These halls took hundreds of year to build, and you would tear them down in moments."

"Sorry." I wanted to add that maybe they shouldn't try to eat their visitors, but I at least had enough self-preservation to hold that inside.

He stood and made his way toward us, the ranks of ogre opening and closing around him.

Okay, that was different than the other ogre. A massive sword, decked with all kinds of jewels on the scabbard was prominently displayed hanging at his side. Maybe that was his status symbol, instead of a useless crown.

"Starren." His voice rumbled when he said her name, anger sharpening his strong voice. "Here to steal from us again?"

She straightened and looked him right in the eye. Yeah, stupid was a family trait.

"I need a favor."

Apparently this was Ferid. Great.

His face twitched, but other than that he gave no sign he'd even heard her.

"We need to find someone, and I was told you may know where she is."

This time he snorted. Somehow I got the feeling that was about as vocal as he got when he found something humorous.

"And why would I help you? You know that coming back here carries a death sentence."

"You'll help us, or I'll tear down your entire hall," I blurted out.

Ferid's gaze moved to me, and I had to force myself not to wiggle under the weight of it.

"You don't know what you're saying. This hall has stood for a thousand years. I will not be the leader that allows it to be destroyed."

Yeah, I hated the blackmail card. But the ends had to justify the means, right? Dan and Nina. Dan and Nina.

"There isn't anything you can do about it. You can't stop me, unless you help us." I could feel the trees tension above us, the roots working their way down, waiting to tear everything apart down here.

Not yet.

The ogre's eyes narrowed, and I didn't even see the signal he gave, but something whistled and boom, I was on the ground, unable to breathe, blood pouring from a small hole in my abdomen.

Several ogre rushed forward and separated Starren and Carver from me.

The ground thundered as Ferid walked over and picked me up by my hair, dangling me in front of him like a limp doll. I bit my lip to keep from screaming, the pain in my scalp rivaling the pain in my gut. Only not moving kept the misery from being excruciating.

Not yet.

The whimper that escaped was embarrassing.

"You're a problem that's easy to fix." He slowly slid his sword out of its sheath. It didn't make a sound.

Okay, now.

Roots burst through the walls. Chunks of ceiling rained down on all of us. The ranks of ogre shifted restlessly, but held their line without even shielding themselves with an arm.

The pause that went through the room was just long enough for a root to grab Ferid's sword hand, the tip burning its way through the top layer of skin on my chest.

I thrashed around, trying to get free, my scalp screaming so loud it completely covered the pain of my mostly healed abdomen.

"Let her go. Let's talk," Starren shouted.

Ferid grunted, putting the full force of his bulk into the sword thrust. It moved forward a millimeter, the pain in my chest now rivaling my hair getting torn out of my head.

More roots lashed forward, pulling at his fingers until the sword clattered to the ground.

I kicked at his armor, bruising my toe through my soiled tennis shoe.

But the trees were angry now. The rage radiated off them. The feeling was the same as it had been up in the forest, right before the forest spirit appeared.

That would be just great. Another thing to worry about.

Ogre were moving toward us now, slow and sluggish as they slashed at roots. This had to stop before someone accidentally got killed.

"Call off your ogres," I got out, teeth clenched.

"Call off your madness," Ferid answered.

Neither of us trusted the other. Someone had to go first.

"Stop!" I shouted, hoping at least half of them would listen. With the ceiling destroyed, the sound vacuum had evaporated, and my voice boomed around the huge chamber.

Instantly all the roots froze.

I blew out a breath in relief.

Ferid studied me there, hanging in front of him, for an eternity. Then he opened his hand and let me drop to the ground.

"What is all this?" he asked.

I didn't have an answer for him. I never did when someone asked me about my freaky traits. I blinked back the tears the pain in my head had caused before answering him. "We need five minutes. Just five. And then we'll leave, and not cause any more damage or pain."

One of the roots took that moment to slap an ogre across the face, knocking him to the ground.

I glared.

It wilted.

"I just need help finding someone. That's it. That's all we want."

Ferid stared through his helmet. "And what do I get in exchange?"

"Starren's sword." I spoke without thinking. It was the only thing we had that he would want. Our lives for a sword? Easy choice.

Starren made an incredulous noise behind me.

It was spur of the moment, and probably stupid, but it seemed like the right thing to do.

"You offer me something I already own? The ore was stolen from me." He stomped on the end of his sword and flipped it into the air. He deftly caught it and held it out, showing me the craftsmanship. "Only those of great authority are allowed to carry a blade made from the ester. It is rare, and when we come into power we must mine it ourselves and forge our own weapon."

He gestured around the huge cavern, and for the first time I actually had a chance to look around. The walls that were still intact were covered by intricate swords, hundreds of them.

"When we die, our sword is never used again, the ore returned to the earth that gave it to us. By taking it, the woman has greatly disrespected us."

Welp. She was definitely not going to be happy, but now I was sure this was the right decision. If I asked the trees for help, maybe they'd collapse this whole place on us, and we'd all die. Me included, because I needed to eat, like, all the time.

"The sword is yours, whether you choose to help us or not."

Starren made a noise in protest. She'd hate me for the rest of the day, but then she'd figure out that it was the only way we were going to get out of this situation. Diplomatically, anyway.

And the other way made me shiver. The ogre did not seem like a people that would give in easily, and killing even one would be too many. I didn't want blood on my hands.

"Please go into more detail about what you need." Ferid's voice was back to almost robotic. I took that as a good sign. He hadn't just demanded the sword.

"I'm looking for a woman named Nara. She'd deaf. The last time I saw her was at Fairbent prison."

He cocked his head, considering his answer. "I know of whom you speak."

Wow, something had finally gone right!

"You give your word as fae, that if I tell you, you'll leave without causing any more damage? Without harming anyone? And you'll leave the sword."

The last bit did not come across as a question. I considered his offer for a moment. Agreeing to something took a serious turn when you didn't have the ability to go back on your word. "If you will give me your word as fae that you will not attempt to hinder us in any way, will not trap us, attack us, anything to stop us from leaving. And that we will have an escort to take us safely to the surface."

He nodded.

"Agreed," we said in unison.

I was actually getting pretty good at this fae stuff, I'd been around them enough I could even mimic their formal talk. Yuck.

Ferid left me standing there and made his way back to his throne, the ogre back in their perfect line making room for him. Once he reached the throne, he dropped into it pretty hard.

I got the feeling he wasn't very happy with our deal. But neither was Starren, so boo hoo. Speaking of.

I glanced back at Starren, who was glaring mutinously at my back. That sword meant a lot to her, but she'd taken what wasn't hers to make it, and it could have gotten us killed. Did I feel guilty? Yeah. But did I also want to survive this? Oh yeah.

Man, it would be nice to have Jaden's level head and support here right now. Wait. Did I... miss him? Not the time.

I went back to Starren and held out my hand. "Sword, please."

She full on glared in my face. *Come on, you know we have to do this.* Maybe she saw my internal begging. Maybe she had a moment of conscience. Maybe she just didn't see another way out of this without dying. But whatever the reason, she drew her sword from its pocket and slowly held it out to me.

Grabbing it before she changed her mind, I nearly trembled in relief. Just because I had said we'd give the sword to Ferid didn't mean that Star would be obligated to listen, and then I'd be in a really bad spot.

"Thank you." I meant it too. We'd come this far, I didn't want to die now.

I walked toward the first row of ogre. They didn't even glance down at me, but they did split down the middle.

Separating myself from Carver and especially Starren didn't seem like a good idea. But then, Ferid did hate Starren, so maybe it would be better for her to not be near him, clogging up his thoughts.

Whether she agreed with my assessment or not, I didn't know, but she did hang back far enough that the ranks of soldiers snapped closed behind me before she was close enough to follow.

Making my way toward the throne, I kept an eye on the roots gently swaying above us. They definitely had minds of their own. It wouldn't be good if they decided I was in some kind of danger and took it upon themselves to protect me.

How would that work? I wouldn't have intentionally broke my word. Were the trees bound to my word? So much I didn't know, and could only find out the hard way.

I had to stop thinking about this. What if I gave them ideas that they acted on?

"So?" I asked Ferid.

He sat on his throne like the thinker, bent over, chin resting in his hand.

"The last I knew, the one called Nara was hiding in Yest Forest."

"How do you know?"

"I keep track of anyone interesting."

Interesting? I didn't know much about Nara, actually. We'd spent some time in prison together, but she couldn't speak.

"Yest Forest?" I repeated. If I got this wrong then we'd be done for.

"I wouldn't travel there if I were you." He held out his hand for the sword.

I put the sword in his massive palm, his giant fingers curling around it. The blade looked more like a dagger sitting there.

"I don't have a choice. I have to find Nara. She has to be able to fix my parents."

Ferid leaned forward until we were eye level, and stared me in the eyes.

I stared right back.

"How can Nara help your parents? Your father has taken over the fae. Your mother is... missing."

Had that been a short pause there, or was it just my imagination? "Not those parents. My dad doesn't give a care about me and my mom disappeared when I was a kid. My actual parents, the ones that took me in, that take care of me every day. Those are my parents." The guilt still got me a little whenever I said that. And that was probably the strongest it had ever come out.

But my dad was my dad. Evil. And my mom... I didn't know what to think about her, so I usually just didn't.

"Hmmm." The sound rumbled in his throat. "You are a strange fae."

"I've been told."

He barked something out that came across more as just sound than words, and two of the ogre in line closest to me snapped even more to attention, though I wasn't sure how that was possible.

"These two will escort you to the surface. Please don't destroy anything else on your way out."

Was he kidding? Hopefully he was kidding. I gave him a weak grin. "I don't have any plans to."

The two ogre moved forward without even a motion from Ferid and herded me away. The rest of the ogre parted, giving Starren and Carver room to follow us.

The two of them crowded in close.

"You owe me," Starren hissed in my ear. "No one else in all of Faerie had a sword made from ore from the HighCrest mines."

"Yeah yeah, you owe me a bunch too, so let's just call it even."

The trip to the surface took entirely too long. Sure, we'd been running on the way down, so it was hard to compare, but it seemed like we walked a mile extra. Maybe it was just the fact that I really, really wanted out of here.

We reached a set of stairs, identical to the ones we'd come down on. But we hadn't passed anywhere in the tunnel where the roots had destroyed the walls, so either they'd walked us around a different way, or these were different stairs.

"The door will open when you reach the top of the stairs," one of the ogre said. They both stopped and went into some kind of stance.

"Thanks for showing us the way." Nina was always so polite, and everyone loved her. Maybe I should try, when it was possible, to be polite too. Maybe.

Neither of the ogre acknowledged I'd spoken.

"Rude."

"Let's just go." Carver steered me toward the stairs, grabbing Starren with his other hand.

I let him, though I kept an eye over our backs the whole time, more than halfway expecting the ogre to change their mind and come after us.

Just like I was wondering about the trees going against my promise earlier, now I wondered if the ogre under Ferid's command could 'disobey' him and break his word, keeping us here after promising our safety.

The stairs stretched on and on forever. This tunnel hadn't been damaged, so the still quiet was back, making my hair stand on end.

But there. The door at the top.

Carver gingerly stepped forward, and just as the ogre had said, the door silently slid open.

We all rushed a bit on our way out into the light, even though it was less bright than the strange lighting underground.

"Whew," I said, dropping to sit in the grass. The door slid closed as soon as Starren stepped out. "I was a little afraid he had some trick up his sleeve."

"Don't be sure yet that there isn't something out here waiting for us. Ogre are tricky, and we are past the point where he said we'd be safe. Even if I wasn't concerned about him, we need to move fast now. Too many fae know we're here. It's going to get back to Father, and Father is going to come after us."

I sat up fast, the grass that had started to rub on my face jerking back at my abrupt sentiment change. "That's not good."

"No."

I jumped to my feet. "Let's get going then." I squinted around us. "This isn't where we entered before."

"No, it isn't." Carver said. "But the real question is, where are we going? We couldn't hear Ferid from where we were standing."

"Yest Forest. Wherever that is. It didn't seem like asking Ferid where it was would be a great idea, so I was hoping one of you two would know how to get there."

Carver's face blanched. "Yest? Are you sure?"

"It's not like I'm going to make up a random name and accidentally pick one that's a real place, Carver. Yes, I'm sure."

"Well that's not good."

"Why's that?"

"Because we have to either spend two weeks going around, or we have to travel straight through the area Father has strongly under his control," Starren said.

Of course. When could anything ever be easy. When did we not have to struggle for every little win. "But we can get there?" Two weeks? Hopefully Wren hadn't been serious about coming after us, or that Cumat would hold his ground and not let her through the portal. Because as much as I wanted Dan and Nina to get their memory back, I'd really rather be there to see it.

"Maybe." Carver shrugged. "But we aren't going to worry about it tonight. It'll be dark soon. We need to find somewhere safe for the night."

"We should get a few miles over with before stopping," Starren said. "We have a lot of ground to cover, and I don't want to be in Faerie any longer than we have to be."

"But if we're stumbling around in the dark, we're going to get killed," Carver said. "Then you'll be here forever. Things around here aren't very safe on a normal day, but all of Faerie is in an uproar right now and fae are getting killed all over the place."

Starren set her jaw, but she agreed. "Fine. But I'm picking the place we stop."

"Fine."

She stalked off. Carver and I followed without a peep. I just hoped she knew which direction we were supposed to be going in.

She didn't make us go far. Far enough from the doorway that the ogre wouldn't immediately stumble on any of our sleeping bodies if they did decide to come after us.

No campfires in Faerie, so we all huddled together under a tree, in silence. The huddling wasn't because of the cold, it was always the perfect temperature, but I wouldn't admit what the real reason was.

"I'll take first watch." There was too much swirling around in my brain to sleep anyway. Might as well make use of it.

"Thanks," Carver said. "Wake me up when it's my turn." He rolled over and was out like a light.

"How does he do that?" I asked Star. "He even slept in Wraith's lair."

She shrugged. "I've always wondered that myself."

It got quiet again. The trees bent branches down to cover us better, and the grass plumped beneath us like a bed.

Thanks.

We sat long enough that I thought Starren fell asleep. But I was wrong.

"I never really had a mom. Not that I remember. I was very young when she left. I'm glad you had Nina, to show you what a mom is supposed to be."

Had? She couldn't just say 'had' like I didn't have her anymore. Like she wasn't my mom any longer. "Have."

"What?" She sounded just genuinely confused, not her normal combative self.

"I have Nina. We're getting her back."

Starren nodded in the dark, the light of what I assumed was the moon gleaming off her unreadable face. "Have. Goodnight."

"Goodnight."

She rolled over, facing away from me.

I pulled my knees tight to my chest so I could bury my face in my jeans. Have. Not had. One way or another, it would be have. *Hold on, Nina. I'm coming.*

CHAPTER THIRTEEN

Time was extremely difficult to keep track of here. We'd been traveling since the sky had begun to brighten, and that had been some time ago.

I'd never thought I'd get tired of fire fruit, but here we were. Very tired of it. I'd snacked on it all day, but all I could think about were cookies. And awesome suppers. And breakfast sandwiches.

I wasn't thinking about Dan and Nina. No, of course not. I couldn't help that thinking about food made me think of all the amazing meals the two of them had cooked for our little family over the years.

Nah. I wasn't thinking about them at all. Only the food.

Starren's pocket only held so much beef jerky. Or, more accurately, our budget had only allowed her to bring so much beef jerky.

No roads in Faerie, so I was completely lost. Not that I wouldn't have been lost anyway, but at least this way I had an excuse.

Thankfully Starren seemed to know exactly where we were going. How she knew, I had no idea since we'd come out of the ground somewhere different than where we'd gone in, but I wasn't questioning her. Even if she didn't know where we were at the moment, we'd have to walk until we found our bearing anyway, so I was just going to choose to believe that she knew where we were. And where we were going.

"We should talk about what we want to do," Carver said. "Right now we're going in the right direction no matter which choice we make, but we should be fairly close to the crossroads. We should know what we're doing before we get there."

"We're going straight through," Starren said, not looking back.

"Just like that. You're just going to make the decision for us, with no discussion?"

"I know what I want, I know what Trish will want, and that makes what you want irrelevant. We're going straight through. I'm not scared of Father."

"I am!" I butted in. "Apparently you don't think you are, or you wouldn't be able to say that, but I think down deep you are. And should be. He's a psychopath. Obviously I don't like either option, but I'm just putting it out there. We should be worried."

"We're going straight through," Starren said. She didn't even slow down.

I grabbed her arm and jerked her around. "Why the hurry? It's been a month. I'm just as eager to get out of Faerie as you are, but risking going anywhere close to Father? Not worth it. We take a little extra time and go around, and we can make sure we actually get it done, and not get grabbed and forced to do some crap for Father that we don't wanna do."

"What about your Wren? I heard her threat. She'll bring humans into Faerie."

"I don't think she's going to do that. Not over a niece she's only spent a few hours with. And you don't either. So tell me the truth."

Starren's shoulders slumped and she wouldn't look me in the eye. "There's something you should know."

Dread rose, clogging my throat. I shook her when she didn't continue right away.

"The memory loss. The longer we wait, the stronger chance it will become permanent."

"What?" I screeched. "We sat around for a month when we could have been trying to help them, and then all of this might be for nothing?" I shoved her away from me. "How could you do that?"

She threw up her hands, stumbling away. "I didn't know, I swear! I was talking with Wraith while you were sleeping, and she told me.

That's why I left. I thought I could get the job done faster on my own, I thought I'd talk to Ferid, nab Nara, and we would head home!"

I crumpled in on myself, leaning into a tree. What if it was already too late? What if we'd risked our lives for no reason? What if we never made it back?

"No," Starren said. It was her turn to grab me. "No. We aren't going there. Get it together. We're going after Nara. We're taking her back with us whether she wants to go or not, and we're getting you your Dan and Nina back."

"Whether she wants to or not sounds-"

"Quiet, Carver," Starren interrupted him.

"She'll want to. She has to want to, we helped her."

"Then she does owe you a debt. Debts are serious to the fae. But that doesn't mean she's going to want to go to the human world. We hear a lot of bad things about that place."

Both Starren and I turned a deadpan stare on him.

"Worse things than this place?" I asked.

"Well, yeah, they're always killing each other and trying to enslave each other, it's in the books Starren brought me."

I stared at him harder. "So that's worse than here, how?"

He blinked several times. "I don't know."

"Exactly. It seems that places are basically the same. Some people just want left alone, like me, and some people want to force their will on everyone else, like Father and The Council. What is wrong with people?"

"Go back, Carver," Starren said. "If that's what you think of Earth, you won't want to go there with us anyway, and that's where we're going to end up."

"Not go to Earth?" Carver sounded truly shocked. "I've been wanting to go there since you brought me my very first book, The Lion, The Witch, and the Wardrobe. I'd really like to meet this Lion, he seems very wise."

"Fiction, Carver," Starren said.

He blinked more. "Oh. I had that one filed with the history books. It's set during World War Two, that's real, isn't it?"

"Yes, that part is real, but it's just the setting," I clarified. "Narnia isn't real."

"How do you know? You take a portal to Earth from Faerie."

Well that was a good point. And one I had no answer for. Moving on. "Straight through the evil psycho's stronghold it is." We didn't have time for anything else.

Carver straightened. "And may the odds be ever in our favor."

We traveled all day, only stopping occasionally to rest. For once I was the one pushing the pace. I hated all this outdoorsy hiking stuff, but now my only motivation wasn't that I wanted to see Dan and Nina as soon as possible. Now we had a ticking time bomb.

I wouldn't let myself think about that. Couldn't, or I'd curl in a ball and never get up, letting myself shrivel away until I died.

We weren't too late. We weren't going to be too late.

The mantra going through my head didn't help as much as I'd have liked.

Starren had been calling mandatory breaks every few hours, so that we could keep our energy up and travel at night. The danger of traveling in the dark was now outweighed by the fact that we were drifting farther and farther into Quintin's territory.

During our last break, they'd napped. I'd brooded. Then finally we'd moved on.

I did not want to have to face my feelings about my maniac father. The one that had played me. Had sent Wade to shoot Nina, even though he knew how much I loved her. The one who had forced Dan and Nina to eat fae food, right in front of a whole crowd of people.

He'd known. There was no other reason he would have made such a big deal out of the fact that they hadn't wanted to try even a bite of anything. He'd known, and he'd pushed them until they hadn't had a choice.

I wanted to dwell on the anger part. But the trees around me showed me what I truly felt.

They drooped and wilted, cracking stems allowing water to flow down and fall to the ground, even with no rain.

Yeah. That was more what I felt.

Mother hadn't wanted me. I went through a whole bunch of foster homes that didn't truly want me. Nice people, but unequipped to deal with an angry, mouthy, teen. My sister hadn't wanted me at first, though I hoped that was changing. My father only wanted me so he could rule the world or something.

The only people who had ever just wanted me were Dan and Nina. And Jaden. But I didn't know what that was and now was not the time to try and figure it out.

A pang hit me at the thought of Jaden. What was he doing right now? I didn't even know what time of day it was to guess. There was some sort of comfort in thinking about him at work, or sitting on the couch watching TV with his little sister, Jaime.

He'd been through enough. He deserved peace.

I glanced up long enough to see Starren checking on me. I gave her a stony look back. We definitely didn't have the talk things out kind of sister relationship.

If we didn't have mutual fear and distaste for our father, would we have even become as good at being sisters as we were now? Probably not.

Nothing in my life was real. I hid who I was from everyone at school, everyone at the gym. Only Dan and Nina knew the real me. Sometimes I felt like they knew the real me better than I did.

They saw me. Not some foster kid, not some freak, me.

And I'd let them. I still wasn't sure how or when that had happened, but I trusted them. Only them.

And Jaden. Who had somehow forgiven me for everything, even though I didn't deserve it. At all.

Ugh, walking gave way too much time for thinking.

"Hey Carver," I said.

"Yeah?"

"What's your favorite book from Earth?"

"We shouldn't be talking," Starren said before he could answer. "Someone could hear us. Or something."

I ground my teeth to keep from letting out some rude, snarky answer, because she was right. And I didn't know which was scarier, 'someone' hearing us, or 'something.' But I needed some kind of distraction.

Hello, trees, you all have anything to say?

They brightened up from their moping and the saplings around us gave a little shiver of joy, but there wasn't any answer.

Seriously. Things had gotten so bad I was talking to plants and expecting them to respond? I really was a weirdo.

But a weirdo with something to get done. People to protect. People to save. *Get it together, Trish.*

A warning brushed through the forest on a whisper from the trees.

People were coming.

I grabbed Starren and motioned toward Carver, putting a finger to my lips and jerking them behind some overgrowth. The brush made like a peacock and fluffed itself out, covering us without difficulty.

Nothing happened for long enough that Starren went from high alert to giving me the stink eye.

I shrugged. The trees hadn't failed me so far. I opened my mouth to tell her that, when something clinked. Something very un-forest like.

Starren snapped to attention. Oh, now she was interested. She pulled a sword from her pocket, one I'd never seen before.

"You have another sword?" I mouthed to her.

She rolled her eyes and mouthed back, "Of course I have backup swords. Don't you?"

"Swords? How many do you have in there?"

She didn't get a chance to answer, because a man in full armor pushed aside a shrub and strode through the forest like he owned it.

Rude. I was starting to feel like I was the one that owned all this. A branch touched my face like it was saying it agreed.

Four people of varying sizes but all in the same armor followed him, and four after them. They streamed by steadily until I lost count.

A whole lot of fae. A whole lot of weird fae. Yeah, I said it, this was weird, even by fae standards. And in matching armor, which was really strange. High fae armies weren't really a thing.

Had they made a whole stash of that armor and hidden it away? There hadn't been an army a couple months ago when we were here, and armor like this didn't get made quickly. This whole thing was bizarre, as far as I knew, fae didn't work well together, and definitely not well enough to work as an army.

"Father's?" I mouthed to Starren.

She just stared grimly ahead, either not noticing or not acknowledging me speaking.

I'd been so focused on how hard all of this was for me, that I'd totally forgotten how terrible it had to be for her. Father had abused her and twisted her mind for years. Manipulated and controlled every aspect of her life, until she had no one in it but him.

So much had changed. She'd changed, to an amazing extent. But that didn't mean that the memories had gone away.

I reached over and squeezed her hand. She shoved my hand away, not looking up from eyes throwing daggers at the soldiers who streamed by.

It was telling, in an odd sort of way, that her rejecting me actually stung. I wouldn't have given a care a couple months ago. Wouldn't have even tried to comfort her, because I knew I would be rejected. But we were becoming real family. Whether she wanted us to or not.

Finally the press of people waned. Like the tail end of a snake, the last set of four disappeared into the next section of trees.

The grass they'd trampled cried out.

I kept an eye on the place where they'd disappeared, and crept out into the open. Kind of. The bush followed me as far as it could reach, like it was still trying to provide cover. I gave it a pat in thanks, then reached a hand down to hover my palm over the crushed grass.

It wiggled, struggling to rise up. More and more it tried, until it popped up to touch my hand, full again.

"You're weird," Starren said, walking past me.

"I know. Were those Father's men?"

"I don't know who else would be raising an army. But I don't know why Father would be either. He has what he wanted. The Council is dead. He rules Faerie unopposed. What is he planning?"

A great question. That I feared the answer to, and I was pretty sure Starren did as well, even if she wouldn't admit it.

"He must have been planning this for a lot longer than we thought." Carver struggled out of the bush. "That armor took months, if not years to make in that amount."

I beamed at him. "That's what I was thinking!"

Starren muttered something.

"What?" I asked.

"He never said anything."

I stopped the beaming. She was hurt that Father had been working on all this and hadn't told her. I'd thought he'd hurt her for the last possible time when she'd switched sides and helped me escape with Dan and Nina. Apparently, like so many other times when it came to Starren, I was wrong.

"I was his second. I did everything he asked. I fought for him, killed for him, bled for him. He never said anything."

She looked broken. I'd seen so many strong emotions from her in the past, but never anything like this.

Carver and I exchanged looks, but neither of us knew what to do.

I stepped forward slowly, trying the hand on the shoulder again. This time she didn't shrug it off. "That man has serious problems, Star. He's crazy."

She looked at me, her eyes bright.

I couldn't quite tell if the bright was caused by tears or more family crazy. I pulled her into a hug, not waiting to see if it was okay. She'd say no, even when she needed it the most. If she didn't like it, she'd go stiff as a board and I'd let go.

But that wasn't what happened. She crumpled into me for a second, her grip around my waist nearly bruising. And then she let go and stepped back. I let her without a fight.

"This is my home," Starren said.

I started to interrupt her, but she held up her hand and I let her get out whatever it was she was trying to say.

"This is my home, and he's destroying it."

"Your home is in Fort Wayne, with me."

She jerked to glare at me, eyes blazing, this time in obvious anger. "You think I want to be stuck there? You think I want to be trapped among all those humans? I only stay because I have to take care of you since you no longer have a family because of me. If we are successful in this mission, which I find highly doubtful, I'll be gone the next day."

"Starren!" Carver said sharply.

That was it. The truth. She couldn't lie. She was only here out of guilt. She didn't want me either. Add another person to the long list. Soon it would be Jaden too. And even if I did get Dan and Nina back, I'd lose them in the same way someday.

"I'm sorry you feel that way," I choked out. "As soon as we find Nara, you're free to go."

I stumbled away from her, blindly going in the direction the soldiers had disappeared in. I didn't even care at the moment if I ran into them. If they caught me and kept me from returning to fix Dan and Nina's memories, they were only saving me trouble. No one wanted me for long. And those two couldn't be an exception to the rule.

"Trish." Starren's voice barely made it through the pounding in my ears. "Trish! Come back, I'm sorry."

But I didn't. I couldn't. Starren could take care of herself. In fact, she was safer without me. I should have seen before now that this should be a solo trip.

I tore off through the woods. The bushes moved for me, the grass springing right back up to cover my tracks. I ran at an angle to the direction the troops had been marching in, avoiding them if I could.

After I couldn't hear Starren calling anymore, I stopped and hid in a bush, its small branches attempting to embrace me.

I shoved them off.

"Which way to Yest?" I asked.

The strange whisper of the trees communicating swept through the forest. It took a moment, but the sound echoed back.

In unison, several trees around me lifted a branch pointing in the same direction.

Fine. I'd always known I'd end up alone. Better sooner than later.

I reached up for the comfort of my sword hilt, and struck out alone.

The super not cool part of traveling alone, other than the extra boring aspect, was that I didn't have anyone to ask important questions. Questions like, are we there yet?

Seriously. I'd tried with the trees, but they'd just seemed confused. Hindsight is 20/20, as Dan liked to say, but I really wished right now that I'd thought to ask Starren how far Yest Forest was *before* I'd stormed off.

It almost made me want to find her, or more likely, let her find me. That was the reason, the real reason. It wasn't like I missed her or anything. We were totally different, raised in completely different worlds, we weren't regular sisters. We shared DNA or whatever, but that was it.

I didn't even really consider us to have the same parents. After all, our bio parents weren't great to us, and I had Dan and Nina, who she barely knew. Yeah, she knew all kinds of facts about them from back when she was blackmailing me to help her find Jaden, but she didn't know them for real. The only time she'd spent time with them was as we traveled from the place The Council met to the tunnel with the portal.

Not enough for someone like Starren to develop any feelings for a person. I mean, did I even know that she had feelings for me? Did she truly think of us as sisters, or was she just with me because of the guilt? She wasn't a guilt type person, maybe it was just the convenience of having someone who understood humans around to help her if she needed it.

"Stupid Starren," I said under my breath.

I marched forward, not paying attention. Stupid me, not just stupid

Starren. I knew what kind of person she was, and I'd still thrown myself into a position to get hurt.

A branch wrapped lightly around my ankle and tugged.

I kicked it loose, shuffling forward.

A vine from a different tree grabbed my wrist and pulled tight.

"What's with you?" I used my free hand to rip the vine off. "Is someone coming?"

The vine wilted a little, but nothing tried to hide me. I listened for a second, but nothing sounded out of the ordinary.

"You're being paranoid, I'm fine."

A root ripped through the ground, tripping me. I kicked it.

"That's enough of that!" Without them actually doing anything, I could feel the trees shrink back. Guilt niggled at me. They'd only ever tried to look out for me. "Sorry," I muttered. But I kept going forward.

I didn't make it far before a wave of dread hit me. I stopped dead, the hair on the back of my neck prickling. I slowly looked around, doing my best to not draw attention to myself. Ha. After that last display, everything in the area knew I was here.

Nothing seemed wrong. The lighting was the same. No scary noises. No bad smell. Nothing the movies and my way too vast experience told me to worry about. I sent a question out through the trees. Even if they weren't able to give me specifics, they still gave me helpful tidbits.

Not this time. This time, there was nothing.

"Uh, guys?" I asked.

Eerie quiet.

I gave a nervous laugh. And here I'd thought I'd be glad to not have to deal with all the weird. Right now the weird felt normal, safe. I scooted backward a few steps, and the feeling of all the plant life around me hit me like a log falling off a truck, nearly knocking me from my feet.

Worry. Relief. Fear.

"What's going on?" I whispered to them.

The closest ones whipped around, but they weren't able to communicate whatever it was that was bothering them.

As an experiment, I crept forward a step. Same as normal. Another step. Still normal. One more step.

Utter mental silence.

What the heck?

I backed up a step again. "Are you all okay?"

They whipped around some more, but they all seemed fine.

"Am I going in the right direction?"

A couple branches pointed in the direction I'd been moving. Not surprising since I'd been following their directions this whole time, but still. I might have been hoping, just a bit, that they had changed their minds.

"Is this it?"

The branches whipped around again. I took that as a yes.

"Welp. Bye then. Take care of yourselves."

And then I stepped into what had to be Yest.

CHAPTER FOURTEEN

Okay. Alright. Maybe this forest wasn't so bad. I'd been walking like ten minutes, and I hadn't died. Always a good sign.

Nothing had ambushed me, nothing was screaming somewhere out in the trees. It was all good.

My anxiety about the situation stemmed from not feeling the plants. That had to be it. Because other than that teensy weensy fact, nothing had changed. The forest looked the same. Same atmosphere. Just quiet.

Maybe it was a good thing. Some peace.

Something snapped in the brush to the left and my heart rate jumped to two hundred as I slammed myself behind a tree.

No. Not a good thing. I could not come up with one single good thing about this situation. Where was Starren when you needed her?

No. None of that either. I didn't need my big sister. I had this well in hand. How big could this forest be, anyway? Just keep walking in the direction the trees had last pointed me in, and it would all be good.

Except I was horrible with directions, even on a good day, and now I was probably turned around.

No more strange noises in the trees. And really, it hadn't been much of a strange noise. It could easily have been a deer or some other woodland creature.

Yeah, good luck convincing myself that was a possibility.

I dusted off imaginary dirt from my hands, squinted at the direction the light came from to get my bearing, and marched forward. Far less confidently than before, but it was something.

Crackling in the woods on my right, totally opposite of the sound direction before, upped my pace, not quite jogging, but definitely much quicker than the timid walk of before.

Where I was trying to get was anyone's guess, but away from here for sure.

Was the disconnect from the forest pumping dread through my soul? Or something else? Just being in the woods in general wasn't a favorite thing of mine. It hadn't been great before I woke up after being dead out in the forest, and then was worse for awhile. After a bit I'd adjusted as the trees and I came to an understanding, and so now I usually did okay. Usually.

Something was watching me.

My breath huffed out faster and faster, my blood pumping. I side-eyed the trees around me, but didn't see anything to worry about. The hair on the back of my neck told me my eyes were lying.

Supposedly it wasn't a good idea to run from a predator. And I hadn't even seen anything to make me think I was being followed. But deep in my gut, I knew, and I had to force my muscles to relax and not spring forward without permission.

I didn't even know enough about Faerie to be scared of anything specific. We'd run into plenty of deadly creatures in the short amount of time I'd spent here, but none of them seemed like the stalk me in the woods type.

If it was Wraith and some kind of practical joke, she was going to regret it. The feeling of dread I was having did feel similar to the type she gave off.

Yet different.

I'd moved into walk-as-fast-as-possible-without-jogging mode without noticing. I probably looked like one of those mom power walkers from back in D.C., but I couldn't seem to bring it back down.

Almost running into a tree, I glared at it. "Thanks for the warning." No response.

Seriously, were all the trees here dead? They looked perfectly healthy. Were they not living in the same way other trees were?

I stopped in my tracks. What if there was another forest spirit here? What if that was why they were acting so strangely? Last time they'd been weird too, but at least they'd still felt full of life.

Angry life, but still life.

Okay, stopping wasn't a good plan. More of an instinct than a plan, but still, certain death.

Rustling started up in earnest just behind me and I bolted.

Something came after me, running just as fast.

I panted, using every iota of strength in my regenerating body.

"Stop, you idiot, it's me!"

I slid to a stop. "Starren?"

"Who else did you expect?" She caught up and bent over to catch her breath.

"Not you. How'd you find me?"

"A tree flipped out and drug us to a spot a half mile ago or so, and then just kept frantically pointing in this direction until we came after you. I thought you were asking for help." She stood up straight, a full on storm across her face. "You idiot, I thought you were dying!"

"Shhh," I threw a finger up to her lips. "I'm not sure that's off the table."

Starren went into warrior mode, still holding onto angry sister mode and doing both at once quite well. "What's going on?"

"I don't know. I just have a bad feeling." Saying it out loud? Yeah, felt stupid. But Starren didn't give me one of her 'you're ridiculous' looks.

"I trust your instincts."

"Where's Carver?"

"He circled ahead in case I couldn't nab you."

"Nab me? Did you think I was going to run from you?"

Starren shrugged. "You did, didn't you?"

"No. I didn't run from *you*..." Not intentionally. "I was running from... something."

Now she looked me in the face instead of keeping watch. "Something?"

"Something."

"Okay, then. We should get moving. There's only one place in Yest I can imagine Nara wanting to hide out. The forest isn't that big." She marched forward.

I hung back. "That's it? You're not going to yell at me about running off?"

She didn't look back, just kept marching. "Oh, you know I'm going to. It's just going to have to wait until I don't have to worry about my volume."

I hurried to catch up. "That's not fair, you've tried to leave me behind a few times."

"Be quiet, Trish, or you're just going to get it now, whatever the consequences."

Getting yelled at for sure now or possibly later wasn't a difficult choice.

"Run!" Carver's voice came through the trees, the near panic far too obvious.

"Carver?" Starren yelled, taking off in the direction his voice had come from. A little ahead and to the right.

The bush in front of us thrashed and Craver fell out. "Run!" He grabbed Starren's hand and tore off, at least in the correct direction. I followed.

A sad baying noise that instantly turned my muscles to jelly started on the right and was picked up on the left. A baying I knew all too well, even after only hearing it once before.

"Vilan!" I yelled to Starren.

She didn't get a chance to respond, because speak of the devil, there he was, standing in front of us.

Starren and Carver skidded to a stop, hardly giving me a chance to follow suit.

"Hello, Trisha," Vilan said. He looked like he just came from a red carpet somewhere, not like he'd been tromping around in the woods. "I've been waiting to find you in a vulnerable spot. My hounds could take you, but I'm not sure what your limits of regeneration are, and your father would be quite displeased with me if I pushed them too far."

He stepped forward, not taking his eyes off me.

With hardly a sound, the brush let a hound slip through on the right. My eyes probably looked as big as my face at the moment. I snapped my attention back to Vilan. There wasn't anything I could do about the hounds without the trees.

Nothing but get injured and heal, over and over again, watching Starren and Carver die.

I sidled up to Starren. "Make a break for it. He wants me. Maybe he won't care what you do."

"Starren, Starren. How the mighty have fallen. I used to envy your position with your father." He held his arms up and laughed. "And now, I have it. How wonderful is that?" He moved forward, the grin so out of place. "Your father will be pleased when I tell him you'll no longer be a problem."

"Uh, I think that means we all need to run," Carver said. "Which is what I was yelling at you to do earlier."

In tandem we took off.

Shoot, shoot, shoot. Of all the things I thought might get me here, Vilan wasn't one of them. How had he found us?

A hound bayed as it took off to the left, herding us right. The other hound yipped in front of us, herding us back.

"You can't run," Vilan's voice floated all over the forest, making it completely unclear where it was coming from. "Once my hounds are on the scent, nothing can stop them."

Starren stumbled and Carver jerked her forward.

Then Vilan was right in front of us. "Boo."

I grabbed Carver, hauling him back away and moving between them. Whether the hounds had brought us back around, or Vilan had somehow gotten ahead of us, I didn't know. At this point I was all turned around.

"I've learned all kinds of interesting human things in the last couple months." Vilan leaned against a tree, that sick grin on his face. Then the grin dropped off, which was worse. Much worse. "All kinds of things I didn't want to know about." He pulled a knife from somewhere in his clothes and tossed it in the air.

We all watched in silence as it flipped through the air before falling like a rock toward the ground. He lightly caught it by the blade and tossed it back up.

"Really, I'd prefer not to know anything about humans. They disgust me. But the frustrating part of the whole thing is that my decision was made for me." He leaned in toward me, gaze nearly boring a hole through my face. "My last few months have been based on a decision made by you. And I really don't like that."

The knife came down again, flashing as it fell. He caught it without looking up. Then the sick grin was back.

"But here we are. I'll take you in to your father, and he'll be so pleased. It might make up for part of the time that was wasted waiting for you to leave Sanctuary." He shrugged. "But then, maybe it won't, and you'll have to make it up to me somehow."

"Trish, do your thing," Starren whispered.

"I can't do my thing," I whispered back. "It isn't working."

Starren looked at me. "Seriously?

"Seriously."

"We're dead."

I inched back away from Vilan, bumping into Carver, who wasn't inching away fast enough.

Vilan tipped his head and smirked at us attempting to get away. "Oh babies..."

The hounds moved out of the foliage, snarling as they stalked toward us.

"Leave the younger girl, I need her. But the other two..."

We ran. We didn't even have to communicate direction or take off, we were just standing there, and then we were running.

I jumped over a root and dodged a limb, reaching for my sword. How it was going to help, I didn't know, but I had to do something.

"Stupid trees!"

A hound nipped at my leg, smoke drifting upward from its open mouth.

"Not that one!" Vilan yelled.

The beast growled but muscled past me. Which wasn't hard, considering how badly I didn't want it to touch me after seeing what had happened back in Fort Wayne.

But no. I couldn't let it past me. Stupid instincts. I needed to stay between the thing and Starren and Carver. I put on a burst of speed and got back between them, the hound being the one to avoid me now. Apparently it knew its touch would hurt me, going against its master's wishes.

The other hound skidded through some brush and nearly knocked into me before righting itself.

I stopped in front of them, making them crash to a stop to avoid hitting me, and held up my hand. "Bad dogs. Bad. Stop right there."

One of them cocked his head in what should have been an adorable way, if he wasn't evil. The other jumped around me and continued after Carver.

"Carver!" Starren shrieked, her voice full of a pain I hadn't heard from her before.

One leap, and Carver would be a dead fae.

A limb lashed out and grabbed the hound around the waist, snatching it out of mid-air. As it died, it threw the thing into another tree.

The hound wailed as bones crunched, and the tree disintegrated into dark ash.

"Yes!" Starren yelled. "That's my sister!"

Was that me? I tried to feel some connection with the trees, but there was nothing. "Wasn't me!"

Starren's face went from an almost smile to it's time to run in the one sentence coming out of my mouth. I couldn't agree more.

The remaining hound howled, a mournful, angry sound that made me shiver down to my bones. She snarled and leapt at me, not seeming to care that her master had ordered her to keep me alive.

A tree branch lashed across her muzzle. It died, but before it even began to wilt, another took its place.

The hound went to war with the forest.

She ran at the closest tree, slashing at it with her front paws. Deep black claw marks tore through the trunk, spreading the darkness until the tree collapsed and turned to ash.

A hand grabbed mine and I almost instinctively punched my sister in the face.

She held a finger to her lips, and jerked me forward.

She was right. This may be our only chance to get away.

I stumbled off behind her, watching over my shoulder as the forest got ripped apart until the hound was out of sight.

An angry inhuman scream blasted through the forest after us. Not a hound. Vilan.

We ran until Carver and Starren couldn't breathe. Even I was gasping a bit. I brushed aside some vines hanging from a tree and motioned Starren and Carver in ahead of me.

"Do those things have a normal dog's sense of smell?" I gasped out at neither one of them in particular.

"Better," Carver gasped back.

"Then we're only here for a moment," Starren said. How did she sound okay again already? She shoved her way around me and peeked out, listening. "What was that back there?"

I grimaced. "I have no idea. But it wasn't me. The trees here won't communicate with me at all, it's like they aren't even alive."

"Like back with the forest spirit?" Carver asked.

"No." I tried to come up with some way to describe the difference, but unless a person had felt it themselves, it was hard to get across. "The trees there felt angry, stirred up, ready to hurt things. But here, it's like they aren't even there. No personality, no opinions, just plants." Ha. Wouldn't Rosie or one of my other friends find that explanation rather weird.

Basically everything about me was weird, so whatever, just par for the course.

The angry yell from before echoed through the forest again. A twinge of sympathy went through me. I'd be devastated if something happened to Storm. But then, I would never ask him to put himself in danger.

"Okay, time to go," Starren said. And she did.

Carver and I followed. The pace Starren set wasn't as brutal as before, but we still moved along at a good clip.

The hound bayed, turning my blood to ice again. She was still alive. And she sounded closer.

Something flashed in the trees beside us. And there was Vilan, somehow his clothes still pristine white.

He lips never moved, but I felt his pull on me, like all the way back in Chicago when I was trying to get the Martans to Sanctuary. And I'd thought life was complicated then.

No. Focus. "Leave us alone!"

Carver took a step in Vilan's direction.

I grabbed him in a death grip, but he struggled against me trying to go to Vilan. "Starren, a little help, please," I got out.

She turned to see what I needed, and was hit from the side by a blur of black.

"NO!" I dropped Carver and jumped at the thing, swinging wildly with my sword.

The trees all around us burst into motion, attacking the hound and Vilan at the same time.

The hound leapt off Starren and bolted to protect her master, tearing at branches and vines in her way. They wove together, making a thatching of living plants. Even that hardly slowed her.

A branch had lashed itself around Vilan, but it didn't last long once the hound arrived. The branches hit at Vilan, repeatedly getting the hound instead as she jumped in the way. Her growls were changing, turning to whimpers.

Vilan stared me in the eyes for a second, and then turned and vanished into the undergrowth.

With him not a threat at the moment, I ran and slid the last distance to Starren's body on the ground. She hadn't disintegrated, but she wasn't moving.

My hand trembled as I reached for hers. Would it be cold, lifeless?

No. Still warm.

I rolled her over, and she blinked at me. I jerked her up into a hug. "You're alive!"

"Hurts," she got out.

I sat her gently back down. "What hurts? Where? How are you still alive? How did you get hurt? Not how, but what kind of injury?" I didn't give her a chance to speak, but I couldn't hold the words back from pouring out of my mouth.

"Ribs. Magic doesn't work on me, but that dog was heavy."

I caught myself before I squeezed her to death. Then I smacked her shoulder. "I thought you were dead."

She gave me a wimpy smile. "Just returning the favor from all of the times you've done that to me. How'd you get the trees to help us? It was you this time, right? You yelled and they jumped."

"Nope." I looked around, suddenly uneasy. "Wasn't me."

"Then who was it?" Carver's voice made me jump. I hadn't heard him come up, and he hadn't interrupted Starren and me.

I squinted at the trees surrounding us. "Maybe these trees are just a little more... alive than most? Like maybe they make their own choices, and that's why I couldn't feel anything coming off of them?"

Carver followed my lead and looked around too, the same discomfort I was feeling showing on his face and in the stiffness of his body. "Are you okay to move, Star? I don't like this place. I don't think we should stay here any longer than we have to."

Starren glowered up at him. "Of course I'm fine. Why wouldn't I be fine?" She tried to stand and went back to the ground, hard.

Carver and I both jumped to help, but the glare stopped us.

"I got this."

And she did. It took her far longer than it should have, but she struggled to her feet.

"Can I take a look?" I asked.

"No."

"You are the most insufferable-"

She limped off, cradling her side. "I'm fine."

And she must truly believe it, or she wouldn't be able to say it.

"You're going to be the death of me," I said without thinking. Oops. Now I sounded like I was trying to be her mom. I hurried to catch up with her, hovering nearby in case she needed support that she would never ask for. "Anything broken?"

"No."

Even that no took a lot of effort. She would probably know if something was broke or not, with everything she'd been through, so I was going to take that as the truth and go on from there. "I was just aiming for Yest, and here we are. Do we have somewhere more specific in mind to look for Nara?"

"If you'd stayed around, we could have told you," Carver said. "There is a place where travelers seek refuge. It's supposedly the only safe place in the forest's borders. We were going to check there first. If Nara isn't there, hopefully someone who can point us in her direction is."

I watched Starren limp along for a second. "How far?"

"At least two miles," Carver answered.

Two miles couldn't be good for Starren. Her lips were pinched, her face white. She looked like her body wanted to pass out, but she was ordering it not to. That was Star alright. What if she had internal injuries that just hadn't showed themselves yet?

I crushed down the panic trying to take over.

"I'll make it," Starren said.

"We should stop for the night. Find somewhere safe. We don't want to get into this safe zone late, if there are guards or anything, they might not think we're friendly." Not too bad an excuse for right off the top of my head. Anything to get her to rest for a bit.

"Everyone is assumed to be unfriendly to everyone in Yest." Starren kept walking like I hadn't tried to get her to stop. "And Carver just told you. There's only one safe place in this entire forest. If we're out here after nightfall, we're dead."

If Starren said we'd be dead, I believed her. It wasn't like she was prone to exaggeration.

"We better keep at it then. It won't be long until dark, and we're going to be slower than normal."

Starren stiffened to nearly straight, then doubled over in pain.

"That's right, you're going to slow us down, we all know it, it's fine, don't stew about it." I almost felt bad, but her bluntness was wearing off on me. Where she was concerned, away. If that was how she needed to communicate, then that was how she probably understood when someone was trying to communicate back.

"It's fine, Starren," Carver said. The frown he sent at me was the most grumpy expression I'd seen on his face, and that was saying something since we'd almost died together at least twice. He still cared about her, whether he wanted to admit it or not.

"We know it's the truth, and it's time we all start being honest with each other. She's my sister and I love her and I'm not going anywhere. We're all in this together."

Starren's eyes widened.

Oops. I'd said I loved her. I'd never done that before. I'd never even thought about it before. But watching that huge beast crush her, not knowing if her ability would stop the destruction just touching it could cause, I'd had a revelation.

It was nowhere near as much as I loved Nina. But, I also relied on Nina for entirely different things than I relied on Starren for. And maybe, just maybe, when I'd been around Starren as much as I'd been around Nina, they might be on more equal ground.

"Fine then, let's just get going." She didn't acknowledge my slipup, but then, I didn't really expect her to. She hadn't shot me straight down, so I'd take that as a win.

We walked about a half mile in silence before the sound of a small group of people moving through the growth made me stop.

Starren heard it too, even in pain and foggy. I should have heard it before her, my senses were a little stronger than hers because of the superhealing body, but she stopped a half second before I did. Carver looked at us both questioningly.

Starren held a finger to her lips, and shrank against a tree. Carver and I followed, crowding in close enough that we both got a look from her, which basically translated to she better not get bumped in the ribs.

A group of four came around a tree. They were obviously looking for someone. Seriously? Could we not get a break?

"Mareena? Starren?" one of the women called.

Oh great. The only person who called me that was Father. Apparently I'd had a name before Trish that Mom hadn't ever called me.

The woman held her hands up, and the men followed her lead. "I know you're right there, hiding near the tree. Please come out, we mean you no harm."

Ha. Even being fae I didn't trust what she was saying was true. Maybe no one in that group was going to hurt us, but there were probably more hiding out somewhere close, waiting for us to come out into the open.

That thought had barely gone through my mind when the tree moved its branches, exposing the three of us to the fae party.

"Hey!" I said.

The tree didn't seem to care.

"I swear that no harm will come to you by my hand or that of any fae in this area. At least until you come speak with our leader."

I shifted uneasily. Until we met with their leader could mean as soon as we got to their camp or whatever, someone took us out.

But Starren was hurt, I didn't have any backup, and I didn't really know what Carver could do.

"Why does she want to see us?"

The woman put her hands down and eyed me. "You'll have to take that up with her."

The leader was a her. Not that unusual with the fae, from what I understood. Whoever it was, if they had Nara they had better be treating her right. I owed her after how my father had treated her, locking her away for who knew what.

Something I would probably be concerned about if she hadn't been so kind to me. She was deaf, and she'd spent quite a bit of the time I'd been in the cell with her teaching me sign language, mostly to keep my mind off of all the crazy going on at that moment.

Who was I kidding. When was my life not crazy?

"If you don't choose to come with us, the trees will be called upon to help," the woman said. It came across pretty smug. Of course, why not. That pretty much sealed our fate.

Starren and Carver didn't seem to have an answer. Getting tossed around by trees right now would be extremely hard on Starren. Ironic that how I usually got my way was being used against me.

"Okay, I'm coming. Don't shoot. Or whatever." I held up my hands and stepped away from the tree.

Starren limped after me, with Carver following her and attempting to look like he wasn't hovering but failing horribly.

I reached the leader. "Why does she want to see us? Who is she? You aren't involved with our father at all? Who's controlling the trees?"

"You can ask her anything you want. We're almost there. And no, I was not sent to help you now by your father." She nodded toward Starren. "Does your sister need assistance?"

The part about father made me relax, just a bit. But she hadn't answered the tree question.

"You sure know a lot about us," Starren said. "And I never need help."

"I know that too, but I still thought I'd offer." She winked at me. "That way I'm less likely to get in trouble." She motioned with her hand and the other fae surrounded us. For protection, or to keep us in line was a call I didn't have enough information to make.

"Get in trouble with who?" She'd set the pace fairly slow, not pushing Starren even after Starren's protests. "And what's with the trees? How do you know so much about us? Is this forest as dangerous after dark as they say?"

She laughed. "Not dangerous for us. The rest of your questions-"

"I know, I know. Ask your leader. Is Nara at your camp?"

"There is a woman named Nara there. She was busy and couldn't come with us, though she wanted to. She thinks highly of you."

That shut me up. She was there. This whole mess was almost over. Soon I'd be back at Dan and Nina's, with life as normal as it had ever been. I teared up, swiping at my eyes so no one noticed. We'd be sitting around the table together eating BLTs soon, or maybe pancakes. I might even go on a bike ride with them, or get Dan to set up a basketball hoop once we moved into a house instead of the apartment.

I didn't even care. As long as I was doing it with them.

After some walking, we moved into a clearing just as the sky was getting dusky. Everywhere in what should have been a clearing, there were living tents, grown out of trees and bushes, neatly set up in rows. Fae moved around the camp, bustling about on whatever their business was.

"What is this?" Starren muttered. "Hey, you," she said to our guide. "You said you didn't work for our father, but he's the only one around here trying to build an army. What gives?"

"Quintin isn't the only one building an army," a voice said from ahead.

With the lighting in the background, I couldn't make out a face. But I knew that voice. I knew it well, even though I hadn't heard it in years.

"Mother?"

CHAPTER FIFTEEN

The world shifted around me, swirling like I was on some ride at the state fair. I'd heard wrong. It had been years since I'd seen my mom, how could I even be sure I knew her voice anymore?

But I did.

I couldn't move, frozen by a few words.

"Trish?" I hardly heard Starren's voice in the distant background.

The woman moved out of the light a bit, and I got my first look at her. She looked exactly like she did in my memories, the good, and the bad.

I blinked aggressively. "Mom?"

"Trisha!" She leapt forward and pulled me into a tight hug. "I've been looking for you for so long! How are you?" She held me at arm's length and looked me over. "Are you hurt? How did you get so tall!"

"I'm fine, Mom, you know I'm always fine."

She hugged me tight again. "I know, I know, and that's something that helped get me through many sleepless nights, worrying about you. But there's more that a mom worries about than physical health, you know? How are you in all the other ways?" She stared, like she truly cared about my answer.

But did she? She'd left me at a children's home. A human children's home, at that. Sure, now I thought that was the best thing that could have happened to me, but at the time, not so much.

"Good," I got out after a moment of awkward silence. "I got in with some great people, they took really good care of me."

"Humans?" she asked, her voice odd.

"Yes?"

Something flashed across her face, but I couldn't tell what it was. Elation? Anger? It had been too long since I'd been around her to know. But it was her. Somehow, she was here.

"I never meant to leave you there. They moved you on too quickly. I had no idea where you were, or how to find you."

I couldn't help the smile that jumped across my face. She was fae. If she said she'd wanted me, then she did. Something niggled at me though. Some of the old doubt, the old hurt. Would it really have been so hard to find me?

"I'm so glad you found me. How did you know where I was?" She tugged me forward, and I stumbled along after her, looking to Starren. Wait, Starren was Mom's daughter too. I'd been so excited that I hadn't even noticed Starren. She was standing back, hunched into herself.

"Starren!" I motioned her forward. She did as I asked and moved toward us, but slowly. Far more slowly than I'd have expected for her getting to see our mom again for the first time in years.

Starren got within range of Mother, and Mother pulled her into a hug too. I didn't even try to stop the grin from stretching my face taut. We were together. For real. A family, without a dad. But who needed him anyway, he was crazy.

"I can't believe this!" Mother said. "The three of us together. And you, Starren, you've grown even more since I've seen you than Trisha has!"

"Maybe that's because you saw me last at three, and her at nine." Her voice came out in a monotone, like she was ordering at some fast food place.

Ouch. "Star," I hissed. "Try not to be yourself."

"No, no, Trisha, she has a right. She can say whatever she'd like." Mom's voice had dropped several levels in the excitement department.

"How about we move inside now. It's getting dark, and I want to truly see those beautiful faces."

I grabbed Starren by the hand, who turned and gave Carver a pleading look. He quickened his pace to stay right beside her, and we all followed Mother into one of the tree tent things.

Inside was almost like Carver's house. So much bigger than it had looked from the outside. We walked down two steps and into a large common room.

"Where'd the guards go?" I asked.

"To their own places." She squeezed my hand. "They know I want some alone time with my girls." She eyed Carver. "And their companion."

"I'm sorry, you were so busy before I felt it rude to interrupt." Carver gave her a slight bow. "My name is Carver."

"Ah, Carver. I know you. Starren still fancy you?"

His face went red, and she laughed.

"Come, sit, rest. You have to be tired after that whole debacle back there."

"How do you know about that?" I asked.

"About Carver?" Mom shooed us into the room. "Let's just say I've been keeping track of some things."

"How did the guard know where to find us?" Starren asked. She moved to sit on a pile of pillows, revealing to the two of us who knew her how much pain she must be in. She would never show weakness like being the first to sit if she wasn't about to collapse.

"I know everything that happens in Yest."

"You knew that we were here this whole time? And you knew Vilan was here too? Why didn't you help us?" Starren's voice was mechanical. She was at the scary point, where she showed no emotions. She only showed zero emotions when she was feeling a hundred, and didn't know which way she wanted to go.

"Of course I knew where you were, Starren. I kept track of you, every moment since I left." Tears filled Mother's eyes, and it was my turn for a hand squeeze. "But with your father being the way he is..." She paused for a second to swipe at her eyes. "Let's just say it wasn't possible for me to come visit."

"You were this close," Starren's whisper came out broken. "This close the entire time, and you never even tried to see me, even after I was old enough to be sent out on my own?"

That stopped me in my tracks. I'd been thinking this whole time of how Mom leaving me had affected my life, and had forgotten that her actions affected Starren too. At least Mom had the decency to look guilty, because I sure couldn't think of one reason that would keep me away from my family if I had the option of being with them.

"I was afraid of your father's influence on you. I didn't know how brainwashed you were. I'm sorry, I should have tried harder."

Of course it wasn't possible. She was a victim here too. Father was crazy, and we all knew it. Pain that had been hiding down deep in my soul pushed its way to the surface and took flight, leaving a weird emptiness inside where it had taken up space. Now I knew. Mother had always wanted me. Had wanted Starren. But she hadn't had a choice.

"We know it wasn't what you wanted, Mom," I said.

Starren stayed quiet. When Mother turned to go grab something from a small table to the side, I glared at Starren. "What's your problem?" I mouthed to her so Mother couldn't hear.

"Why are you so stupid?" she mouthed back.

Well if this wasn't exactly how my family always operated, I'd be shocked. Of course Starren and I were on different sides of this. We were on opposite sides of everything.

Mother came back and handed me a bowl of some food.

"Still always hungry, I assume?"

I chuckled awkwardly, but dug into the food. Oh, to have real food again. And this stuff was good, whatever it was.

"Carver, Starren, would you like something to eat? To drink?"

"We don't need your food," Starren said. "We're here for a reason. Let us speak with Nara."

"Nara is already in her home for the night. We aren't going to bother her. But soon, I promise."

As eager as I was to help Dan and Nina, we weren't going anywhere tonight. Not after seeing Vilan. He was probably out there lurking, waiting for us to leave Yest. Or worse. He'd left to go and report to

Father, who would bring even more people down on our heads. But it would be nice to know if Nara could help. I'd sleep better tonight if I talked with her, if she told me she'd leave with me in the morning and we could head back. I could be hugging Nina a day from now. Or just a little more, depending on how long it took us to get out of Faerie. We couldn't wait any longer. If Starren was right and there was some kind of time frame for helping them...

"Are you sure she would mind us popping in for just a second? Just so I could talk to her, figure out a plan?"

Mother's face did that same weird twitch thing it did earlier. "Wouldn't you rather stay here and talk with me? We have so much to catch up on. We hardly know each other anymore."

"Whose fault is that?" Starren said. She kept her voice low, just loud enough that I could hear with my extra good hearing.

I frowned at her, but I did have to agree to a certain extent. How hard would it have been to find me, really? I'd ended back up at Waterton Heights like five times. That was five times that it would have been pretty easy to scoop me up, because they lasted months each.

"I'd really like to talk with Nara. I don't know how much you know, but I seriously need her help. She could save some people who are important to my health." True enough to say it, but not the full truth. Why hadn't I wanted to tell her the full truth? I didn't even know. But something held me back. She was my mom, and I should be able to fully trust her. But she was also fae. Fae always had their own agenda behind everything.

"Is it going to affect your health tonight if you don't go and see her right away?"

Did mental or emotional health count? Apparently not, because I couldn't force myself to say yes.

"It's settled then. Rest tonight. You need to tell me all about your quest, and your journey here." She moved over to the pillows near Starren and sat down, patting the cushion next to her. "How did you get into Faerie? I'd heard Quintin has everything locked down."

"A friend had a way that Quintin hadn't gotten blocked yet." Now why was I being evasive? I didn't even know.

Starren gave me a look that I couldn't quite interpret, but it seemed like approval. I hoped.

But mother didn't look super happy about it. "Well, tell me about your life on Earth then. What's it like? Do you have any friends there?"

This was starting to feel like when Starren grilled me about my life looking for blackmail targets before we'd known we were sisters. She'd have done it at that point even if she'd known we shared parents, we hadn't gotten along great back then.

"Oh, you know, lots of acquaintances. What's going on out here in the middle of nowhere?" I said. "And how do you not get killed by the trees?"

"Just acquaintances? How about these people you're trying to help?"

Starren started to say something but I interrupted. "There's a nice reward."

"Ah, my smart girls, taking care of themselves. It's so terrible that your father drove you out of Faerie. I could kill him for that."

A shiver went down my spine. That didn't sound like sarcasm, and obviously wasn't a lie, so that left the truth. And the other truth. I didn't know my mom at all. I'd only seen one side of her as a kid. The side that had kept me a bit at arm's length, but loved me. How many other sides did she have?

"But then, there are a lot of fae who would love to kill your father. He has a following, yes, but he's also made a lot of enemies. Especially with his new, idiotic plan."

Now Starren was on the hook. I could tell by how she was so casual, and so fake. Father meant more to her than to me. She'd known him much better. But part of him meaning more wasn't in a good way. He'd treated her horribly, and I'd hoped she never have to truly think about him again.

"We're not joining you against Father," Starren said.

I kicked her leg before remembering she'd been recently injured. She ignored me and kept talking.

"What have you ever done for us? Nothing. You haven't cared about us, helped us, even checked on us. You've ignored me my entire life, and Trish more than half of hers. If one of us were drowning I doubt you'd even put forth the effort to throw a rope."

"Star," Carver said.

"But I protected you with the trees here." Mother looked teary eyed. "And if Vilan ever shows his face in Yest again, I won't be so kind as to allow him to leave with his life this time. I care very much. I don't know how to be a good mother."

"That was you? You can control the trees? You controlled the trees, from here?" How had I not known about this? Had she always been able to control plants, even back when I traveled with her? Maybe that was why we mostly stuck to nature, like Yosemite.

It only made sense, since most fae got their powers at eighteen that she'd already had it when we were on Earth together. Why hadn't anyone told me? Everyone had acted like I was freak because of what I could do. But maybe that was more because I could heal, also? Or maybe, they didn't know.

Mother turned her back for a moment, like she was getting herself under control.

"Did you know she could do that?" I mouthed to Starren.

"Until you did it back at that farm house, I didn't know anyone could do that."

Mom turned back with a smile, still teary eyed. That seemed odd. Fae didn't like others knowing what they felt. "You'll find out some wonderful things are possible, as you grow into your gift."

Some wonderful things? There were already a ton of wonderful things. But being able to control trees miles away? To know what was going on by communicating over such a distance? Crazy.

"I'll teach you all about it. You're going to surpass me so quickly, since you'll have me to help you. I didn't have anyone to teach me, my mother didn't have a gift and my father could only tell if someone was telling a lie, not very useful in Faerie."

"We won't be here long enough for you to help her learn anything." Starren shifted on the pillows, wincing as she tried to get comfortable. "We're leaving in the morning after we talk with Nara. Either way she answers us, we won't have a reason to stay."

Mother looked hurt. I kicked Starren again, this time not caring if it hurt.

"Surely me being here is a reason to stay, even if it isn't a great reason?"

"No." Starren's face was deadpan.

"Starren!" I said this time.

"It's fine, Trisha," Mother said. "She'd been hurt. It's built up, grown, and it's coming out in hurtful ways."

I'd been hurt too. But not in the same way. Mom had left me, but I'd always thought there had to be a reason. I'd convinced myself that she was protecting me. But I didn't have any evidence of that. Would asking her now make me horrible? If we left in the morning, this may be my only chance. I was choosing Dan and Nina over her. Was I okay with that? She had to have had a good reason to abandon me. She was my mother. She loved me. But I had to know. "Why did you leave me? At Waterton Heights."

"Oh my girl, I didn't want to. If there had been any other way, it never would have happened. Your father was close to finding us, close to taking you from me. I couldn't let that happen. So I left you somewhere I knew you would be safe, planning on going back for you. It didn't work out like that."

Convenient to blame it on Father. Convenient, and also pretty safe. She had to have a good guess of how I felt about the man. If she'd been living this close to his home, she had to know the things he'd done to Starren. Known and hadn't done anything about it.

I looked at Starren, sitting tight-lipped and pale faced. Not from the physical pain, though there was plenty of that. No, it was the emotional pain. If I chose to let Mom influence me, I'd lose Starren. And probably Dan and Nina.

But this was my mom. She'd been there for me, took care of me. Loved me, right? The physical act of trying so hard to remember how I'd felt back with Mom made my head spin. I dropped down to sit on the pillows next to Starren. She had loved me. I'd always known that. She was my mom, so that meant she loved me, that's how it was supposed to work. I'd only found out later that the version of love I understood was human, not fae. Fae didn't love in the same way. They could, obviously, because I did. Jaden did. But the whole concept was foreign to the fae race.

Nina. That was a mother's love. Not just providing for my physical needs, but caring about every single thing in my life. How was I supposed to remember how my mom had treated me so long ago?

You didn't remember the situation, but you remembered how people made you feel. That saying hadn't meant much to me when I'd read it somewhere a month ago. But now it popped to the surface.

Mom had made me feel small. We'd had some good times, but there had always been something... It had been part of the reason it had been so hard for me to connect with Nina. That had been quite the battle, in the beginning. Me not wanting to have any connections, her just chipping away at my walls, piece by tiny piece until there was an avalanche and stupid me figured out that she loved me, and I loved her.

"I really need to speak to Nara. Just so I know what's going on. I like having a plan."

"Back to Nara, then?" Mom looked sad. Ouch. But we had to get back, as soon as we could. I couldn't risk Dan and Nina. I could come back and visit Mom, or she could come to me.

Someone knocked on the door, startling me enough I almost fell off my pillow.

The fae guard from before stuck her head in. "I'm sorry to bother you, but you're needed out here."

Mom sighed and nodded in acknowledgement. "I'm sorry, but seeing Nara just isn't possible tonight." She stood and smiled. "I'll be back as soon as I see what this is about, and then we can talk some more." She came over and pulled me up for another tight hug.

And then she left.

"Just like that she's gone?" I asked no one.

"Typical," Starren muttered. "I trust her almost as much as I trust Father."

"Don't say that." I glared. "She isn't like Father. At all. She's a leader and probably has things she needs to look after."

Starren glared back, hers much more practiced than mine. "No.

She's dangerous, and I don't like any of this. You should go and check the door."

I almost did. But then I stopped myself. This was my mom. The woman who'd taken care of me when I was little. Who I'd dreamed about since the moment she'd left me behind. She had her reasons, she had to.

"You're just jealous because she took me when she left, and not you. Don't tell me to not trust her, I have to have a few people I can trust, and right now it's just you and Jaden!"

Carver looked insulted.

"And Carver."

"That's not true, Trish. I'm not jealous. I don't feel anything toward our mother that could be confused with affection. She's just as conniving as Father, but better at hiding it. I would be glad that she didn't take me with you when she left, except for the fact that we lost years being sisters. Father and Mother don't care anything about us except for how we can help them in their little games. But at least now I have one person I know I can count on."

"Hey!" Carver said.

"Two people I can count on."

"We're going to have to agree to disagree on this one, Star." The fact that she knew she could count on me calmed me down a bit. "I know you think you're telling the truth, but I think you're just jaded toward Mother because she had to leave you. I'm sure she didn't want to. We haven't even let her tell us her side of the story yet."

Starren's face went hard. "That would be very entertaining. To see how she dodged around the truth, unable to lie but not wanting to offend you. At some point you'll see that I'm right. And I hope it's not too late for you when the time comes. Or too late for me."

I seethed in silence for a minute. Mom had our best interests at heart. That's what a mom did. It was part of the job description. She wanted us, she had to. It had been Father who had forced her hand.

"How are the ribs?" I ground out.

"Been better." Not a lie, but no real information either.

A knock on the door made us all jump. Man, we needed some rest, and somewhere we could actually unwind a bit.

Mom poked her head in the door. "Still up for some together time?"

"Of course!" I said. Starren's words still stung a little. Mom needed to get in here. The best way for Star to see how wrong she was would be to actually spend time with the woman.

"Did I miss anything?" Mom asked.

"Nothing you need to hear about." I smiled to distract her from Starren pouting over on her pillow.

"Good." She shut the door behind her and walked over. "Now, where were we?"

"We were talking about Nara, and how you won't let us see her," Starren growled.

"I spoke to Nara. She isn't receiving any visitors tonight, and will see you tomorrow."

There was one way that I could prove Mom wasn't just here because she thought we could help against Father. I could show Starren how wrong she was. "Mom?"

She looked up from concentrating on Starren.

"Do you love me? Do you love Starren?"

"You know I care about you." She looked me in the eye when she said it, willing me to believe her. But I'd gotten to know the fae over the last year, and I didn't like what I'd found out.

"Yes, I get that. But do you love us? Would you give your life for either of us?"

"Not wanting to die doesn't mean a person doesn't love you."

She was avoiding the subject. Avoiding the subject meant bad things. Abort, if I wanted to not prove Starren right. Abort. But the truth was more important. She loved us. She was our mom. She just wasn't good at saying it. I got that. It had taken me forever until I was able to say it to Nina, and I still struggled telling Dan. I needed to know.

"You're right. It doesn't. You hardly know us, so I guess I could understand not wanting to die for us. But I love you. And I can say that without any effort. Can you say it back?"

She looked down, like she was shocked and figuring out what to say.

Typical of the fae to have every kind of lie figured out but not expect the truth, or a direct question.

Starren struggled, trying to stand.

I jumped over and put out a hand to help her, Carver on the other side.

"I think we'd better be going then," I said.

Starren nodded, staring Mother down.

Carver kept his mouth shut, but moved under Starren's arm to help steady her. She had to be exhausted, and in a ton of pain. Was it really fair of me to ask her to leave a nice, safe, comfortable, place to spend the night? I looked at her, trying to communicate with my eyes.

She nodded.

I took that to mean she agreed, and hoped that she actually understood what she was agreeing to.

"I'd like to speak to Nara, please. And then I think we'll be leaving. We're on a tight schedule."

Mother looked up then, and the anger on her face showed right through her mask. "I don't think that's a good idea. I care about you, and I wouldn't want you to get hurt. Yest is a dangerous place, even in the day. At night? You never know what will happen."

I shifted uncomfortably. "Even with your control of the trees?"

She smirked. "Especially with my control of the trees. I think it's best you spend the night, think things over. Because I care about you, I don't want to see anything happen to you." She turned and headed for the door.

Funny how she kept adding how much she cared about us.

"You sound just like father," Starren said quietly.

Mother whipped around, rage covering her face. "I am nothing like your father, and you had better never say that again." The tent made out of live plants around us creaked and groaned, branches reaching toward us. Mother slapped one down as it dove for Starren's face.

I moved in front of Starren and Carver, my hand on the hilt of my sword.

The branches writhed around us, and my heart dropped. This was how they acted when I let my anger get out of control. This was how people felt. Like they were going to die.

"Stop," I yelled. "That's not going to help anything."

The vines and branches slowed, and mother's posture loosened a little.

I pried my fingers off my sword hilt one by one. This was the woman I'd spent nights crying myself to sleep over? That I'd tried to remain loyal to instead of Nina? That I had longed and watched for? Why?

"You're not going anywhere tonight. We'll discuss this in the morning." She walked out and limbs immediately covered the door so tightly I wouldn't be able to get even a finger through.

The three of us stood there in shocked silence for a moment, leaning on each other.

"Well," Carver said, "I didn't think this was possible, but it might be that your dad is more rational than your mom."

Starren sighed and hobbled back toward the cushions. "I'd have never have guessed either. Not in a million years did I think that someone could be as crazy as Father. But I guess crazy attracts crazy." She fell to the cushions. "The jury's still out though. I haven't known her long enough to truly believe she's worse than father." She raised an eyebrow at Carver and me standing there, and somehow felt taller than both of us even though she was seated almost on the ground. "Well, what are you waiting for? Find us a way out of here."

Duh, what were we waiting for? A rescue? Not likely. The fae here were probably just like the fae under Father. They were too scared to do anything he didn't like, and now it seemed like Mom was a lot more similar to him than I would want. That put everything she said and did into the suspect category.

I walked over to a wall, poking at it while I kept an eye on Starren. If she was showing this much pain, she must be in a ton of it because normally no one would be able to tell.

Carver hovered near her until she glared at him. Then he moved over near me and pretended to knock at the walls while he also watched Starren like a hawk.

"These trees definitely aren't going to cooperate like the ones at Carver's." In fact, with some of the things Mom had said, I was a little worried that they were keeping an eye on us for her. I pulled out my sword and gave the wood an experimental whack.

The tree threw the sword back at me, cutting right through a strand of hair and getting close enough it could have taken my ear off.

I froze, speechless for a second. "Don't try that." I walked around the wall, checking half-heartedly for any other kind of exit. Mom wasn't an idiot. There wasn't going to be an exit. But I still had to check. "You think she'll let us go in the morning, right?"

"I wouldn't count on it." Starren's tone was grim, her face set.

"She has to. We don't know how much time we have before Dan and Nina…" I couldn't say the rest out loud. Carver and Starren knew what I meant.

"It's that stupid prophecy," Starren said. "Whoever has the girl wins the war. She's not going to let you go if you might be useful."

I shivered. "What war?"

Starren looked at me but didn't answer, her lips white.

"I think your parents…" Carver drifted off mid-sentence.

Yeah. I did too.

I threw myself down on the pillows next to Starren. "This is stupid. I can't do anything Mom can't do, so why does she need me? And why did that soldier lady call me Mareena in the woods? Mom's never called me that."

Starren sat bolt upright, sucked in a breath of air because sitting up that fast when you're injured is stupid, and grabbed my forearm. As soon as she did, my ribs began to ache. Her eyes widened, and she let go.

The pain was instantly gone.

"What just happened?" Carver asked.

"We can explore that later," Starren said. "The important thing right now is that I think that was a message. From Father. He knows where we are, and he's coming for us." She bit her lip, eyes glossy as she stared off into space. "How could I have missed that? It was so obvious. Father always called you Mareena to me, but everywhere else I'd heard you called Trish. I just assumed Mother called you Mareena as well, but of course she didn't. She wouldn't have wanted to slip up in front of anyone, or had you confused as a child. Of course she always called you Trish."

That was more than I normally heard from Starren in a day. Unless I was getting chewed for something, of course. But she was right, and I didn't know how to feel about it. Even with her fit of temper, Father scared me far more than Mother. Mother at least 'cared' about us, whatever that meant. "So now what?" When Starren wasn't paying attention, I reached down and touched her arm. Instantly the pain was back in my ribs. Bad, but livable.

Starren glared and jerked her arm away, and then bit her lip to keep from crying out.

"What is happening?" Carver asked again. "The father thing, important, but we'll get to that in a bit, what is going on between the two of you?"

"I think I can feel her pain when I touch her," I answered when Starren sat there tight-lipped. "Is that what's going on?"

"More than that, actually." Starren crumpled a little. "When we're touching, my pain is cut in half."

"Seriously?" I asked. I reached forward and she weakly slapped my hand away.

"I'm fine."

"No, you're not. You could at least use a break while we figure out what to do."

She crumpled a little more and didn't fight back this time when I grabbed her wrist.

Instant pain hit me in the ribs and I hissed. "This is half your pain?"

She shrugged. "Ribs are the worst."

Carver stared at us. "How are you doing that?"

"I don't know."

"That's normal," Starren said. "She does weird stuff she didn't know she could do. Usually it's a problem for me, at least this time it's beneficial."

"Hey, I thought it was pretty beneficial when you had me killed and it didn't stick, thank you very much. And I knew I healed, just didn't know it was to that extent."

Starren rolled her eyes. "Yeah, yeah, you're never going to let that go, are you."

"Starren!" Carver said. "I wouldn't let it go either! You had your sister killed?"

"I didn't know for sure she was my sister at the time. And only killed on Earth, it should have just brought her to Faerie like it does everyone else. But no, she always has to be different."

It was a good thing I was starting to understand Starren's hard to see inflections. She thought she was being funny. Or, it seemed like it.

"Maybe you should find these things out BEFORE you have people murdered," Carver said.

"Yeah, I figured that out on my own, thanks."

I sat down next to Starren, being careful not to lose my grip or jostle either of our ribs. I didn't actually have the damage she did, but I didn't know how that worked since I didn't even know I could do this until now. Which would freak me out if I let myself think about it, so I wasn't going to go there. Nope. No thinking. Could I take her injury intentionally like I'd taken Nina's by accident? "Hold on, I'm going to try something. Let me know if you feel anything... weird."

"Weird?" Starren's voice was a little high. She'd put up with a lot of weird from me on the daily, so me saying it might be weird probably didn't have the greatest effect on her.

"Not weird, weird, good weird." A bad explanation, but it was going to have to do. I closed my eyes and concentrated. I waited for the weird light to go down my hand, with the warmth and everything. But no. Nothing. I squeezed my eyes tighter, pulling a breath in through my nose in an attempt to center myself.

"Is something supposed to be happening?" Carver asked.

"Hush." Of course something was supposed to be happening. I wasn't doing random meditation.

Random meditation. As if. But yeah, that's what it looked like, because nothing whatsoever was happening. I opened an eye just a crack. Nope. No glowy light. No strange warmth. My hand wasn't stuck to Starren's arm like someone had let Jaime free with a glue gun and no supervision.

"Well shoot."

"It was a good try," Starren said. She'd seen what had happened with Nina, and had probably figured out what I was trying to do even before I started doing it.

"What were you trying?" Carver sounded frustrated. It would be annoying to be on the outside of all of the stuff Starren and I shared.

Hey. My sister and I actually shared quite a few secrets. Not what boy we liked or that we'd snuck into an R-rated movie like my friends kinds of secrets, but it made me strangely happy anyway. Maybe we would wind up being a family, if we ever got Dan and Nina back. Dan and Nina. If Mom held us here too long, I'd lose them. In fact, I could be losing them right now. I jumped up and let go of Starren's arm, pacing over by the wall. "We need to find a way out of here."

"Uh yeah, we've been saying that, but that doesn't answer my question," Carver answered.

"Where did your mind just go?" Starren asked.

"Way too complicated," I answered. "But the end point was that we could lose Dan and Nina if we hang out here too long." I stopped and crossed my arms. "I know, I know, we've been through that. But I can't keep from going back to it."

Starren struggled to her feet. "That's true. But I'm not sure thinking like that is going to help. You need to learn to shut off your feelings until you get a job done."

I threw my hands up in the air. "I'm trying! But it isn't you who could lose their family at any time!"

"Can I not?" She stared at me until I shifted uncomfortably. Father had been her only family. And though I truly believed she would have left him at some point on her own, she'd left him for me. Put herself in danger, ruined her reputation, gave up her standing with the fae, for me.

"Sorry," I muttered. It didn't sound sincere. One of my many character flaws. But being unable to truly apologize was slowly going way. It would probably be my last habit to break. As a foster kid, you never admitted you were wrong. It was dangerous. Or at least it felt like it.

"Would someone please explain to me what's going on," Carver said.

"Trisha has healed another person in the past," Starren answered.

"She was trying again, but doesn't seem to have full control of that aspect of her powers yet."

"Oh," Carver said. "Neat."

Starren had failed to mention the part of me healing a person where I had to take their wound on myself. Not pleasant, but since I healed usually within an hour of most wounds, worth it. I was going to have to work on that, being able to do it on command. But I didn't know where to start. I could ask Mother. She may know.

Or I might be giving her insight she didn't already have. A shiver went through me. The less she knew about my abilities, the better. She knew I could heal, and it sounded like she knew I could communicate with the trees, but I didn't know how specific her knowledge was. For some reason that made me uncomfortable.

Movement even worse than before, Starren shambled over to the wall. She inspected the doorway. "Hmmm." She moved past it, going over every crack and cranny in the place, then made her way back to the door.

Pulling a small knife from her pocket, she shaved off a piece of the branch covering the door. It lashed out at her. Normally she'd have no problem dodging something like that, but with her injuries she stumbled as she got out of the way, nearly taking a hit in the gut. "Ouch!" She kicked the door. The branch kicked back. Her glare didn't seem to intimidate the tree like it did everyone else. It was almost funny. If anything could be funny at the moment.

"That's not going to work," Carver said.

"Obviously." Starren got grumpy when she felt out of control. She was used to forcing things to go her way. I almost felt bad for her, but I only had so much emotional energy and I was feeling bad enough for me at the moment that I didn't have any to spare.

"What if she keeps us here? What if she doesn't let us go back?" I leaned on the wall, trying not to tear up. "Dan and Nina won't even know I'm missing. No one will care." No one but Jaden. Jaden was probably flipping out right now. He was a positive, happy guy, and it took a lot to get him to freak out, but I'd been missing for awhile now. I didn't even know how long without counting it up, and I didn't have the energy at the moment. Maybe Rosie would miss me. Wren wouldn't, but she'd probably always wonder. Was her threat to come after us real?

It didn't matter. If she even found a way into Faerie, she'd never find her way to us.

Dan and Nina may not know to miss me, but I sure could use them right now. Dan's calm and Nina's peace and love. How was I supposed to go through life without that, now that I'd had a taste? More than a taste. A buffet, for years, even before I appreciated it. Man I'd been dumb back when I'd first moved in with them.

The missing Jaden so much was the part that surprised me. We weren't a thing. Hadn't even talked about being a thing. But he was always there for me, his quiet, peaceful presence making the bad stuff seem not as bad. If only he were here now. But then I'd just have another person to worry about.

How did I come to need so many people? I was supposed to need no one, be my own person, solve my own problems. But things had changed. Sure, I was still very independent. Probably too independent. But the reliance on others didn't seem like a terrible thing anymore, now that I actually knew some people that were worthy of that trust. And that was the scariest thought so far.

"We aren't getting out of here," Carver said. He grabbed Starren who had moved to a different section of wall while I wasn't paying attention and was beating at it with the hilt of her sword. "We should just get some rest. Make a plan. We aren't getting out of here on our own, and we aren't getting through that forest without some thought. Even if we fight our way out of here right this minute, your mother's trees aren't going to let us past."

Ouch. He was right. Mom had a control of the trees here that even I couldn't understand. They didn't feel alive, didn't seem happy around her like the plants always acted when I was around. Her hold on them was crazy.

Maybe there was a way I could break through to them. Convince them to help us, or at least let us through.

"Rest is a good idea," I said, intentionally yawning so Starren didn't catch on that I felt fine and just wanted her to relax for a bit. Her guilt at what had happened with Dan and Nina was probably what was pushing her, along with the fact that whether she wanted to or not, she cared about me now, and cared about my emotional well-being even when she didn't understand it.

"Fine. But I still think we should take turns keeping watch." Starren shuffled to her pillows and slowly dropped down onto a pile, shifting around until she had a pillow under her arm supporting her ribs. "Wake me up when it's my turn." She closed her eyes.

I shook my head at Carver and the tip of his mouth turned up in the first half smile I'd seen in awhile.

"I'll take her watch," I mouthed.

He nodded and made his way over to the pillows. He stacked extra pillows around Starren, making a wall between them so he didn't accidentally bump her in her sleep, and laid down. It wasn't long before light snores were filling the room.

Good. They both needed it. I was lucky and didn't need it as much as a normal human or fae. I moved to the door and laid my hand against a branch. Time for me to see what I could do about the trees.

Night went by faster than I'd expected, but not as quickly as I'd hoped. I'd had zero progress with trying to communicate with the trees here. They still blocked me out, acting like they weren't alive when I obviously knew for sure they were. That much control... How long would it take me learning from Mother to be able to do things like that?

It didn't really matter. After last night, I was out of here as soon as possible.

Without waking Carver and Starren, I stood and stretched, my whole body creaking and cracking, which was extremely unusual. My fault though. I'd fallen asleep in that meditation position while trying to get the tree to at least acknowledge me. Good thing there wasn't a real reason to stand guard. It wasn't like anything was getting in without Mom, and obviously we weren't getting out.

The branches across the door suddenly slithered off the frame. I tensed, waiting for someone to come bursting through.

Waiting. Waiting. Nothing.

I stepped over, internally debating with myself if this was a good idea or not. A quick glance showed Starren and Carver hadn't been bothered by the light sounds the branches had made while they disappeared.

Let them sleep, safe, until I figured out what was going on.

Opening the door a crack, I slipped my head out, glancing both ways, waiting for something to jump me. Nothing did. I pushed the door open a little more, considering going and getting Starren.

But no. No reason to. Mom was sitting at a table made of polished wood, drinking a cup of something. "Morning, dear, come on over."

I inched out, checking over my shoulder for Starren.

"Don't bother them, let's have a talk, shall we? Just you and me."

Okay. A talk with my mom. I'd dreamed about this for years. Longed to see her again. Here was my chance. We'd all been tired last night, grumpy. Maybe she wasn't as bad as she'd made herself look. Ha. I'd tried the same line of thinking with Father, and look where that got me. Imprisoned. What was with Faerie and getting myself locked up?

It was a short walk to the table, but I drug it out as long as possible.

"How'd you sleep? There were plenty of pillows, weren't there?"

"Yeah." I skipped the first part. She didn't need to know I'd hardly slept, and what sleep I had gotten had been uncomfortable and full of nightmares.

"Oh now, Trisha. Don't sound like that. Just talk things through with me." She patted the bench beside her, and pulled over another mug. "Coffee? Something I learned to love while hiding from your father on Earth. Now I can't hardly live without it."

"No, thanks," I mumbled. I moved over and sat on the opposite side of the table. As I made contact with the wood, a shiver of distress went through it, straight into me. I shivered in response, the feeling instantly gone but leaving strong reverberations behind.

Mother must have seen something cross my face, because when I looked up, she was staring at me. And now I knew how a rabbit felt right before an eagle snatched it into the sky in one of Starren's documentaries.

"Um, yeah, what did you want to talk about?" A question was a good distraction, because I did not like her looking at me like that. I reached out toward the bench/table, trying to see if it could respond. Small bursts of uncomfortableness went through me, but not the almost despair of before.

"You, of course."

"Huh?" Oops. Way too distracted. "How about we talk about me after we talk to Nara?"

A muscle in her face twitched, but she kept herself together pretty well. "We'll get to that soon. She went on an early morning patrol and won't be available for a little while." She took a drink of her coffee and sat the cup down. It sparkled in the light. It was made out of something weird, something familiar... Oh! The rocks that I'd stolen from the dead troll's pocket what seemed like forever ago.

"Like it?" Mom asked. "It's made of stones from the Crystal Lake. They're said to bring good luck, and maybe the favor of a mythical creature." She laughed, putting me at ease even though I didn't want to be. She hadn't laughed often when I was a kid, but I'd always loved it when she had. "Mythical creatures. Some would say you and I are mythical creatures, and yet here we are."

"What do you want from me?" It came out more blunt than I'd meant it to. But then, I'd always been a pretty blunt person. "Why did you lock us up?"

"What do all mothers want from their children?"

And there it was. A question for a question. The fae way. Deception and lying without telling a non-truth.

"I want you to be happy." She looked sincere. I wanted to believe her. But it was too vague. She wanted me to be happy. Okay, did that mean she'd try to make me happy? That she wished I was happy here? That my happiness only mattered if it went along with her plan?

There was no way to know.

"Great. Then let me see Nara, so I can get some stuff handled, and I'll be happy."

Mom stood and walked around the table to lean over me. She

smiled, but it wasn't a smile I liked. Then she cupped my face in one palm. "You'll see her when I say you'll see her." Then she stood and sauntered over to a smaller table I hadn't noticed, packed with food. All kinds of yummy fae food.

My stomach growled loudly. "Traitor," I hissed at it. It should be sad and frustrated like the rest of me.

Motioning me over, Mom held out a plate. It looked like it was made of clay maybe, but I wasn't an expert. Or even a beginner, really.

I stood, and the same feeling of distress went through me, like a sad call. I laid my hand on the table, and it warmed beneath my palm, but I couldn't understand what it was trying to say. I made my way over to Mom.

She handed me a plate and started piling her own high.

I went back and sat on the bench, feeling the warmth of the non-visible sun, relaxing, letting my mind try to wander. It was the only way I knew how to get in touch with a plant, but really difficult to do at the moment.

The tree felt... odd. Not in control. Like what it was doing for Mom wasn't voluntary. It wasn't her friend, didn't feel any affection toward her like the plants always seemed to feel toward me.

Mother had started on her food, seeming to enjoy it almost as much as I always did. While she was busy, I concentrated, doing my best to figure out how to get through to the tree when it didn't feel like it had a choice.

There. More of its feelings flooded me. It just wanted to be a tree. Once the floodgate was open, I couldn't hold back the cries that poured through, so loud I could almost hear them with my actual ears instead of just feeling them. None of the trees here were working with Mother. She was forcing everything they were doing for her. The entire camp.

Dizziness hit me and I closed my eyes, bracing myself on the table. The trees called for help, to be let free of the awkward positions Mother had forced them into to serve her needs. She hadn't even asked, just came in with brute force.

"And that's my plan for the day." Her voice leaked in over the sounds of the trees trying to straighten, to reach for the sky again like they were made to do. "Trish, were you listening?"

"Ah, sorry. Got distracted. This food just looks so good."

Mother frowned. "Then why haven't you taken a bite?"

Great question. I shoved a spoonful of something into my mouth, plastering on a fake grin. "So good."

Is everything okay? I whispered in my mind, like Mom could hear me. *What's wrong?*

The tree making up the table didn't answer, but the feeling of distress grew.

"So. Tell me about your life, Trisha." Mom leaned forward, staring at me intently, gripping her coffee mug way too tight.

"Ah, not really sure what to tell you. I'm living in the human world, but you knew that."

Mom nodded impatiently.

"I'm going to school right now, and working a little when I can. Just odd jobs for people."

"Do you have any plans for the future?"

Plans for the future had always included Dan and Nina. So no, other than getting them back, I didn't really have any plans. Nina had tried to get me to look at colleges in Fort Wayne, but Dan had told me I didn't have to go if I didn't want to, that there were plenty of good jobs without it. But that's where we'd left things. That's where we'd been right before that fateful trip, the one that had gained me a sister and lost me my parents.

I looked up from being distracted. Mom was still staring, to the point it made my skin itch. "No. No real plans."

"That's not a bad thing." She reached forward and placed her hand on mine, the one holding the spoon. "Maybe that means you'll think about staying? Here with me, I mean."

Warning bells went off in my head. That's exactly what Father had tried. Crazy, evil Father. He'd wanted me to stay too, and Starren said it was because of the stupid prophecy. Whoever had made it needed a swift kick.

I pulled my hand out from under Mother's and dropped the spoon onto the plate, bracing myself on the wooden bench. The wood warmed beneath my hand. "Where'd you get this table?" It didn't come out as nonchalant as I would have liked. I usually was proud of the fact that I was blunt about everything, but something told me I was walking a line and should probably figure out how to be a bit more fae.

"Oh, you know how it is, the trees being so helpful. This one makes a nice breakfast area, don't you think?"

Two different sentences. A pause in the middle so they weren't technically connected.

Suddenly the wood under my palm flowed up and over, trapping my hand. My vision went dark. I was the forest. I could feel the roots, snaking under the ground for miles, everything interconnected. Someone was here. In the dark. Soldiers were making their way through. A call, an order. Kill. But trees were peaceful. Didn't like the violence. I wasn't going to harm anyone, especially when they weren't a threat. But the order came through so strongly I almost couldn't resist. My roots creaked and groaned as I fought the urge to reach down and rip them apart.

My brothers and sisters lost control first. Tearing through the soldiers.

I gasped as I came back into myself, my eyes wet with tears. Had she made the trees murder people? Had she forced them against their will?

"Trisha?" Mother asked. "What happened? Is everything okay?"

"Is it alright if I take breakfast to Starren and Carver? They're probably starving. It's been awhile since we really ate well."

"Yes, of course. I was planning on them eating here with us, but it might be better for Starren to rest even more. Make sure you take enough for you too, you hardly ate anything."

I nodded like I agreed, rushing to get my back turned to her. How could she? How could I believe that she would? What was wrong with one of us? Maybe the trees could lie. I shouldn't just believe what I'd seen. Maybe I'd misunderstood it. "Starren needs as much rest as she can get, especially with us leaving after we talk with Nara." Calculated. I was becoming calculated in every word I said. I hated it. I hated all of this.

"I'll let you know when Nara is available."

No commitment. No timeline. No way I could hold her to anything.

I heaped two plates with food, doing my best to keep my face from turning beet red, the anger wanting out. Take care of Starren and Carver. That's what I had to think of at the moment, so I didn't dwell on the fact that my own mother knew what I needed and didn't want to provide it because she wanted something from me. Nope, stop thinking about it. Think about the food, getting the food to the others. Starren might not want much, but hopefully Carver would, and I didn't know what he liked. So he was getting a bunch of options.

Making my way back to our prison cell, I brushed my hand over the table. It wiggled a bit in response, almost like the plants back when I was first learning about my powers, after I'd woken up in the forest recovering from taking a bullet. *I'll be back.* I had no idea what I was going to do for the poor thing, but I couldn't leave it without giving it some kind of hope. Did trees hope? No idea.

I shuffled slowly toward the tent thing I'd spent the night in, looking around, hoping to see Nara, but more importantly, getting an idea where everything was. Maybe Nara wasn't ever going to 'become available.' For all I knew, she was a prisoner here too. No one had stated otherwise. Or even worse, maybe she was here, but dead. I shoved that thought down pronto. We were not going to work so hard to get here and not even get to find out if she could help or not. Or someone else with her ability. There had to be another, right? I mean I was supposed to be rare, but there were at least two of us.

It would be so much better if there was only one. Mom hadn't heard of the great power, great responsibility thing, apparently.

And what was going on with the whole Mareena thing? That still freaked me out a bit, even though it seemed like nothing was going to come of it. Maybe that lady had known me before Mom had taken me and run, before my name had been changed to Trish, and I just didn't remember her.

This was all so complicated.

How I missed running in the door at home, dropping my book bag and heading straight for the kitchen to see what Nina had made for me while I was at school. To hear Dan's 'Hey kiddo, how was school?' again... Just to feel safe.

I had to shut those thoughts down pronto or I'd become a sniveling mess.

At least fifteen tents. No one out and about though, strange with how big the tents were. They should be able to hold at least ten people each. Ten each and at least fifteen tents? Not what humans would call an army by any means, but the fae were different. The fae couldn't stand each other long enough to gather like this. Definitely not long enough that they would need shelters, even if Mom could form them instantly. I hadn't seen her do it, but with the other things she could do it seemed like a fair assumption.

Both my parents were forming an army. And I was smack dab in the middle of it all. I shivered, glancing back over my shoulder.

Mom watched me. She held up a hand in a wave when she saw me looking. I smiled, but my hands were too full to wave back. A branch reached ahead of me and opened the door, before I even tried to juggle the plates around.

Helpful, or a show of power? Not that she really needed one of those.

Maybe the tents were empty, and that was why I hadn't seen anyone around. The people last night could have just been reporting in or something. Maybe Mom had gone ahead to make this place. But she'd sounded like she'd been here awhile when she was talking with Starren, and even Carver on the other side of Faerie had known to avoid Yest.

Wait. The forest spirit. That couldn't have been her that had gotten the trees so angry. No. I stumbled, not paying attention to my footing, my muscles weak.

No. It hadn't been her. I would choose to believe it wasn't her until proven otherwise. Innocent until proven guilty. But deep down, my stomach clenched.

Carver was up when I finally paid enough attention to where I was going. Starren was still asleep, which told me how injured she actually was. Had Mom even tried to help her? I'd been so excited to see her the night before, I hadn't even thought to ask about a healer. I was a terrible sister.

Carver grinned at the sight of the food, and took one plate right out of my hands. I sat down beside Starren and placed the plate beside her. I'd lost all appetite. I couldn't have an evil dad, and an evil mom. What would that say about me? Nina would say it meant nothing, but genes did matter, didn't they? I picked at the fringe of one of the pillows. Starren wasn't evil. Self-centered, yes. Obnoxious and not good at anything social? Absolutely. But she wasn't evil.

I'd spent years longing for my mom. And now I knew who she actually was.

"Everything alright?" Carver asked quietly.

"I just want to go home." I needed Nara. Like, right now. And I needed to get Starren somewhere safe until she was back to not only being able to take care of herself, but everyone else too.

"Think we should wake her up?" Carver nodded at Starren.

"I think she'll be mad as is, and really mad if we don't. So it just depends on the level of mad you want to deal with."

He grimaced, then leaned forward to gently take Starren's hand. "Star? Hey you, time to get up. We have an escape-slash-kidnapping to plan." He looked at me. "Are you planning on kidnapping Nara if you have to?"

"No!" But he brought up a great point, one that I'd been literally ignoring. Even though she owed us, Nara could totally say no. If she wasn't the type to pay back her debts, we were in a load of hurt. Could I make her? Complete desperation was very motivating. Disgust for myself rose up so hard I nearly lost what little breakfast I'd eaten. I would not become my parents. "Let's just find her first. I tried to pin Mom down to actually saying she's here, but I couldn't get that much out of her. Just that she knows where she is."

"She's here," Starren mumbled. She struggled into a sitting position and grabbed her head. "Don't ask me how I know. I can't think right now. But something tells me she's here."

"There are at least fifteen of these tents. But I didn't see a single person. Do you think they're out on patrol?"

"That, or Mother has them locked in like she did us, so she had you to herself."

Ouch. That sounded creepy.

"Or they all slept in." It came out even more lame than I'd thought it would. But I'd grasp at any straw at the moment.

Starren snorted, then noticed my face. "Oh, thought that was a joke."

"Yeah, a joke." I smiled, but it even felt weak. No way it was convincing anyone.

Carver gave me a sympathetic look, which just made me annoyed. I didn't need anyone's sympathy. I just needed some help.

"So what's the plan? How are we going to get in touch with Nara if Mom isn't going to let us?" I popped a small piece of an unknown fruit into my mouth and walked over to look out the door, which was still open. "And sorry I forgot to ask. How are you feeling?" She'd hate it that I asked. On the outside, anyway. But that didn't change that I needed to start being a better sister. So far I'd just let her be the big sister and hadn't worried much about her. That was going to change.

"Better than last night." She didn't say thanks, but she at least didn't glare at me. That was something. We were going to learn how to be real sisters, even if it took ten of these disasters. Hopefully we didn't have any more relatives I didn't know about who were terrible people too.

Wasn't that a scary thought.

"Do you need me to..." I gestured toward her.

She gripped her ribs defensively. "No."

It was Starren. No use trying to argue. "At least eat."

She reached for the plate and grabbed a fire fruit to nibble. I made a mental note. I'd seen her eating them a lot. She must really like them. That was something a sister should know. Nina knew exactly which cookies to make for me after school, what food to have around when I was having a bad day. Apparently humans showed affection through food, and that was something I could totally get behind.

"But you did straight up ask about Nara?" Carver said.

"Yes. Same vague answer. She's around but can't talk." I eyed the tree branches around us warily, and moved in close to Carver and Starren. "You don't think she's here but dead, do you?"

Starren shifted uncomfortably. "Mother did say we could talk to her, but never said anything about her answering. That I can remember." Which implied that she knew she wasn't at her best, but wasn't going to admit it out loud.

"No, she's alive, stop freaking yourself out until we have something to freak out about," Carver said.

I gave our surroundings a pointed stare and lifted an eyebrow.

"Yeah, being locked up isn't ideal, but so far I don't think we need to worry about our safety."

"Just Dan and Nina's memories possibly being gone forever because we take too long." It came out more caustic than I'd meant it to, but every time I thought about the fact that this could be my permanent way of life, my stomach almost turned inside out and I had to hold in the vomit. I'd gotten through the last couple months on hope. I wouldn't let anything change that. Even if the hope shrank by the day.

"We obviously aren't locked up now." Starren nodded toward the open doorway. "What happens if you try to walk through there?"

I moved back to the doorway for a second, studying it, and then cautiously put a foot through. Nothing.

Starren struggled to her feet. I frowned at the plate she left on the floor, still heaping over even after I'd nibbled at it too. Starren ignored my face. "Let's go have a talk with Mother, shall we?"

Chat with Mother. Again. How wonderful. But it had to be done.

We walked out together, Carver more obvious in his hovering than I. Starren, of course, acted like she was completely fine other than walking just a tad more stiffly than her normal cat movements, while ignoring the both of us.

Mother was waiting for us at the strange table. She hadn't moved a bit since I'd left her awhile ago. She was even looking in our direction when we stepped out of the tent, completely attentive. Shoot. I probably should have told Starren about the table's vibe back when we had some privacy. I didn't know if it meant anything or not, and she was a lot more likely to.

"Ah, there you are," Mother said when we got close enough she didn't have to be loud. "Feeling any better today? Did you get any food down? Injuries like that can make your appetite go right out the window, but it's important you keep up your strength."

See, she did care. Starren might be the expert on our Father, and I admittedly should have listened to her earlier in that whole situation, but I knew Mom way better than she did. She probably wouldn't even have recognized her if they'd met in passing before today. Mom wasn't evil. She cared about people. Or at least about me. Us. She wasn't crazy, just had grown up fae. We could fix the results of that. I hoped. A nine year old always wanted to believe the best about their parents, and when I was around her, I was nine again.

We moved toward Mom slowly. Starren could have moved faster, so I checked to see what was up and noticed her counting housing units and checking out the perimeter. Trees. That was what the perimeter was, and at the moment, that was a huge disadvantage.

I waited until Starren carefully settled herself in at the table, keeping an eye on her. She wouldn't admit she needed anything until she was about to collapse, and I didn't plan on letting her get that far.

"Good morning," Mother said, like the last time she'd seen Starren had been a normal mother/daughter interaction. But then, maybe it was. For the fae.

"Where's Nara?" Starren asked. I would have kicked her, but she was wounded enough at the moment.

"Here, getting some rest after a night of protecting us all. You wouldn't want to force her away from that, would you?"

Starren ground her teeth. "Yes, I would."

"Does she know we're here?" I asked.

"*Yes,*" a voice said in my head.

I jerked, looking around. "*Who is this?*" I asked back, in my head.

"Is everything okay, dear?" Mother asked.

She was staring at me, along with Starren and Carver.

"Everything's fine."

She watched me, like she didn't believe me. "If you say so." Then she went back to Starren. "You didn't answer my question about your injuries. How are you feeling this morning?"

"You tell me where Nara is exactly, and I'll answer any question you want." Oh boy, Starren was getting intense. That was a serious promise for a fae to make.

Mother's face went calculating. "Any question? And you'll answer it as soon as I ask it?"

"*Say no,*" the voice in my head said.

Starren started to speak.

"That won't be necessary," I interrupted. "I think we're good." I opened my eyes wide, trying to communicate. Starren eyed me back, but closed her mouth. We might not agree on much, but we trusted each other, and that was far more than most fae had.

"*Fifth tent, on the forest wall.*" The voice was feminine, but I'd never heard it before. Somehow it seemed to know me.

"What brings this change of heart?" Mom asked.

I shrugged. "Oh, you know Starren, always proud enough to get herself in trouble."

"You know that you should put your trust in me, right?" Her question used 'should' instead of 'can.' Starren was right. Mother couldn't be trusted. The revelation was like a punch to the gut. She'd showed it several times, but I'd just ignored it. A ping-pong ball at a tournament had more stability than my feelings at the moment.

The table stretched under my hand, groaning as it tried to regain more of its natural shape. I laid a palm on it. If only there were some way I could help. But I didn't even have any ideas.

Mother's face went blank for a moment, then she slapped the table, standing like that was her intent the whole time. "Did you finish your plates of food? There's an abundance, so have all that you want. Can't have anyone saying I don't take care of my own daughters." Her grin was forced. Frustrated. Something wasn't going her way, and I didn't even know what. She made her way over to the other table, and grabbed a platter. Stomping back over, she dropped it onto our table, sending it clattering toward the edge. "There you go. You can take it with you. I think it would be best if you went back to rest for a bit. Can't let Starren irritate her injuries any more than she already has."

Back to rest. In our cell. "*Are you locked up too?*" I asked the voice. No answer.

Mother politely but firmly herded us toward our cell, the whole while pretending not to. But we knew. All three of us. If any of us stepped out of line, we'd get put right back in place very quickly.

And, at this point, getting put back in place wasn't something I wanted to test. How far would she go if we disobeyed her?

"Don't try it. I'll come to you, as soon as I can." The voice wasn't familiar. I hadn't ever heard it before, that I could remember. *"And don't say anything to your friends about me, the walls have ears."*

Okay, that I didn't like. I understood, because Mom seemed to know everything about everything around here, and if I, who was just learning about this stuff, had stumbled into seeing things back with the forest spirit, I could imagine what Mom could do. But still, it didn't sit well, keeping it from Starren. Her trust was hard earned, and I finally felt like I was there. Not even just a partnership, but real sisters. For sure on my end, and seemingly on hers.

"As long as it isn't affecting anyone and I don't have a way to get my point across without Mother overhearing, I'll do that. But I can't even tell anyone who you are anyway; you haven't told me your name."

And there it was again. Silence. At least I was getting better at not reacting so strongly when whoever it was decided to jump into my thoughts. Otherwise Starren and Carver would probably assume I was going crazy.

Well. That might not be a bad assumption. But why not believe the voice in my head? Fae had all kinds of abilities, this could easily be one of them. But why did she keep going silent?

Mom ushered us into our tent, but stayed at the entrance. "There are a couple of things I need to take care of. I'll be back soon."

"Mom?" I asked.

She turned back to me. "Yes, dear?"

"On our way here, we went through a forest. It was so angry. The trees were killing travelers. Did you have anything to do with that?" I'd done it now. I'd asked something that would make her mad enough she'd never let us leave. Something that would make up my mind about who my mother truly was. But I had to know.

"Of course I angered the trees there. As far as I know, you and I are the only two capable of doing it." She beamed at me. "I was hoping you'd inherit my power, but it doesn't always work like that. I'm so glad it did. I'll show you how to do it someday, once you have some other important things under control." And then she turned and left.

I pinched my nose, trying to keep myself together. She'd done that. Caused all that pain. And she was proud of it. Wanted to teach me how to do the same thing.

The door closed behind her, and her footsteps rushed away, very unlike everything I'd seen of her so far. Had something happened we hadn't noticed? At this point I almost didn't care. I just needed to get out of here.

"Something's wrong," Starren said. "She needs info from us. Needs us to believe she cares about us. Things were going well. Why would she lock us back up?"

Her questions made sense. But I had enough to think about at the moment. Oh, and the whole walls have ears thing. I pointed at a wall and held my finger up to my lips.

"What?" Carver asked.

"Oh, nothing. Which food was your favorite?" I answered.

He looked at me like I was crazy, but Starren seemed to catch on, moving over to inspect the wood.

"I love that grey mush stuff. I forget what Father called it."

"Ipsish," Starren said absently, staring at the wall.

"Yeah, that's the stuff. Delicious."

Carver watched me like I had a screw loose. And maybe I did, hearing voices in my head and all. But it was only one voice. That made me feel a bit better about the whole thing.

I patted my ear and then pointed at the wall again. It didn't change the way he looked at me.

"Just wait until you try Yaymat." Starren poked the wall, but nothing happened. "It's only allowed at special occasions, and it's to die for."

"It's to die for is pretty serious for a fae."

Starren looked at me, face deadpan. "I know."

Outside, the sound of running feet went past our hut. "Did you hear that?" I rushed over to the door, in case it was my new friend. Hopefully friend.

Shouting started, but the words were indistinguishable.

"I do now." Starren moved over to stand beside me, hand lightly on her sword hilt. "There's usually only one reason for that."

She stopped for a dramatic pause. When we got home I was throwing the TV out.

"Yes?"

"We're under attack."

CHAPTER SIXTEEN

Wonderful, just what we needed. Not. "Do you think Mother's okay?"

"Did you see how easily she took out those hounds? From miles away?" Carver asked. "I'd say she's fine."

"I think this proves my theory correct, though," Starren said. "Father knows we're here. He's probably sent someone after us."

A whistling went by outside, followed by a rather loud boom, shaking the ground. I reached out to steady Starren, and got a glare for my efforts. A large amount of screaming started on the other side of the wall, both the scared kind and the attacking kind.

"Correction. He's sent lots of someone's after us."

"We can't just jump to a conclusion like that, Star," Carver said. "They may have been about to attack anyway."

"How many battles between fae factions can you remember, Carver?"

He paused. "None."

"And how about your father? He kept the histories, right?"

"Ah, none. I don't remember a time when the fae were open about their in-fighting."

Starren grimaced. "That's what I thought. The solider who brought us in yesterday had no reason to call Trish Mareena. Father sent her, and now that she's reported to him, he sent her help." Her face suddenly went white, and she gripped my outstretched arm. "This is important enough that he may even have come himself."

And now the blood was draining from my face as well. I never wanted to see my father again. After the last time we'd been here, and after what he'd done to Dan and Nina... How he'd had Wade act like he cared and help us escape, only to shoot Nina in the gut...

Mother obviously had her faults. But she couldn't be worse than Father.

"How are they getting past the trees?" Carver's question gave me something to focus on.

"Father knows a fae who can stop any other's power from working in a certain space. He must be here, blocking the trees."

Of course he did. Which meant whoever it was could block my powers as well. No super healing, yay. Not that I wasn't used to that from Sanctuary, but Sanctuary wasn't usually dangerous. No more dangerous for me than any human.

"We need to get out of here." Starren started poking at the walls again.

"Yeah, we've been saying that since last night. Look where it's gotten us. Here, that's where, in the exact same place."

"Mother's distracted now though. See if you can talk to the tree trapping us in here."

That was an interesting thought. Mom seemed so powerful that there was nothing I could do against her, but that power had to end somewhere. Right in the middle of a battle seemed like a good place for that. At this point I'd rather Mom won, but not enough that I'd stick around to find out in what might be our only chance at escape.

I put my hand on the door, and this time I could feel the roots holding it closed. Before they'd felt dead. A small amount of progress, at least. The roots were angry, like the table outside, twisted into a shape they didn't want to hold, going against their nature. I comforted them, like I had back with the forest spirit.

The door budged. "Yes!" I shouted. It hadn't moved even enough to put my fingers through, but it was something. I'd take about anything at this point.

"Did you get it?" Starren asked from the other side of the room.

"If we were cockroaches," Carver answered. "Cockroaches are a real thing, right?"

"Does that really matter right now?" Starren asked.

"No, guess not."

"Yes, Carver," I answered. "They're a real thing." Then I closed out whatever the two of them started to argue about and concentrated on the door. Starren came up beside me, still at it with Carver, but watching over my shoulder enough to annoy me. "Could you back off a little?"

She threw her hands up in the air. "Pardon me for caring if we get out of this mess or not."

Whatever. We'd deal with all the grumpy later. Right now, our lives may depend on me convincing this tree to let us out. A shiver went through me. The other two's lives. I was in no danger of dying as long as Mother and Father both thought they needed me to defeat the other. The thought made me work twice as fast. I would not be trapped again. I would not lose another person I cared about.

The door shifted open another inch, screeching and protesting the entire way. It was open far enough now that I could get a glimpse outside. Starren and Carver plastered themselves to the door frame to see as well, the three of us probably looking pretty comical in a different situation.

Every tent must have been completely full to the brim of the amount of people that they could hold. How had Mother convinced this many people to fight for her? But there were more of Father's fae. Far more, dressed in their shiny armor. Small battles raged all around the camp, centered around a man in black robes. Any time a branch came within thirty feet of him, it dropped to the ground like normal firewood. Inside that circle, Mother's forces battled Father's.

One of the fae stepped just a bit too far from the man in the middle, and a branch grabbed him, tossing him high and out over the forest, where he was snatched up by another branch.

"Oh wow, that had to hurt." Carver cringed for the fae, but I ignored it all.

Father wasn't going to get us. To get me. I wouldn't let him. I'd die before I became his puppet. I needed out of here, now. The room spun a bit, and I righted myself using the branches wrapped across the door. My nails bit into the soft wood as I frantically clawed at it. "Let us out!" I screamed through the small crack. No one even looked our way.

"Hang on. I'm coming." The voice didn't ease the fear I could physically feel going through my veins. If Father had someone along with him that could cut me off from my powers, I wouldn't be able to stop him from dragging me away. From locking me up. From making me do his dirty work, like he'd done to Starren for years. I couldn't live like that. And after a bit of time, I wouldn't have any reason not to, with no Dan and Nina to go home to.

And Jaden. I'd lose Jaden. Whatever we could have been, I'd never find out. And it was my fault, because he'd repeatedly made sure I knew that he was just waiting for me to be ready.

"Keep it together," Starren snapped. "Get to work on that tree."

I shook my head, using the physical act to try and clear it a bit. Starren's grumpiness had done a better job of that than I could myself. "Please," I begged the tree, wherever it was that these roots were attached. "Please. I need to get out of here. I have to."

The root loosened a little, the door falling open about six inches.

"Thank you. Almost there. Just a bit more, please."

Starren and Carver crowded in closer, pushing me part way out the door.

It creaked with our combined weight, and let go, spilling us all outside. Carver and I jumped up instantly, but Starren took a little longer. We both grabbed her under the arms and drug her around behind our hut where there wasn't any fighting going on. Yet.

"Let's get out of here," Carver said.

"You guys go, get in the trees out of sight, I have something I have to do."

Starren glared at me. "What could you possibly need to do here? If it has something to do with Mother or Father, you need to let it go."

"It isn't them."

Starren sighed. "Dan and Nina. We don't even know where to start looking for Nara, Trish. She could be in any of the structures around here, or even not here at all. We need to get free, then figure out a plan." She started for the trees like that was the end of the discussion. She should know me better than that by now.

"I've been talking to someone here. They say they can help."

"Been talking with someone?" Starren asked. "Like, in your head?"

She shouldn't be surprised. She had to know that some fae could do that. I hadn't known, but she should have.

"You idiot. That's so dangerous!" Starren clenched her hand into a fist like she'd barely kept herself from smacking me. "If you answer them, you open a doorway!"

"Um, what?"

"We don't have time for this." She gestured back toward where the sounds of fighting were getting louder. "Either we're going to get grabbed and taken to Father, or Mother is going to find us, and trust me, she'd be very unhappy the tree obeyed you over her. I can't see that ending well."

"Right." Now that she mentioned it, it did seem like that was something that Mother wouldn't be too happy about. "We just have to go to the fifth hut, just in case."

Starren's face went all stubborn.

Two could play that game.

"Go on. I'm not leaving without finding out." And I took off. If it was anyone else, I wouldn't have been able to leave them in danger like this, but even injured, Starren could take care of herself.

I skidded around a hut, nearly running into the fae that had called me Mareena the day before when she'd come to escort us to the clearing. She was surrounded by Father's soldiers. Well. That was nice to have confirmation about. Kind of.

"Hi." It came out pretty lame.

"Mareena. Good. Your father is expecting you."

I inched backward. "Oh, really? Is he here?"

"No. He was unable to make it. But he'll be waiting for you when we return." She waved a hand and two of the soldiers stepped toward me. She smiled. "This was easier than I'd thought. Everyone makes it sound like you would be difficult to bring back, but you've made it so easy."

I turned on my heel and ran. I didn't even care where to at the moment. Anywhere would be better than back to Father. I'd even take running into Mother right now. I wouldn't really be happy about it, but I'd figure it out.

"Come on, guys, help a girl out, would you?" I asked the trees. A small rumble went through them, like they were waking up to my voice. But I still didn't have much influence. Did that mean something had happened to Mom? My heart dropped before my head remembered that she was probably a really bad person. Even then it didn't matter. She was my mom.

I dodged back and forth between huts until I was back to the one I'd been locked up in. Shoot, shoot, now what? The soldiers were a little slow because of the armor, but they were not far behind.

The table from before wriggled a little, catching my attention.

Soldiers careened out of the woods ahead of me, slashing at the trees. I tripped, nearly falling as I changed trajectory. And there, the guy with the ability blocker. He wasn't far either. I was trapped between them all.

The poor little table writhed, probably trying to defend Mother. I rushed over to make a stand on top of it, because there was no way they were taking me back to Father. I pulled my sword and vaulted off the bench onto the table.

The lady chasing me stopped long enough to laugh. "Do you really believe in your swordsmanship skills that much?"

"Better than not trying anything," I spat back. I glanced around quickly for Starren and Carver, and an odd mixture of elation and disappointment went through me when I couldn't find them.

A tug on my ankle made me look down. The table had deformed enough to put a root up and grab my attention. I tried to pull my ankle free, but it just gripped tighter. I jerked, waving my sword at it. "Let me go. I don't want to hurt you."

It didn't listen. Instead, it started pulling downward.

"Hey, seriously, let me go."

"Raiena is doing something!" The fae lady shouted, and started to run forward.

A long time since I'd heard my mother's name. But it didn't feel like she was involved.

Then the root jerked sideways, knocking me from my feet. I landed on the table hard enough to knock the breath out of me. Then it snapped closed around me like a clam shell.

Trying to wiggle my sword around, I slapped at the wood with my free hand. "Hey! Let me out! Let me out, now!"

The tree didn't listen. In fact, it just closed in tighter, the branches wrapping around me to the point I almost couldn't breathe. Or, it felt like I couldn't breathe. It was too tight. Would this be how I died, died?

The branches finally adjusted around me where they wanted to be, settling in like a boa patiently squeezing the life out of its prey. But then, it made a viewing hole, so I could see out, but kept leaves in front of it so no one would notice.

Was it... trying to help?

I tentatively reached out to see if it would communicate with me. No. It still couldn't. But it felt... determined. Apparently protecting me fell enough under what Mom would want that the tree could find some wiggle room to leave the position she'd forced it into.

"Thank you," I whispered.

The soldiers were hacking at the branches. The poor tree groaned. It wasn't going to last long.

"*Stop.*" It was the voice, in my head. But the soldiers listened to it. "*You're all very sleepy.*" I wanted to rub my ears, to try to figure out if the voice was inside my head or out, but I still couldn't move. "*You all need to rest. You're about to die from lack of sleep. It's as if you haven't slept in weeks.*" Intention must have meant something, because the soldiers dropped like flies, but I didn't feel anything. "*You can let her go now,*" the voice told the tree. And it did.

I rolled out like I'd been trapped in a carpet and someone pulled the edge. I slammed into someone's legs, and scrambled to my feet, barely avoiding cutting myself on my own sword. Starren's words made the hair on my neck stand up. I'd let this woman, whoever she was, into my head willingly. It was probably time for another fight. I gripped my sword in both hands and lifted it to meet whatever new threat this was.

Except... I knew that face. "Nara?" I gaped.

She grinned at me, completely a different person than the one I'd met a few months ago. So much healthier out here in the sunlight. Freedom looked good on her.

"You look so good! Are you doing okay? Are people treating you okay? We need to get out of here!"

"I'm fine, silly."

The voice, it was her all along. I hadn't known it, because I'd never heard it before. Why hadn't she spoken to me like this back at the prison?

"The blockers. No powers worked there, and this is part of mine."

I'd thought she'd needed my help, and here she was, as or more powerful than me. Wait a sec. I hadn't said that last part 'out loud.'

"You don't have to. Once you answered me, you opened up your thoughts to me, just like your sister said."

Oh crap. Oh double crap. She was in my head? Knew all my thoughts? There were a lot of thoughts that went through this stupid brain that I didn't want anyone to know about. Did she know all of my past? The stupid things I'd done? The people I cared about?

"No, I haven't dug into any of that. I'll do my best to respect your privacy. But current thoughts like this when we're connected, those I can't filter. Now let's get out of here before these soldiers wake. It might not work on them a second time. Or the ability blocker may come back this way, and then we'd be in trouble."

"Thank you!" I called to the tree that had helped me, then rushed toward the section of trees I'd shooed Carver and Starren into. Hopefully that hadn't been a terrible decision. It seemed like Mom should be busy enough at the moment to not notice them, but I really didn't know where her power ended. It was a shame, I could have learned a lot from her. But I'd much rather learn it on my own than with a person like that.

After hitting the treeline, I paused for a second, sending out a little wave of concentration to the trees, just to see if they would respond. I could feel a slight consciousness, like they knew what I was trying to do, but there was no real answer. Even in the middle of a battle Mother had a firm hold over the forest here.

Starren popped out from behind a tree, her blade instantly at

Nara's neck. The suddenness of her arrival had Nara and me jumping into each other.

"Who is this?" Starren asked.

"Nara," I nodded toward Starren. "This is Starren. And somewhere around here is Carver."

Nara nodded toward Starren. *"Then my debt is paid."* She smiled and put an arm out. I bumped it awkwardly, not really remembering what I was supposed to do with that. *"Farewell, and be safe."* She turned to leave.

"Wait, no!"

She paused.

"I need your help. I'm not sure we can get past the trees."

"I'm on your side, in this, needing freedom. But I'm on your mother's side in everything else. She gave me a family, and I'm indebted to her. She may be in trouble right now, I must go and make sure Quintin's forces scatter. My debt is paid, and you no longer need me. It's time to part ways."

Oh shoot, she was right. A twinge went through me. Mom could be in real danger. She was crazy powerful, yes, but Father had to know what she could do, and he wasn't the sort to waste resources without being sure of a result. Her life may very well be on the line.

But she'd chosen her path. She'd dabbled in all this, after power just like all the rest of the fae. Dan and Nina had gotten where they were while trying to help me. Trying to save a life. There was no comparison. Father wouldn't have Mother killed. At least, I didn't want to believe he could. I'd just have to go with that for now, because they'd already proven there wasn't much I could do against them without the trees' help.

"That doesn't work for me." I winced at how strongly that came out. "The time to part ways thing. I can't leave without you. I need your help. At home. And then I'll consider your debt more than paid. How good are you with those mind games of yours?"

"Pretty good." It didn't sound haughty, just a matter of fact. She studied me for a moment. *"What do you need?"*

She hadn't right out refused. That was something. Not much, but I'd take any kind of hope right now. "Do you remember how I was looking for Starren when we met?"

She nodded.

"I wasn't the only one. I had help. Human help. They ate some food Father forced on them, and now they've lost their memory."

Nara's face went blank at the mention of humans. If she was one of those fae that hated humans for no reason, or just thought they were lesser, we were in trouble. She leaned in close. *"You brought humans here? Are you crazy?"*

I gave her a sickly smile. "Somewhat. Or so I've heard. It wasn't really a choice I made. They wouldn't let me come without them, and I had to come because Starren needed me."

"Stop saying that," Starren hissed from beside me.

Oops, yeah, she wouldn't like that one at all.

Nara studied me long enough it felt awkward. Really. But I took it, because at this point there was no way for me to force her to help, and no way we were leaving Faerie unless she let us. Starren might not be affected by her mind power, but I most likely was.

"If I help you, will you have a real, honest discussion with your mother? To find out she isn't the horrible person you seem to think she is."

"I thought you weren't going to read my mind," I muttered.

She just gave me a look.

"Fine, fine! I'll have a talk with my mom." Ha. I didn't say when. Maybe when I was two hundred I'd be ready to talk to her again. If her and Father didn't succeed in killing each other by then.

"Wait here. I have someone who can help us." Nara took off back toward the clearing.

"Wait!" She heard me. She had to have. But she didn't even slow. "That's just great."

"You know she's probably going to get help, right," Starren said. "You know what kind of help."

I knew. But I had to trust her a bit, just out of desperation.

"Is it safe?" Carver's voice came from somewhere out in the trees.

"Yes, come on out." Starren motioned toward where the voice had come from. "I told him to stay back there and be ready to go for help."

"All this moving around can't have been good for your injuries. Let me help, while we're waiting for Nara."

Starren gave me the glare.

I gave it back.

"Okay, fine. But don't tell anyone. And hurry up and get started before Carver gets back."

I moved over to grab her hand quickly, without giving her time to change her mind. The pain hit me much harder than the night before, making me jerk a bit at the suddenness of it attacking my ribs. "Star! This is so much worse!"

"Injuries always get more sore when you're active," she answered in a monotone. "But you wouldn't know that, would you. You never have them for long."

"Oh stop with that stuff. Yeah, I have a different ability than you, but yours is pretty cool too. Like right now, Nara could totally mess with my mind if she wants, but she couldn't with you. That's pretty awesome. For you, that is."

"You know what, you're right. I guess I should be the chosen one, huh?" She huffed and leaned back against a tree, distancing herself from me but not severing our connection. "But seriously, you are right about one thing. I make the decisions until Nara is out of the picture, since I can't be sure it's you and not her influencing you."

"Ah, no." I wasn't going to just blanket give her permission to be in charge. She did have a good point, but she also didn't have much empathy or compassion, so sometimes her choices were terrible.

"But at least actually take my advice seriously right now." She wasn't fighting back very hard. She must have known what my answer was going to be, and tried it anyway. "In case you aren't thinking straight. We should come up with some kind of code word while Nara isn't here, and you'll just have to make sure you don't think of it."

"Uh, ladies, is there a problem?" Carver asked.

We both ignored him.

"Oh, so easy, just don't think about it."

"Not thinking should be easy for you. It's your default mode."

Okay, now things were getting just plain mean. "Just because we think differently doesn't mean I'm not thinking, Starren. I think all the time. But I shut it down, and you know why? Because for years and years nothing could go my way. But then I got Dan and Nina. And then Jaden. And now you. And I just want things to go my way. Stop insulting me, I can't help it if I grew up on Earth all dumb while Father trained you to be some kind of super soldier here."

"Trish," Starren interrupted.

"I'm not done. You can't get me this mad and then not let me have my say. I know growing up here was terrible, but my childhood wasn't great either, I-"

"Trish!"

"I said I'm not done, you can listen for once!"

Starren kicked me, and I whirled to see what she was pointing at.

No. It couldn't be. The only person that rivaled my father on my never want to see again list. Dark blond hair. I knew the color of his eyes, even far enough away I couldn't see them. "He sent Wade?" It came out as a whisper, but Starren quickly squeezed my hand in sympathy anyway. "He sent Wade?" This time it came out much stronger, angrier. "He sent Wade!" My scream echoed off the trees. If I'd stopped to think about it I would have worried he would hear, but I was too angry.

He was in the clearing, slicing through Mother's troops. Did Father really think it was a good idea to send the person I hated most in the entire world here to bring me back?

"Keep it together, Trish. We don't have time for this."

My blood started to boil, my vision nearly fogging over. I was back in the woods, holding Nina's lifeless body, feeling her go cold. The colder she felt, the hotter my skin burned. "He sent Wade."

"Think of those people," Carver said. "Let it go. The ones you want to save."

He wasn't helping. It was them I was thinking about. Dan crying as he clutched Nina to his chest. Wade had shot her. And she'd died. Or close enough that I hadn't been able to tell the difference. If it was up to him, I wouldn't even be able to see her in passing right now. I took a step in his direction.

"Not now, Trish. Come on. Like you always say, Dan and Nina. Say it." Starren's voice slowed me a little, but not enough.

I couldn't even bring myself to turn back. She grabbed me, spinning me around to face her. I struggled, but not hard enough to hurt her with her injuries, and turned to watch Wade over my shoulder. I wouldn't lose sight of him.

"Come on." Starren shook me. "Say it out loud. Dan and Nina."

I glanced at her for a second, before looking back at Wade fighting his way toward us.

"Dan and Nina," Starren repeated.

"Dan and Nina," I said. Something about their names made the rage in my gut unravel. Just a bit. They'd forgiven Wade. And they were waiting for me.

"Come on. We need to get somewhere he won't see us."

I growled, but turned to follow her. Wade would have to wait. If I went after him, I'd lose my chance of getting out of here. We needed to get out of sight. I could let Nara know where we hid telepathically. If I could figure out how to open the connection, there had been quite a few times when she hadn't answered me before.

We moved into the woods until we were far enough away to no longer see the clearing, but close enough to see the spot we'd been waiting for Nara. When she came back, we'd be ready. Then we could get out of this stinking place before I lost my cool and tracked Wade down. Maybe it was a good thing that the trees weren't listening to me right now. If they felt what I felt at the moment, they'd be murdering someone. Someone specific.

I'd hardly been able to keep them back the last time we'd parted ways, and I'd been in a better spot then, and in front of Nina, who I would do anything not to disappoint.

I hadn't let go of Starren's arm. She pretended to try to shake me off a couple times, but I knew better. She was hurting enough she didn't insist. And I was using the pain to keep myself grounded. At least grounded enough not to snap.

Where was Nara? At least Wade was out of sight, because if I had to sit here watching him while I waited, it would not turn out well. Even while we stood around doing nothing, I could hardly keep my thoughts from going down to him, fighting, ruining other lives. Did he think we could reconcile? Did he think we were going to be friends again? Or did he not care, too brain-washed by my father.

It shouldn't matter, but it did. I would never forgive him. I'd gotten over him shooting me when I'd learned why, when everything had been explained to me. But him shooting Nina? No. That was never going away. And his 'explanation' had only made it worse. He'd better not come anywhere close to me without that ability blocking guy around, or he'd find out just how much I despised him.

"Ah, Trish," Carver said. "Are you upset about something?"

"None of your business." Just because we were traveling together didn't mean he got to ask questions like that. And he should know the answer anyway. He was different, but not dumb.

"It's about to become my business." He pointed up.

The tree branches were roiling around, tangling and untangling, trees flailing against each other.

"Oops. I wasn't worried about that because I thought they weren't listening." I couldn't just get a chance to work through things. Somehow I always had to just be okay. If I wasn't okay, someone could get hurt. "Talk about something."

"Like what?" Carver asked, eyes wide.

"I don't know, I don't really care, just talk about something."

"She needs to get her mind off Wade," Starren said. "Though it is interesting that when you're angry enough, you are able to get through to the trees. Maybe we should experiment with that."

"I'm not some experiment, Starren."

"I know, I know, I just meant that maybe we'll be able to use that. Unless..." she stopped, then looked away from me.

"Unless what?"

"There's the possibility that the trees are responding to you because they no longer have another master."

No longer have another master? Did she mean... "No. Mom's fine. She's too strong for anything to happen to her."

Starren shrugged. "Father always has everything planned, even the minuscule. He wouldn't have risked sending troops here if he didn't think he was going to win. Wade probably isn't the only ace up his sleeve."

I dropped her hand and took a step in Mom's direction on purely instinct. She was terrible. She might even be evil. But she was my mom. What if she was dead? I'd longed for her for so many years, and now I'd found her. I would have left without a thought if I knew she was safe, but now...

"Leave it, Trish. I shouldn't have said anything."

But she was right. I didn't know if my anger had overpowered Mother's ability, or if she was in trouble, or even dead. Somehow it didn't seem like a kid would be able to overpower an adult fae, who had used their ability for years and knew how to control it and what they were capable of.

"I'm going down there."

"Really?" Carver asked. "We just got away."

"I'm not doing anything, I'm just looking." I didn't give them a chance to truly try to stop me. I shoved off the tree I'd been leaning on and took off back toward the clearing.

"Trish, wait!" Starren yelled. "I'm coming with you!"

Nope. She was injured and I wasn't going to wait. I wasn't going to let her get hurt worse. I didn't know how to control that thing that had saved Nina, and I didn't know if I'd ever be able to do it again. I wouldn't risk her, not for Mother.

It wasn't far to the edge of the trees. The clearing looked like the battleground that it was. The huts had come apart, probably in Mom's defense. Bodies littered the ground, and tree limbs covered the earth.

The trees all around the clearing looked shorn, branches and limbs hacked off. Some sliced straight through, and I really didn't want to meet who, or what, was able to do that.

Nothing moved in immediate sight, but the sounds of fighting came from the other side of the clearing, on the far side of the trees that had once been forced into huts.

Did I really want to get involved in this? Over Mom, who hadn't even looked for me in years? Who'd used me, abandoned Starren? But then a scarier thought hit. What if something happened to Nara?

I ran toward the sound, jumping over fallen weapons, avoiding looking at the bodies even though I wanted to know if one of them was Mom. I just couldn't. Or Nara. If something happened to Nara, I was screwed. I couldn't stay in Faerie any longer looking for someone else who could help. Not with both Mother and Father looking for me.

Between the two of them, they had eyes and ears everywhere from the look of things.

I rounded a hut just in time to see a fae slide off Wade's blade. Behind him, the ability blocker stood, a ring of guards around him. At least it looked like Mom had stopped forcing the trees to attack, only to get chopped to bits when they entered the circle. I frantically searched for Nara, or Mom, who Nara had gone to check on. I only was looking for Mom to see if Nara was fighting beside her, that was it. Not because I wanted to know if she was okay. Of course not. I didn't need another crazy sociopath in my life.

There, just outside the circle. Mom directed trees, destroying any soldier foolish enough to step out of the circle, or to allow the circle to move on without them.

"Raiena."

That voice. Echoing out across the clearing. It caused everyone to pause. The name wasn't yelled, but the voice carried.

I cringed down, scurrying to find something, anything to hide behind. Father was here. He moved out of the forest. The trees leapt at him, but he didn't seem to notice or care as the fae guard around him hacked and burned the branches and limbs to pieces.

"Give me the girl." The way he said it made me sink even lower into the one patch of grass I could find that wasn't razed. The girl. He couldn't even be bothered to say my name.

"No, Quintin. She's mine."

This may possibly be the worst custody battle ever.

My instinct was to just go out there and let them have it. Maybe some yelling would knock some sense into them. But then my brain kicked in, and I realized how utterly stupid that would be. One of them would come out on top, and which ever one did would be after me next. We really needed to get out of here.

"Nara, where are you?" I wasn't really sure if I was asking myself or her, but I didn't expect an answer. It hadn't worked like that so far.

"I grabbed a friend who can help. Meet me at your hut."

I nearly fell out of my little patch of grass. I didn't care who the friend was or what they were for, we were getting out of here. We'd have to book it back, no stopping for food, no sleeping, whatever it took. If we ran out of time and got back and there was nothing Nara could do, I'd never forgive Mom for the time she'd held us captive.

Shoot, I never should have left Starren and Carver. I jumped up and charged back toward the woods where I'd left them, but didn't get far before Carver popped out of hiding behind a burned out shell of a tree.

"Carver!" I yelled. "Don't scare me like that! I told you to stay in the woods."

Carver shrugged. "You also left me with Starren. Starren does what Starren wants."

"You know that's right," Starren said, hobbling over to stand by Carver. She looked like she was in pretty poor shape. She had to be hurting so bad right now.

"Nara is ready to go. She said to meet her near our hut."

Starren didn't answer, just got a head start wobbling toward the hut. I moved up beside her and grabbed her arm before she could protest. The pain nearly knocked me to my knees and I bit down hard enough I almost cracked a tooth.

"This is half your pain?"

Starren straightened a little and moved forward at a better clip. "Yep."

"Not-healing is terrible."

"Yep."

When we got to the hut, Nara was already there, waiting, with an older fae, probably in his fifties. If he was human. He might actually be two hundred for all I knew.

"Who's your friend?" Starren asked when we were within earshot.

"You don't need to know his name," Nara answered. She must have been speaking in all of our heads, because Starren got that muleish look on her face. At least she didn't get lippy. Maybe the pain was good for something. *"Are you ready to go?"* Nara asked. *"This is it though. After this I'm done. Fae pay their debts."*

"Ready and waiting. Where is the closest portal? It's going to take us days if we have to make it back to the one we brought in."

Nara didn't answer. She stared into my eyes and my memories of having breakfast with Dan and Nina at the apartment, playing games, watching TV, doing homework while they cooked supper together, all flashed before my eyes. I blinked back tears. Seeing the things I had lost was even worse than just remembering. She turned to the man for a second, they stared at each other, and then he nodded.

He lifted his hands and started swirling them around in a circular motion. At first nothing happened, but then, bluish sparks formed into a portal.

"Whaaa?" I said. "That easy?"

"Unless you'd prefer to walk. I don't have much time, so if you do prefer to walk, I'll just meet you there in a week."

"No, no, let's go."

"You first," she gestured toward the portal. *"I'll be back soon, keep it open. But go and see if you can help Raiena,"* I heard her tell the guy through our connection.

Wait a second. This seemed too easy. What did I really know about Nara? Nothing. Nothing except that we'd met in prison, and I still didn't know why she was there. Father had put her there, so that was a mark in her favor.

"You don't have time for this decision. Make your choice, quickly."

"Trish?" That voice, I hadn't heard it in awhile. And now was too soon. I whirled to face Wade. "Trish!"

"Let's go," I said. I turned to go through the portal. An arrow whizzed by my head, going right past and hitting the portal dead center, disappearing.

"Hey!" I yelled at Wade.

"That was a warning, you know I could have hit you."

"Just go," Starren said.

She was right. I didn't have time for this, even if I'd rather stay and have him squeezed to death.

He reached for another arrow.

I dove through the portal.

CHAPTER SEVENTEEN

Bam, I hit the floor at home. Home home, as in Dan and Nina's apartment home, not the smelly place where Starren and I had been living for awhile. An arrow quivered in the wall across from me.

A carton of eggs hit the ground, and I jerked around to see Nina standing by the fridge, mouth open, hands still in place like she was holding the eggs.

"What the–"

Dan jumped up from the counter and dove in front of Nina, pulling a cooking knife from a stand and brandishing it in front of him. "Who are you?"

I didn't get time to answer. Nara flew through the portal, landing on top of me. I shoved her off and stood, just in time to catch Starren and get her out of the way before Carver came through.

"What's going on here?" Dan roared.

"Trish?"

The sound of my name almost brought tears to my eyes, and I thought for just a second that they'd remembered on their own before I realized it wasn't Nina. And that it was coming from down the hall. "Aunt Wren?" I yelled back.

"You know these people?" Nina called to Wren.

"Yes," Wren answered, coming in from the living room and running forward to grab me into a hug, squeezing me tight. "And so do you. Are you okay, Trish? I've been frantic but had no idea what to do. I was about ready to start making some calls."

"I'm fine, Wren. Thank you."

"Those two?" Nara asked. She sounded impatient. But she did have a war to get back to.

"Yes, those two."

Nara stepped forward, and Dan stepped to meet her.

"It's okay, Dan. They're friends," Wren said. She sent me the eyes, like she was asking if this was the right move.

To someone who didn't know him, her words wouldn't have seemed to have an effect. But I did know him, and saw the slight relaxation around the eyes, a little of the tightness leaving his shoulders. "What do you want? How did you just appear like that?"

Nara looked deep into his eyes, and he looked back, hypnotized.

"What's she doing?" Nina asked. She moved forward like she was going to try and stop whatever was happening, but Wren grabbed her around the shoulders and pulled her back. Nina struggled, but she was no match for her little sister.

I waited, tapping my hand against my thigh, then bouncing on my heels. How long did this take? Was anything even happening? What if after all that, we were too late? "Can you help them?" The words burst from my mouth. I couldn't stop them.

She kept her eyes on his. *"The memories are still there, just blocked. I can reroute around the block, and the memories will be able to be accessed again."*

Nara took her eyes away, and Dan broke free. He blinked, then grabbed his head, groaning.

"Dan?" I asked anxiously, hovering in close but not wanting to touch him until I knew it had worked.

He didn't answer.

It hadn't worked. I was going to be alone forever. It hadn't worked, I'd lost my parents, my real parents. My life would be the terrible mess it had been the last couple months forever. I'd die alone someday, after having to move away because I wasn't aging at the same rate humans did.

"Trish?"

"Dan?" I asked back, my voice hoarse.

"Who is Trish? Why does everyone keep saying 'Trish,' like that should mean something to us?" Nina asked.

"Just wait a second, honey," Dan told Nina, and then pulled me into a bone-crushing hug, squeezing me until I couldn't breathe, and not letting go.

"Dan, what are you doing?" Nina nearly squawked.

Nara moved in on her.

Nervously, Nina picked at her shirt. "Dan? Wren? What's going on?"

"It'll be fine." I pulled free from Dan's tight grip and faced Nina. "I promise. Just a minute, and you'll understand everything."

And then she caught Nara's eyes, and went wherever it was that people went while staring.

I clutched Dan's arm so hard he probably lost all feeling. He didn't seem to mind, and watched Nara carefully, like he was ready to step in at any moment. I couldn't blame him. I knew her and still didn't really like the thought of her poking around in Nina's head. She could learn all kinds of important things to pass on to Mom. But I didn't have a choice if I wanted Nina back, and I wanted Nina back more than anything I could imagine.

There it was. Nara stepped back, breaking eye contact with Nina. *That should do it. Is my debt to you fully repaid?"*

"Trish?" Nina asked, just like Dan had.

"Paid in full," I managed to croak out before jumping Nina.

She was leaning in hard at the same time as I was, and we hit, crashing to the floor, holding each other so tight that I didn't even think about trying to breathe. This was it. We'd made it in time. I had them back, my family. We could be a family again. Dan and Nina, Cray, Starren. And Jaden, however he fit in. As soon as I'd seen enough of Nina, I was going over to visit Jaden.

I laughed. Like seeing enough of Nina was possible at this point.

"Farewell," Nara said. She turned toward the portal.

"Wait! You don't have to go back. You don't have to be her prisoner."

"For once I'm making my own decisions. Your mother is good to me. Think about that next time you're angry with her." And without waiting for an answer she stepped back through the portal. It snapped closed behind her. Good riddance. Not for her, but for the severing of that last connection with Faerie.

"Who was that?" Dan asked.

Nina just kept hugging me. Tight enough that I couldn't even answer Dan. At least he wasn't freaked out about the portal anymore, now that he knew what it was again.

The warmth of the kitchen seeped into my bones, and the familiar smells of Dan's cologne mixing with the waft of cookies made my soul settle a little.

"Could someone answer me, please?" Dan asked.

Starren was looking pale, sitting against the wall. Carver stared at Dan like the human was about to try to hunt him down and eat him. This was probably the first human he'd ever actually seen. It had taken forever for me to get Cray to stop freaking out, hopefully it would go quicker with Carver since he loved human books.

I shoved Nina off, just enough to be able to speak without actually letting go. "She's a friend I made in Faerie last time we were there."

"Last time? We were only there one time."

"You were only there one time," I answered.

"Time for me to get in on this," Wren said, dropping to the floor and surrounding Nina and me in a tight embrace. "I'm so glad this is all over. Trish, if you ever treat me like that again, I'm going to kill you myself."

"Wait a second, you two have met?" Nina asked. "How did that happen? When did you go to Faerie again? What did we miss? I remember the last few months, but you aren't in them, did someone do something to us to make us forget you during that time?" Her face froze for a second. "No. I saw you. I saw you at Rebecca's apartment building, and I didn't know who you were. I treated you so badly!"

"Nina, you couldn't treat anyone badly. You just didn't know who I was at the time. It's all good." And it was all good. A few painful memories couldn't stand up to the fact that I had my family back. I'd look back on that, and not even care. It just made this moment so much sweeter.

She pushed me back, really looking at me. "What happened to you? Your clothes are burnt and shredded. If someone did this to you…"

"I'll tell you all about it." And I would. I practically needed therapy after everything with my mom.

I snuggled in for another hug. How had I not noticed how much I missed contact? I used to hate hugs as much as Starren did, but now I never wanted out of this one.

"Can we talk?" Starren asked. Very un-Starren like, to ask something so politely.

"Now?" I asked. Couldn't whatever it was wait?

"Now." She was so serious. It made me actually take notice and give Nina a squeeze before getting up and following her down the hallway a bit.

"Hurry up, though," Wren called after us. "We need to hear about this trip!"

"You got it!" I hollered back.

Carver trailed us as we moved to almost where my old room was, like he wasn't quite sure he was invited, but he also didn't want to hang around with the humans either.

"What does this mean for me?" Starren asked as soon as we were out of earshot of the kitchen.

I stared at her blankly. "What do you mean?"

"You aren't going to want to live in that apartment. You don't need me anymore. What does this mean for me? I can't afford that crappy apartment alone. And I don't know if Carver is staying, and even if he is, he doesn't have a job."

Carver snorted. "Of course I'm staying. And how hard can it be to get a job?"

"We'll figure you out in a bit, Carver, but Star, you know you're staying with us. What you don't know yet is that you just gained two family members. You'll love them, even more than you love me." I smiled. "They're much more loveable. And as for the living situation, we've been going to move for awhile anyway, and there's a guest room."

"What would I want with a guest room?"

"It's somewhere you could call yours, but not be tied down." I understood all too well the panic that came with feeling like you didn't have an out, that you were committed to something. I also understood that if I could get her to move in, she'd end up loving Dan and Nina whether she wanted to or not. They were irresistible.

She thought long and hard about it. I could practically see her brain working. "When can we get our stuff? I want out of that apartment as soon as possible. But just until I find something better. I'm not going to stay in this human town and rot forever."

So she said now. But I'd be able to convince her differently, I was sure of it. Or maybe Father or Mother would win whatever it was they were fighting about and lose interest in us, and we'd be able to go wherever we wanted again. Not that I was ever going to want to be anywhere but here.

"Oh shoot, I should text Jaden. He's going to be so mad."

"So mad." Starren agreed.

I pulled my phone out of my backpack where it had spent the entire trip to Faerie. Dead.

"I'm just going to run over and see him."

Starren smirked. "You do that."

"Shut up."

She raised her hands. "I didn't say anything."

"Yeah, yeah."

Normally I'd just yell where I was going to Nina and head for the door, but that wasn't going to happen for awhile. I walked in and gave her a hug.

"Everything alright?" she asked.

"Everything is great. I'm going to run over and see Jaden. Back in a few."

Nina frowned for a second. "Seriously? After not seeing you forever?"

"It was forever for me, not for you," I reminded her.

Her smile took up her whole face, and she swatted at me. "Okay. What about Cray?"

Shoot, I'd been so focused on Jaden, I'd forgotten how important this whole thing would be to Cray. He loved Dan and Nina too. "Would you text him?"

"Sure will. Hurry back. We have a ton to catch up on."

"Starren can get the party started." I rushed to the door. The more I thought about it, now that I had Dan and Nina back and I could actually think, the more I missed Jaden. Hopefully he was home. I didn't even know what time of day, or day of the week it was. If he was at work I was going to be seriously disappointed.

I trotted down the stairs and went outside, checking real quick to see if Storm was around. No sign of him, but I'd been gone and he didn't know to wait here instead of at the other apartment.

I jogged toward the Martan's, hurrying because I wanted to see him, because I wanted to get back to Dan and Nina, and because it was cold. Amazing how quickly I settled right back into being home, being safe.

Seeing Jaden was going to be amazing. I'd missed him far more than I'd have dreamed. I should have known I would though, because he was the only person outside of my little family that I truly trusted. Who'd seen the real me, the one that was a complete and utter mess, and yet still came back anyway. He was an amazing guy, and I didn't really want to overlook that anymore.

I walked down the alley beside his apartment building, taking the shortcut I always took.

Halfway through, I finally noticed two figures waiting at the end. I slowed until I could make them out.

Mother. And Father. Standing together. The world was about to end. What were they doing here? And not fighting? Something was seriously wrong. I should run. But where would I go? They couldn't be here. This was my safe space. This was home. Sanctuary. But they were. And there was no way I was going to let them follow me home. I'd just gotten Dan and Nina back, I wouldn't risk losing them permanently, which I knew would happen if either of those two figured out how much I cared about my fosters. Better to just get this over with.

"Trisha dear, we need to talk."

"Don't listen to her, Mareena. It's I who needs to speak with you."

Here. Both of them, here, in Sanctuary. The old fae laws about no violence in Sanctuary were the only thing keeping them from killing each other, and somehow that didn't seem like it was enough to last for long. Was it possible to break Sanctuary, just no one did it? Or was there something physical that prevented them? I didn't want to find out. I wiped my sweaty palms on my jeans, and moved a bit closer, though still far out of range.

"You know how much I care about you," Mom said. She smiled and held out her hand.

"Yes. She does know. She knows you care not at all. Ignore her Mareena. You know the things I can offer you. Power. Wealth. Whatever you want."

I crossed my arms in front of my chest. "I have no desire to go with either of you. Fight it out, and let me know who wins." I turned to leave, and then thought better of it. "On second thought, I'll find out who wins from someone else. I never want to see either of you again."

"Oh honey," Mom said, sounding sad. "It's so cute that you think you have that option. You see, your Father and I have very different plans for the human world, and we both need you to help us make those plans happen. You can only serve one. Our views of how the fae and human worlds should interact are not compatible with each other. Don't you want to be a family again? Me and you?"

Plans for the human world? They weren't just going to destroy Faerie? I shivered. Of course not. When was any dictator ever happy with what they had. "I have a family. One that actually cares about me for me."

Then I did start to leave. I couldn't stop them. I couldn't do anything but try to live my life. I had Dan and Nina back, and that's all I needed. Those two would have to either work together, which wouldn't happen, or call a truce, which also wouldn't happen, before they could try to take on the human world. We were safe.

Nara's voice went through my head. *I wouldn't be so sure about that.*

Growing up, it was impossible to catch Cassie Greutman without a book in her hand, even at the most inappropriate times. Since then with the rise of ebooks, it's only gotten worse. With her full-time job of caring for over thirty horses, some of that has changed to audiobooks, but you can bet there is always some type of story rattling around in her brain. She has always loved stories in any format, whether that is a movie, video game, or book form, and hopes to tell stories that catch a person's imagination and interest like so many have done for her.

A finalist in the Cinematic Book Competition with Screencraft out of over 1200 entries, and five star ratings with Reader's Favorite, and a win with The Indie Author Project, Cassie has been throwing all of the extra time she has into building worlds for everyone to enjoy. When she isn't stuck in a book, of course.

I so hope you enjoyed Trish's latest adventure! The next chapter in her life, Premonition, is already out!

Follow me on Facebook and TikTok for updates on new stories:

https://www.facebook.com/cassiegreutman/

https://www.tiktok.com/@cassiegreutman

Or join my newsletter for a free short story about Trish first coming to live with Dan and Nina:

https://dl.bookfunnel.com/pq98nn1jof

If you'd like early access to stories as I write them and behind the scenes posts, check out:
https://reamstories.com/page/lh4u19l5l3

www.ingramcontent.com/pod-product-compliance
Lightning Source LLC
Chambersburg PA
CBHW070504300726
48975CB00007B/2319